"Well, we know where it ended. The question is where did it begin?"

"We aren't going to figure that out now." DeeJay turned, and as she did so, her boot caught on something, maybe a root, and she started to fall.

Instantly, strong arms caught her and the next thing she knew she was pressed against Cade's chest. Layers of down prevented it from being in any way intimate, but when she looked up into his eyes, no amount of down could prevent the hot arc of hunger that speared through her.

A flare in his gaze seemed to answer her.

"Cade?" she said breathlessly, the question almost lost as the treetops stirred in a sudden wind. It didn't matter. She didn't know what she was asking anyway.

"Damn," he said quietly. Apparently he knew the answer because he leaned in and kissed her.

***

Be sure to check out the rest of the
Conard County: The Next Generation miniseries!

***

If you're on Twitter, tell us what you
think of Harlequin Romantic Suspense!
#HarlequinRomSuspense

Dear Reader,

Falling in love is one of the biggest risks we take in life. It's the emotional equivalent of jumping out of an airplane without a parachute and trusting your jump partner to catch you and carry you down. When we're young, we leap into it with joy. When we get a little older, if we've had some bad experiences, we're not as quick to take that leap. Maybe we refuse to take it again.

But at the root of love is trust—trusting someone enough to be utterly vulnerable to them, because when we truly love we become emotionally naked. All the walls are down, all the defenses lowered. With a single word or act, we might be devastated.

DeeJay and Cade both have reasons not to trust, DeeJay more than most. But when they are partnered to help catch a serial killer, those defenses must be breached. As partners they must rely on one another completely, and that reliance requires the first seeds of trust. Preoccupation with the case gets them through at the beginning, but in the end love saves them both.

Enjoy!

Rachel

UNDERCOVER HUNTER

Rachel Lee

◆H◆ HARLEQUIN® ROMANTIC SUSPENSE

Recycling programs
for this product may
not exist in your area.

ISBN-13: 978-0-373-27901-2

Undercover Hunter

Printed in U.S.A.

Rachel Lee was hooked on writing by the age of twelve and practiced her craft as she moved from place to place all over the United States. This *New York Times* bestselling author now resides in Florida and has the joy of writing full-time.

Books by Rachel Lee

Harlequin Romantic Suspense

Conard County: The Next Generation

The Final Mission
Just a Cowboy
The Rescue Pilot
Guardian in Disguise
The Widow's Protector
Rancher's Deadly Risk
What She Saw
Rocky Mountain Lawman
Killer's Prey
Deadly Hunter
Defending the Eyewitness
Snowstorm Confessions

Harlequin Special Edition

The Widow of Conard County
Thanksgiving Daddy
Reuniting with the Rancher

Visit the Author Profile page at Harlequin.com for more titles

Prologue

Calvin Sweet knew he was taking some big chances, but risks always invigorated him. Coming back to his home in Conard County was the first of the new risks. Five years ago he'd left for bigger cities because the law seemed to be closing in on him.

Returning to the site where he had hung his trophies was a huge risk, too, although he could claim he was out for a hike in the autumn mountains before the first snows fell. There was nothing left, anyway. The law had taken it all away, and the sight filled him with both sorrow and bitterness. Anger, too. They had no right to take away his hard work, his triumphs, his mementos. His boys. He knew his mother would be proud of what he'd done, but the proof that he'd appeased her was gone.

They'd taken it all away. After five years all that was left were some remnants of cargo netting rotting in the tree limbs, the remains of a few sawed-off ropes.

But he could close his eyes and remember, and remembering filled him with joy and a sense of his own huge power, the power to purify them forever. Calvin had saved them.

Unlike his boys, he was filled with great purpose, a purpose handed down to him by his mother.

From earliest childhood he had been fascinated by spiders and their webs. He had spent hours watching as insect after insect fell victim to those silken strands, struggling mightily until they were stung and then wrapped up helplessly to await their fate. Each corpse on the web had been a trophy, marking the spider's victory. No one ever escaped.

No one had escaped him, either.

But his boys were gone, carried away to a different fate on cold slabs and cold holes in the ground. Honored no more, at least not by him.

He stood for a while, remembering, then turned to begin the trek back to the ranch. A small ranch, left to him after his mother's death long ago, but it was isolated enough to pursue his calling, and without his mother around it would be even more private. He considered it a bonus that construction at the new ski resort had begun. An influx of people for the jobs made his return even less remarkable.

These past years, moving from city to city before he could be found, he'd had to give up a lot of his boys, which had left him feeling incomplete and unsatisfied. Certainly there'd been no spiderwebs. Well, he could rebuild his triumphs here. Not in the woods, perhaps, since they'd found his first group, but maybe in the barn loft, out of sight? He needed to think about it.

He really wanted his web again, his carefully preserved trophies. He wanted what every spider wanted, and he'd find a way. The need was growing stronger. He needed to act again, and he needed to honor those who sustained his soul. He also needed to carry out his mission of purification. Sometimes, though, he lost track of what mattered more: his mission or his need. In those moments, he felt a little confused, but eventually he righted himself.

A cautious part of his mind warned him to wait a little longer, to make sure his plan would work. Soon that voice would give way to the compulsion that filled him, making the whole world seem luminescent, especially the chosen one.

But for now he suppressed the need. He wasn't stupid. In fact, he was quite smart, as proved by the fact that no one had come for him yet. He knew he was committing crimes. He just didn't care. His mission was bigger and more important than mere mortal laws.

He was himself chosen, just like a spider, to be exactly what he was.

Chosen. He liked that word. It fit both him and his boys. They were all chosen to perform the dance of death together, to reach the ultimate purity. To sacrifice the ordinary for the extraordinary.

So he quashed his growing need to act and focused his attention on another part of his life. He had a job now, on the crisis hotline. Calvin had worked at them before, which had gotten him a job almost the instant he walked in the door. Five evenings a week for four hours he answered telephones and talked with distressed people: victims of rape, of domestic abuse, and the ones who interested him the most, the desperate boys.

He was whistling now as he walked back down the mountain to his truck. A spiderweb was beginning to take shape in his mind, one for his barn loft that no one would see, ever. It was enough that he could admire it and savor the gifts there. That he could bask in the purity of his successful missions.

The impulse to hunt eased, and soon he was in control again. He liked control. He liked controlling himself and others, even as he fulfilled his purpose. Self-control was everything, as his mother had often reminded him.

Like the spider, he was not hasty to act. It would have to be the right person at the right time, and the time was not yet right. The right times were coming to him more often now as he grew in strength.

But first he had to build his web.

Chapter 1

In January beneath a leaden sky, special agents Cade Bankston and DeeJay Dawkins rocketed down an empty state highway toward the town of Conard City, Wyoming. They had been summoned to find a serial killer.

Cade had been to Conard City a few times years ago, very briefly, and had found it unremarkable but pleasant. DeeJay had never seen it. Given her background, he wondered how she would react. But then he couldn't figure out what the hell a woman with her past was doing working as a criminal investigator for the state of Wyoming. As a former military cop for an elite MP unit, she should have had her pick of jobs.

Maybe it was that prickly nature of hers that caused her problems. Certainly they'd had a few near-fights over the past three days, and they'd only just been made partners. If there was something, imagined or real, for DeeJay to object to, then she seemed to find it.

The red car they were driving was kind of sporty for the country, but that was the idea. To look like outsiders rather than insiders. To act as cover for a couple of investigators pretending to be married travel writers.

That "married" was still the biggest bone of contention between them. Not that it had been their decision. Nope. None of this had been their decision, and if they could just wrap their heads around that part, maybe the spats would ease up.

He kept his attention on the road. Snow blanketed the open spaces around them, although it was still a thin blanket. Plenty of brush stuck up through it, and tumbleweeds tossed like agitated prisoners against the barbed wire that had snared them. If there was life out here that was mobile, it had found somewhere to hide. Even the ranch houses were invisible from the road, although occasionally a sign pointed the way or smoke from a woodstove signaled in the distance.

He glanced at his companion. Well, okay, partner. He'd never wanted another female partner again, but that was a subject he wasn't about to explore again, now or later. He just didn't like it and didn't want it, had learned it contained huge pitfalls. Now here he was with a woman stapled to his side for the duration.

She'd have been pretty enough if he hadn't already discovered she was a prickly pear cactus with enough sharp spines to leave a man in ribbons. Inky black hair, high, wide cheekbones that bespoke some Native American ancestry, a straight nose that was just right for her face and a mouth that, damn it, looked like it was begging for a kiss. Even when it was compressed in disapproval, which it often was as far as he could tell. And that inventory didn't even get to her figure, a great figure for someone who was in the peak of physical conditioning, which she clearly was. He liked women who were fit.

He clapped his eyes back on the empty road and schooled his thoughts to a safer area. The woman in the passenger seat was off-limits, no caveats, no exceptions. And she was probably still stewing because he was driving.

That had been their first disagreement of the day. Just the opening salvo. The next battle had ensued over the choice of radio station. He liked country music while he was driving. Turned out she liked NPR. Now why would that surprise him? Thing was, when he was driving he preferred to escape into fantasies about losing the woman, the truck and the dog rather than listen to real-world discussions that usually riled him up because he mostly didn't like the way the world was going these days.

So no radio at all. Some compromise.

Then there had been the disagreement about where to get coffee. Crap, that beat it all to hell. She wanted the expensive place; he'd have been happy with any roadside diner. So he took her to the chain coffee shop and then she'd ordered ordinary coffee. Not a fancy drink, just a gigantic cup of black and strong. Same as him. So why the argument?

He hoped they found this serial killer soon, preferably before one of them killed the other in a shoot-out at high noon.

"I need to eat," she announced. Her first words in 250 miles.

Not *we* need to eat. No, just announcing her own wishes. Of course, maybe she was used to that. He'd heard she'd been an officer, kind of way up there or something. Maybe she said *jump* and was used to having everyone do it. Well, he wasn't used to jumping and wasn't about to begin.

"You see a place to stop?" he asked mildly enough. Not exactly a courteous response on his part, and even he knew it. But he figured if he gave DeeJay Dawkins an inch, she'd take a country mile.

"Next place," she replied.

"Greasy spoons from here on out." He hoped she'd object to that. After all, she was the type who went to specialty coffee shops to get ordinary coffee. Next he'd be hearing about organic food restaurants and how she lived on fresh salads.

She shocked him by saying, "Fine."

Man, the conversation in this car was a real crowd-pleaser. The thought of having to share a house with her until they finished this investigation made him want to change jobs. Except he mostly liked his job, so he wasn't going to let anyone, especially her, make him throw it away.

Focus on the job, he reminded himself. Not the partner. They were after a serial killer, or at least the local sheriff thought so. One who was taking adolescent boys. No bodies yet, but apparently it had happened a few years ago, too, then abruptly stopped. They didn't find the evidence until later. Much later. Now the sheriff feared it was starting again.

Not unusual. Some serial killers were fairly smart. They often changed locales and evaded the law until they died. Or they went to prison for a while for some unrelated crime and their trail went cold. If the sheriff was right, they couldn't hope for a stupid killer this time, because that would be a really idiotic assumption on their part.

It had happened before; now it was happening again,

and half a decade was a long time for a copycat to suddenly show up. Ergo, it had to be the same creep.

Around a tight bend in the road, settled into a hollow almost out of sight, he spied a roadhouse. One of those places that somehow hung on in the middle of nowhere, serving people who lived too far from a town to want to make a lengthy trip for a drink, some socializing and a lousy sandwich or overcooked burger.

Without a word, he flipped on the turn signal and nosed them in. Only a couple of dusty pickups sat in the gravel lot, but the open sign blinked red neon at them. Rusty, ancient-looking signs announced beer, food and cigarettes. Sort of an outdated convenience store, except there'd be a bar. There was always a bar. He just hoped the place didn't house any trouble right now. He and DeeJay, dressed in brand-new Western clothing and boots to fit their assumed roles, might as well be wearing neon signs of their own: dude alert.

He climbed out and waited. DeeJay followed a moment later. He'd already learned not to open a car door for her, even though they were supposed to look married. He hadn't fought that one much, though, except to annoy her.

She came to the head of the car, and he watched her size up the place with experienced eyes. Then she glanced at him, and her dark gaze seemed to say, *We can handle them.*

Yeah, they could. If it became necessary and it probably wouldn't. He wondered how many times in her career as an MP she'd had to walk into places like these, probably a hell of a lot more crowded with drunks. Maybe not much, if she'd been an officer. How the hell would he know? She wasn't talking, and he was damned if he would ask.

When they reached the battered door, at least she didn't argue about him opening it. He was on the left. He'd have let anyone on the left open it given the way it swung. He walked in behind her and took it all in, familiar from countless places in the past. Wood everywhere, darkened, stained and scratched by the years. A long bar, also scratched and stained, stools that had needed to be replaced forty years ago, the stench of stale alcohol, tobacco, sweat and other things he didn't care to pick out. No scouring in the world would get rid of those odors now.

The jukebox was wailing some bluegrass, the bartender, maybe owner, looked like a leftover from gold-rush days. A number of old men gathered at a corner table, watching them suspiciously.

DeeJay took one look around, then strode up to the bar as if she owned the place. Cade stayed by the door. The Native ancestry stamped on her face could still cause problems in some parts. He waited to see how she'd be received.

"Coffee," she said to the bartender, "and a menu. Please."

The gray-bearded man hesitated only a moment, his old pale eyes darting to Cade, then he grabbed a ceramic cup from the stack on the counter and filled it from what looked like a fresh pot. He carried it to DeeJay, then slapped down a plastic-covered menu that was probably sticky. Weren't they always?

Cade meandered over to take a seat by DeeJay. The bartender had issued the message *We don't want no problems here.*

Good enough for him. He ordered his own coffee, and agreed silently with DeeJay that a burger was probably the safest thing to choose, not that the menu was big. Soon the smell of frying beef rose from the griddle and it was like someone let the tension out of the room.

Lunch without problems. Always a good way to go.

Then DeeJay astonished him almost to speechlessness. She lifted her head from her burger and said, "This is a great burger. Just the way I like them."

The bartender froze and stared at her. He probably received a compliment once every hundred years or so.

DeeJay pushed her jacket out of the way, reached into her hip pocket and pulled out one of the phony business cards they had for this trip. "We're travel writers," she said. "We write about great places to stop. If you have a card, I'd like to tell folks about your burgers."

Now the bartender's jaw dropped. Silence fell from the far end of the room, except for Hank Williams Sr. wailing tinnily about cheatin' hearts. You could almost hear the ice in the room crack as it thawed.

"Ain't got no card," the bartender said. "Take one of them menus, iffen you want."

"I'll do that," DeeJay said. "Thanks."

For her efforts they both received a complimentary piece of apple pie.

Cade let DeeJay pay, figuring this wasn't the time or place to get into an argument about who was buying lunch, and it was all the state's money anyway. When at last they stepped back outside, he drew in lungfuls of fresh cold air and remarked, "Great job." He didn't even sound grudging.

"The pie crust was heavy," she remarked, her only response.

Stifling a sigh, he climbed back in behind the wheel and set them once again on the road to Conard City.

However long it took to catch this killer, it was going to be too long.

* * *

DeeJay didn't care for men. It was one thing to have a fling with one, another to work with one. In a single instant she'd seen the resistance in Cade Bankston's eyes when he'd heard they were to be partnered, and that had been all she'd needed. He was a macho meathead who couldn't accept that women were as capable as men. Like that pinheaded CO who had turned her life into a living hell because he didn't think a woman was qualified to command an MP unit. That freaking martinet had wanted every *i* dotted, and it damn well better be dotted clearly enough. But he wasn't the only one. There'd been the CO in Afghanistan who'd warned her that if she filed a rape charge her career was over. And the series of them who had been infuriated when she insisted on investigating the rapes of other soldiers. There'd also been too many men working for her who didn't get why they should take orders from her. And then there'd been the guy who had forced her out.

They hadn't all been bad, but enough of them had that DeeJay had a real burn on for men. A guy got one chance with her. Bankston had torched his.

Still, she had to work with him. She wasn't ready to nuke any bridges on this job. There was a killer to catch, although she still didn't understand what lamebrain had come up with the idea that they had to pretend to be married. Wouldn't it have been enough that they were working together on a travel story?

She looked down at the thin gold band on her ring finger, courtesy of an evidence locker somewhere, and wished she could fling it out the window.

She glanced occasionally at Bankston, taking in his square jaw and chiseled face from the side. His hair was a light brown, a little wavy, and he had a pair of aquama-

rine eyes that she would have admired in any other setting. He probably believed he set women's hearts aflutter,
and maybe he did. For a guy who must be pushing toward
forty, he took good care of himself.

All she knew about him, though, was that he had a lot
of experience and had been with the criminal investigation unit for most of that time. She'd heard that he'd once
been a beat cop in a major metro area, but she didn't have
any idea which one. It wasn't a whole lot to go on.

She did know, however, that he didn't want to be working with her, and she didn't want him any closer than the
job required. When they'd received the news that they
were pairing up for this, she'd seen it clear as anything in
his eyes. If he'd been a mule, he'd have dug in his heels
and brayed. She had to give him some credit for taking
an order he didn't like, but she wouldn't give him any
more than that.

Nor did she feel as if she needed to prove herself to him.
She'd proved herself countless times in a much tougher
organization, and she'd learned the hard way that con-
ciliatory women were considered weak, and tough ones
were called bitches. She preferred being a bitch. At least
no one tried to take advantage of her that way.

Stifling a sigh, she wished this drive would come to
an end. Looking out the window, with the mountains still
purple in the distance, had begun to bore her. She wasn't
used to sitting still for so long.

She glanced again at Cade and decided that maybe she
should back off him a little. She'd made her position clear
repeatedly over the past few days, but they still had to
work together. The question was how much she needed to
back off. Except for their disagreement about who would
drive, he'd done his share of backing off. And she'd let him
drive only because he'd made the logical argument that

he knew this country and these roads. It had been clear at that point that he wasn't insisting because he thought the man should always drive.

Okay, give him back a point, but after that expression when they'd been told they were working together, he still had a lot of points to earn.

"I guess that you don't know much about the sheriff we're working with, unless someone gave you a dossier," he said, disturbing the endless silence between them, a silence filled with the humming of the car engine and tires on the road.

"Not a thing," she admitted reluctantly, wondering if she had been deliberately left out of some loop. Men often tried that with her.

"He's good," Cade said. "Not your average elected official whose chief accomplishment has been kissing babies."

Despite herself, she almost wanted to laugh. Even as an MP she'd had to deal with that kind of local law enforcement occasionally.

"He's former DEA," Cade went on. "Undercover operative until a car bomb nearly killed him and wiped out his entire family. He still carries the scars."

DeeJay swore quietly. She knew a lot of stories of car bombs all too well. Some of them had involved families.

"Yeah," Cade answered, apparently hearing her. "Anyway, long story short. He came here to heal, got hired as a crime-scene investigator, and years ago when the old sheriff retired, he was elected. Folks still call him the new sheriff."

"Of course." That didn't surprise her at all.

"His name is Gage Dalton. Runs a tight ship. His predecessor, Nate Tate, was sheriff for forty years and still sticks his finger in the pie. Let him. There's no one and nothing he doesn't know about this county."

"Except who the killer is."

"Obviously."

DeeJay hesitated. Then, offering a slender olive branch, she said, "Sounds like a couple of good men to have on our side."

"The best. The deputies are good, too. Nate started a trend of inviting his old military pals to come this way. He was Special Forces. Anyway, they joke sometimes that they have more Special Forces types in Conard County than most military bases. Makes for an interesting and sometimes useful mix."

He was trying to tell her to be careful of stepping on toes, she realized. Trying to warn her that she'd be meeting men with backgrounds similar to hers and who shouldn't be casually dismissed. Or wisely dismissed. While she resented the implication that she made a habit of stepping on toes, she'd certainly been stepping on his since their first meeting. Since she couldn't just come out and say that she only stepped on toes she meant to break, she decided to take it as a good omen that he was trying to fill her in. Much as it killed her, she said, "Thank you."

"The sheriff knows we're both coming. It'll be up to him to decide who to trust with that information, but from what little I know of him, I doubt he'll trust very many. They're already working the case, though, and as you know we're here by invitation."

"Got it. Been there, done that before."

"I guess you have."

She hesitated, then asked, "You read my jacket?"

"That stuff's private. What I know about you is exactly nothing."

That wasn't good, she thought. They were partnered and both of them had to have some basis for trusting each other's instincts, as far as the investigation went. They didn't have to like each other, just to develop a professional trust. Partners could succeed no other way. But she still had a burr.

"You didn't want to partner with a woman," she said.

"No." He didn't varnish it. "Nothing to do with you personally. Bad experience once."

"I could say the same about working with men, only more than once."

She felt him glance at her before he spoke. "Then I suggest we focus on the badge and not the packages we're wearing. I trained at Quantico and I've been a cop in one shape or another for seventeen years."

She gave a short nod. "I did Quantico, too. Twelve years as a cop, mostly in investigations. All over the world."

"Good. Well, we're entering a different world here. You let me know if it reminds you of any place you've been before. People in this town are pretty tight. Just about everyone's going to be upset about the missing boys. Then there's a ski resort they started to build this past summer. Some new people from that. Some who came with the semiconductor plant and didn't leave when it died. But most folks were born here and will be buried here. That kind of place."

"I've been in villages like that." She'd run into them in the Appalachians on a couple of cases involving military personnel, and overseas in Iraq and Afghanistan. Tight, cliquish and distrusting of outsiders. How was that going to help them?

She looked out the side window again, feeling as if the day's gloom was settling into her bones. Some nuts were impossible to crack, and this sounded like one. How the hell were a couple of pretend travel writers going to get any real information from anyone? It would give them the freedom to move around without suspicion, but little else.

The more she thought about it, the less she liked this whole cover story. Profiling, in which they'd both been trained, could only get you so far. After that, you needed solid information.

"You know," she said presently, "this cover story stinks. The whole town is going to be upset because kids are disappearing. Does anyone think they're going to want to talk about that with travel writers?"

He didn't answer for a minute. The car noises seemed to grow louder until he spoke. "That crossed my mind. But you tell me, Dawkins, how else we can insert a couple of strangers into a small community like this? No matter how we do it, we're going to stand out and nobody's going to want to talk. This cover story at least elevates us above a couple of dubious drifters and doesn't give away our real mission."

He was right. "So we back up the local law. I can deal."

"Yeah. They'll probably give us most of the information. We're the ones who need to help pull it together. And who knows? We're talking about one thing and looking for another. We might learn something useful just by keeping our eyes and ears open."

"You mean the unsub could slip up."

"We can hope."

Amazing how much of law enforcement came down to someone slipping up and someone else having the wit to notice the slip. She drummed her fingers on her thigh. They had been called up because of their training in profiling. She didn't have the highest regard for it, but it could occasionally provide some useful directions to an investigation.

She spoke as they passed the sign announcing that they were entering Conard County. "We'd better get on a first-name basis fast."

"Yeah. Why'd you tell that barkeep that you were going to tout his burgers? He'll be looking for an article."

"Nah. He has a business card and a story to tell. That'll make him happy. He'll brag and our cover will be established."

"True."

She guessed that was an olive branch from him.

Calvin Sweet finished arranging his latest trophy and stood back in the barn loft to admire it. Three of them now hung from the commercial fish netting he'd acquired on his travels.

He liked that netting. It was better than the cargo net he'd used before, thinner, made of highly durable plastic. As close as he was going to get to a spiderweb unless he took the time to weave one himself.

His three trophies, wrapped in clear plastic painter's drop cloth, hung beautifully like ornaments, visible but slightly hidden in their protective cases. Mysterious, like the life force he had taken from them. Holy now that they'd been saved.

Backing up, he settled on a bale of hay to admire his handiwork. His private collection, growing steadily, a work of art. He hoped that someday someone other than himself would be able to admire it. It had taken a lot of work and thought. Hunting for something more to his liking than rope cargo net had actually taken quite a while. There were a surprising number of different kinds of fishnets and netting, and he'd had to do research until he could walk into that place on the East Coast and order exactly what he wanted.

Even the clear plastic drop cloths were problematic, as he had to be careful not to buy too many at any one place. He'd driven many miles buying two or three at a time to make the stack that now stood in a corner of the old tack room. Always paying in cash, too.

Then there were the plastic, disposable restraints. Easy enough to come by if you ordered them online, a hundred at a time. Figuring out how to avoid leaving that trail had cost him as much time and effort as any other part. He'd been delighted when he'd learned he could buy them in smaller quantities at some sex shops, and for cash. That had meant a lot of traveling, too, and going into places that he was certain were evil.

But he liked the flexible ties better than tape, which damaged the skin and looked ugly, and better than rope, which could stretch and be wiggled out of. Imagine his surprise when he'd learned that most rope stretched on purpose so it wouldn't snap.

But now here he was, his trail concealed, his beautiful web in operation, three offerings to admire. It had been worth it. All of it.

He had saved these three from miserable futures full of heartbreak, hard work, illness and sin. He had set them free. He had kept them pure.

And in setting them free he had purified himself, made himself stronger with their unsullied energy. Just like the spider, who could poison her prey and then eat it without suffering from the poison. Receiving only the nutrition.

His spirit had been fed. Now he honored those who had fed him, acknowledging their gifts.

It was essential to be grateful for these gifts. Gratitude filled him with a righteous light and reminded him how important his boys were, thus endowing them with the importance they deserved.

They had served him well.

He would honor them just as well.

But then the watch on his wrist beeped, reminding him

it was time to get ready. He had a shift on the crisis line tonight, and no way would he miss it.

There was more than one way he could help others.

Satisfied, he rose and climbed down the ladder, locked the barn and headed to the house.

Nights brought him many good things. Tonight he might have the chance to help a mistreated woman. Life was good to him and he was great.

He needed nothing more.

Chapter 2

The town looked as buttoned-down as a military base under a black flag warning, DeeJay thought as they tooled down tree-lined streets beneath the skeletal fingers of leafless branches. Snow berms lined the streets from the plows, and lawns lay beneath an icy blanket of white. Holiday decorations, unlit now, hung from the light poles, awaiting the people who would remember to take them down.

"Do you know where this house is?" she asked.

Cade nodded. "Near the downtown. The guy next door is the landlord. We'll get the key from him."

If he was home. But she kept that thought to herself. "There's no one about." The winter night had fallen a while ago, but it was still early. "Is it always this quiet?"

"I doubt it, but like I said, I've only been here briefly a few times and that was long ago."

"So people are hunkering down because of the kidnappings?"

"Maybe so. Once we talk to Gage we'll get a better idea."

Her eyes never stopped moving as she surveyed the streets, the town she could see, the emptiness that made it seem more like a ghost town. Lights glowed from inside the houses, but that didn't change the sense of abandonment. She'd seen frightened towns before and this was a frightened town. Frightened for their young boys. It was enough.

She itched to get on the job, to catch the scent and start her work. The time between the last two disappearances had been just over two weeks. The current victim had disappeared four days ago. They didn't have a whole lot of time.

She'd learned patience as an investigator, however. Impatience could lead to mistakes and oversights. These could not be allowed. She drew a deep breath and let relaxation pour through her. Time. It always took time.

"Do we have any idea of his cycle?" she asked.

"The killer? Not sure. He was escalating somewhat before he vanished, and he seems to be escalating again. It's hard to be sure with only three missing kids, though. You read the report?"

Of course she had, but it had mostly been a description of events five years earlier. Little enough about the present except that it appeared to be happening again. Since Cade had been in these parts for at least a decade, she couldn't help wondering if he knew more than was in the report. If so, they were going to have a meeting of minds very soon. If not…well, they were starting on equal footing. "The more frequently he acts, the more likely he'll slip up." On the other hand, that put some very real pressure on them to figure out something fast.

"We'll find out." He pulled a left turn onto an even narrower street, this one devoid of pole decorations, although a few houses still sported lights along the eaves. Barnstable Street.

"There it is."

Unmistakable, she thought. It was the only house on the street that was completely dark. Not very big, either, which could be good or bad, depending. Her mind ticked over impressions, cataloguing them for later.

He stopped the car at the end of a plowed driveway, no heaped snow blocking it. "I'll get the key."

She didn't answer, just climbed out. He paused, then switched off the ignition and set the brake. She didn't explain her actions, felt no need to, but she was damned if she was going to start letting him cut her out of anything, however small.

She was a tall woman, but Cade was even taller. As they mounted the three salted steps side by side, the wind bit at them with frigid teeth. It was freaking cold this evening, like the breath of an advancing ice age. Even with her hood pulled up, the chill found ways to snap at her ears.

Cade knocked, a courteous knock rather than a police banging, and soon the front door opened to reveal a beautiful and very pregnant young woman. "You must be the Dentons?" she said.

Cade nodded. "I'm Cade, and this is my…wife, Dee-Jay." DeeJay hoped she was the only one who noted that hesitation. To her it sounded too obvious to miss.

"Come in," the woman said, smiling. "I'm Kelly Jackson. You'll freeze out there waiting for me to get the key."

So they stepped into a tiny foyer where the wood floor was covered in a bright braid rug and a few photos hung on the walls. "How about some coffee?" Kelly asked. "You must have had a long drive. Hank should be back soon. He's helping with the search parties."

DeeJay could smell roasting pork from the kitchen and

guessed dinner was cooking for Hank. Then it struck her. This woman was talking about search parties to a couple of travel writers. What's more, they weren't supposed to be clued in.

As they were ushered into the front room and waved to seats on the sofa, she asked, "Search parties?"

"We've had a boy go missing," Kelly answered, her smile fading. "Just twelve years old. Let me get that coffee."

Kelly returned quickly carrying a tray that held three mugs and a coffeepot. "You'll like the house," she said. "I know you might not be here very long, but it's where I first lived when I moved here." Her face seemed to shadow, but then it brightened. "A real estate agent rented it to me when Hank was away for a few weeks. I thought Hank was going to have a cow when he found out. The place was in terrible shape. I don't think you ever saw a man move so fast to repair things. He hadn't intended to rent it out so soon."

DeeJay thanked her for the coffee. "How long did you live there?"

Kelly laughed again, seeming to relax. She sat in an armchair across from them. "Long enough to finish out my divorce and marry Hank. Just long enough to fix it up a bit. The furnishings aren't top-of-the-line, but they'll serve you."

"What's Hank do?" Cade asked.

"He'll tell you he's just a cowboy."

DeeJay hooked on the way she said it. "But?"

"Hank will never be *just* anything."

DeeJay was sure Kelly believed that, but she also sensed there was more of a backstory. No way to ask. "So he's out searching for this boy?"

"A lot of people are." Kelly's face darkened again. "I

might as well tell you, since you're going to run into it anyway. You picked a bad time to write a travel piece about us. Even with the new ski resort opening next fall."

"Why?" DeeJay asked gently.

Kelly shook her blond head. "This is the third boy to disappear since late fall. And some are talking about how this happened before I moved here. People are scared. Whether they talk to you about it or not, you're going to sense their fear."

Five minutes later they were parked in the short drive-way of the dark little house. Kelly assured them that Hank had turned up the heat that morning so they should be warm. Everything was ready for them, including the phone.

Cade drummed his fingers on the steering wheel. "Want to unload the suitcases first or find a place to eat?"

"Greasy spoon?" she asked, quoting him from earlier.

"One of the best."

"Then let's eat first. As cold as it is tonight, I don't want to settle into warmth and then have to go out again. When do we meet the sheriff?"

"Soon. With the search going on, I can't say any better than that." He pulled away from the house, rounded a block and headed in toward the center of town. The houses grew bigger and some even boasted decent-sized yards.

If you blinked, DeeJay thought, you could miss the entire center of town with its flashing red stoplight. It had the kind of charm most old small towns boasted, along with the inevitable seediness. It could have been almost anywhere in the country or anywhere in the past century.

Whatever tourism might come to Conard County from the ski resort, the town hadn't yet given in. No cheesy T-shirt shops, no cowboy-hat shaped neon announcing Western clothing. No upscale boutiques. No touristy stuff at all. The town hadn't yet wakened to its new status. Maybe it never would.

They parked at a place called the City Diner. "It's empty," she remarked before they climbed out of the car. "That's not a good sign."

"This place has a great rep," Cade answered. "And remember, people are either out searching for a boy or they're locked inside where it's safe."

Three boys missing and the town feared they had a killer in their midst. Not understanding the mentality of most serial killers, they wouldn't get that anyone other than a young boy would probably be safe. And that was wise, because there had been a few who had had no particular victim type, and hadn't cared whom they had chosen for their ritual.

"Ramirez," Cade said, almost as if he were reading her mind. "That guy ran the gamut in his victims."

"But as far as we know, this one doesn't."

"So far."

"Maybe more like Gacy."

"Maybe."

Inside, the diner looked ancient, with seats patched with tape and tables that were scratched past all shine but clearly clean. The menus weren't even sticky, but the woman who waited on them was something else. If she'd ever had a charming bone in her body, it had abandoned ship a long time ago. Crockery clattered, cups slammed, hot coffee filled them and splashed a bit, and all without any communication beyond indeterminate grunts. Mavis apparently wasn't much for talking.

Then came the platters overflowing with steak sandwiches and enough fries for an army. The dinner salads in their tiny bowls almost disappeared beside them.

It was then they discovered that Mavis could talk.

"You them travel writers?"

"Yes," Cade and DeeJay answered together.

"Humph. Bad time to be coming to these parts. Don't know if I like that whole ski thing, neither. We were getting along just fine."

"You'll get more business," Cade pointed out.

"Already got all the business we want, and some that we don't." With that, Mavis stomped away.

Cade and DeeJay exchanged looks, the first real understanding that had passed between them. It arced almost electrically, and both quickly glanced down at their plates.

"So everybody knows who we are," DeeJay remarked, picking up a half a steak sandwich that by itself would have fed three men.

"At least we won't seem suspicious."

"Maybe not." But she had her doubts. Strangers in a frightened town always caused suspicion. They really had their work cut out for them.

The house created its own set of problems for them. It was tiny, with one small bedroom. DeeJay insisted she sleep on the couch because she was shorter, and this time Cade didn't offer an argument.

They'd brought home hefty containers full of leftovers, but they'd also made a stop at the grocery for coffee. No day would be complete without it. At least they agreed on that much. Cade picked up a few other odds and ends for snacking while DeeJay selected some energy bars. Even frozen, they'd be edible, and right now they were utterly in the dark about how they were going to handle a case they knew very little about.

Back at the house, they brewed a pot in a decent drip coffeemaker, then sat down to pass the time. Being here in support of local law meant they had to await directions. And all of this undercover stuff was designed to lull the perp. If he caught wind that two state investigators had been brought in, he might disappear again. The pressure to catch him was heavy, almost creeping along DeeJay's nerve endings. She suspected Cade was feeling much the same.

"There are crimes and then there are crimes," she remarked.

"I read you loud and clear," he answered.

"These sick twists make my skin crawl. I've dealt with all kinds of crimes. Just like you. I can understand most of them. People get mad. They want money. Lots of reasons that fit human understanding. Hell, most of us have probably felt an urge or two in our lives but haven't acted on it."

"True."

"But these guys…they *like* it. They're playing out some bizarre fantasy and compulsion. They never stop until they're dead or in jail. All that stuff they poured into us at Quantico? It still doesn't make sense to me."

"I don't think it ever can."

"If it ever does, I may cash in my chips."

He surprised her with a quiet laugh.

She looked at him, something she'd been trying to avoid by pretending a fascination for the pattern in the curtains or the back of her hands. "I didn't mean that to be funny."

"I know you didn't. I laughed because my reaction is the same. It's bad enough we have to try to understand enough to predict him. That's as much understanding as I ever want to have."

"More than enough. And we start as usual with the same bare-bones outline. Probably male, most likely white, late twenties to early thirties, drives a car that doesn't stand out…" She trailed off. "A lot of blanks to fill in."

"It could be a woman."

"Quit reminding me we can't eliminate anyone."

At that he laughed freely, and as much as she didn't like most men, she joined in. It felt good, released tension, and she hoped he was beginning to feel less resentful of having a woman for a partner.

In fairness, he couldn't feel any more resentful of her than she felt of him. She sighed as the laughter died. Somewhere in the depths of the house the heat kicked on. First came a wave of chilly air, followed by warmer air that smelled a little musty.

The doorbell rang. She let him answer it. She heard Cade and another man exchange a few words, then Cade ushered in the sheriff along with a blast of cold air. The first thing that struck her was that one side of his face had been burned and showed old, shiny scar tissue. The next was that he limped, and occasionally pain flickered across his face. The car bomb.

"Gage Dalton," he said, pulling off his glove and offering his hand. She rose and shook it. Cade took his jacket while DeeJay introduced herself. And even though it was a female thing to do, which she usually avoided, she asked if he wanted coffee.

"Always," he answered promptly.

"I'll get it," Cade said.

DeeJay waved Gage Dalton to a chair and didn't miss the way he winced as he sat.

"Long day," Gage said.

She didn't want to dally on niceties. "When did the boy disappear?"

"Four days ago, after school. His dad was in town to buy supplies at the feed store and told the boy he'd pick him up after school. When he got there, the boy was gone and the dad assumed they must have crossed wires and he'd taken the bus home after all. But the bus arrived, and no kid."

DeeJay nodded, seeing it all so clearly. "No one saw him on the bus?"

"Nope. So it had to have happened while he was waiting for his dad."

"How old is he?"

"Twelve."

Cade returned with the coffee. Given the size of the house, he couldn't have missed any of the conversation. "So these kids are fitting a profile? Not an age group?"

"That's how it's looking. I can show you all the photos, from this time and last time. He's picking the small skinny boys, all of them with dark hair so far. He's definitely choosing by physical appearance."

"I guess that tells us something," Cade muttered as he passed DeeJay her coffee and sat at the other end of the couch.

For a minute, no one said anything. Gage stretched out a leg and rubbed it absently, a gesture that had become unconscious through long experience. DeeJay recognized the signs. The sheriff was looking off into space, shaking his head slowly.

"It really chapped me that we didn't catch up with him last time. He was gone by the time we found his trophies out in the mountain. Sickening. And not a damn thing to link anyone to it."

"He likes taking risks," DeeJay said. "He must know that everyone has figured out he's back, and that everyone is being watchful. He must get a real thrill from riding close to the edge of discovery."

"Meaning?" Gage asked.

"He'd not hiding. He's out in plain sight."

Cade nodded. "She's probably right. At this point I'm

inclined to say he's making contact with these kids before-hand. In some capacity that makes him seem trustworthy."

Gage nodded. "We figure he's got to be a local. Only problem with that is that locals leave all the time because they can't find work here. A lot of them came back with the jobs at the ski resort. Not much narrowing we can do that way." He sighed. "But if he seems trustworthy to the kids…" He trailed off. These kinds of questions always trailed off in an investigation like this. Trying to over-look nothing meant often coming up against the lack of answers.

DeeJay spoke. "Tell us exactly what happened the other day. Were other kids or adults around? Did anybody see the boy before he disappeared?"

"Nobody remembers seeing a thing," Gage answered. "The buses had come and gone, the walkers had headed home, the teachers were back inside or gone for the day. One of them questioned him when he was standing out front, but he answered he was waiting for his dad. He re-fused her offer to wait inside. That's it. Dad was a little late and by the time he arrived, no kid."

Cade and DeeJay exchanged looks. DeeJay spoke. "Our perp had to be somewhere he could see when the kid was alone. Completely alone. How big a time frame was that?"

"Maybe ten minutes," Gage answered. "The teacher remembers the approximate time she spoke to him. The dad came along about ten minutes later."

"Planned," said Cade flatly. "Not a target of oppor-tunity."

"That's the way I'm figuring it," Gage said. "Hardly anybody knew that boy was going to be waiting there in-stead of taking the bus. He *had* brought a note to school that morning asking that he be excused from taking the bus home. A couple of school officials knew, the teacher that talked to him knew, maybe some of his friends. We checked the whereabouts of the administrators and teachers for the entire time between dismissal and his disappearance and came up blank."

"Vehicles on the street or parking lot?"

"Lots. Teachers. Administration. Plenty of cover for one vehicle. Nobody would notice it unless it didn't fit at all."

DeeJay leaned forward, holding her mug in both hands. "How often do kids wait for a ride like that?"

"At this time of year? Almost never. It's too dang cold and we were having some thick snow that day."

"More cover," she remarked. "Okay, our perp must have found out that kid would be out there. Question is, how? And why was the dad late?"

Gage sighed and ran his fingers through his hair. "When he came out of the feed store, he had a flat tire."

Cade looked at DeeJay. "Organized," he said.

"Highly organized," she agreed. "Leaves nothing to chance, but likes riding the edge. We need to go over those files again." She looked at the sheriff. "Is everything in the file you sent to the state?"

"Pretty much. I didn't include victim photos, but everything else is there."

Cade spoke. "We need anything else surrounding the other disappearances that you or someone else can remember. I know this goes back a long way, but it helps us focus on what we need to think about."

"You got it."

DeeJay gave him a smile that was nearly a grimace. "We'd like to be able to point you in a direction that's more specific than late twenties, early thirties..."

Gage surprised her by laughing, a raspy sound. "We've all heard the basics. Useless. So believe me, I'm going to be racking my brains and everyone else's for every sliver I can come up with. In the meantime, I can establish your bona fides. Stop by the office in the morning, and it'll be all over town that you two are on the side of the angels. There's only one thing folks are talking about right now, and they might drop another splinter into this morass that'll help you. As long as they know you're okay."

"In this town," DeeJay remarked after the sheriff left, "I suspect it takes more than a few days to win local trust."

"Most likely. But let's get out those files and burn some midnight oil. Maybe we'll get a clue. Mostly I'd like to see if we can get a sense of his time cycle. Is he speeding up? Maybe, maybe not. But at least we'll have some idea how long we have before the next kid goes missing."

"We've got to stop it before then."

Cade nodded, his aquamarine eyes regarding her with something close to genuine warmth. "I'm praying for it."

At midnight, Calvin Sweet signed out from the crisis response center. One woman was leaving at the same time, and he offered to see her safely to her car.

"Thanks, Calvin," Dory Patterson said, and patted his cheek. He was a handsome, pleasant young man, and she was just old enough to get away with the gesture. "You're very thoughtful."

"Well, people are afraid," he said. "Terrible thing about that boy disappearing."

"Yes, it is," she answered as they stepped outside onto the crunchy snow. "At least you don't have to worry."

Calvin simply smiled, savoring his secret.

"But then, neither do I," she remarked.

He shook his head. "If there's one thing I've learned from working crisis hotlines, it's that women are at risk.

Better to be escorted to your car. It's the least I can do. I'm parked, what, fifteen feet away?"

Dory laughed, a surprisingly girlish sound from a woman who must have been pushing fifty. "I appreciate it. I'm sure you've seen more of the big bad world than I have."

"Big cities," he admitted. "More opportunities for trouble."

"Well, you do a great job on the phones. I've heard you. But it must seem awfully slow here after working in bigger places."

He stood and waited while she unlocked her car. "You know, Dory, I'm happiest when we aren't needed at all. Makes you wonder about the human race when the calls are coming in constantly."

"I bet it would." She slid into the driver's seat and looked up at him. "I'm glad you didn't come back for a construction job. We needed you here." Then she paused. "I realize it was a long time ago, but I *am* sorry about your mother's passing. She was a good woman."

"Yes, she was," Calvin agreed.

He stepped back and watched Dory drive away, amazed at how little of the truth ever got out. No one in this crummy place had any idea how he had been treated by that woman, how many times he'd had an "accident" that was no accident. He didn't miss his mother at all.

Climbing into his truck, he wondered if he might not be getting a little revenge on all the people who had been so blind. No, he decided he wasn't. His purpose was higher than that.

But he was aware of the urge starting to grow in him again, stalking him like a living thing. And this time he felt himself wanting a woman. No. He shook himself. Too soon.

Damn, he was thinking about taking a woman again. He hated it every time that urge arose. It might provide additional concealment, or it could prove his undoing. Nor did he understand exactly how it fit his mission, which unnerved him a bit.

The sky had cleared and a carpet of stars, brilliant as diamonds, filled it as he drove away from the town's lights. Maybe the Egyptians had been right. Maybe each one of his boys had become a star up there now. He turned the idea around and decided he liked it. They were pure now, gleaming lights showing the way. Yes.

When he got home, he almost hiked out to his barn to enjoy his trophies for a few minutes, but the wind cut hard and stole his breath. It could wait for morning. They wouldn't get lonely anymore. He had saved them from that.

Once inside, though, he felt a shift in his perspective. Light and color seemed brighter.

It was too soon.

The warning came from someplace deep inside him. In the city it had been different. He'd been able to hunt more often. In cities people disappeared all the time. He was well aware that out here they didn't. And while he didn't mind taking some risks, he was in no hurry to leave this place. He hadn't yet filled his web. He didn't want to leave the job half-done.

Sitting in an old rocker, he began to rock, trying to still the urges inside him. He knew he couldn't afford to lose control of them. His mission would never be completed if he did something stupid. The mind must control the need, always. It was a sign of his strength that he could.

He was getting stronger, he reminded himself. With each boy, he gained power and purity, but he was a long way from done.

He forced his mind to other things and lit on something he'd heard at the call center that night. There were two travel writers in town, a married couple. Bad timing for the town, he thought with sour pleasure. Search parties going out every day, everyone looking over their shoulders...

He leaned back and smiled, the urge easing. He'd caused that. A sign of his growing power. He was approaching utter control of himself.

His thoughts trailed back to those travel writers he'd heard about. Who the hell would miss one of them? Nobody around here. He wondered if the woman looked anything like his mother.

Yeah, if it came to that...

But it wouldn't. Not yet. He was still in control of himself and, when he thought about it, most of the people around. He saw them as puppets on strings, little marionettes. He could make them afraid, very afraid. He could make them spend their days searching the countryside for a missing boy instead of pursuing their regular lives.

Power. It was a great thing. Taking a woman would enhance it even though it wouldn't fulfill his mission. He'd done it twice before and found a wholly different kind of satisfaction.

Something to think about.

Rocking slowly, he smiled into the darkened room. Damn, he was good.

Chapter 3

Cade woke early in the morning, despite having sat up until just after two combing over every bit in the file with DeeJay. It was a sadly thin file, one they needed to pad out. But you could never be sure when some little item might open a door in your thinking.

He sat in the kitchen while coffee brewed, facts and details running around in his head like skittering mice. Not much in the way of pattern yet, not enough for predicting much.

Sighing, he rubbed his eyes. DeeJay, he reluctantly admitted, was turning out to be an okay partner. While she was absorbed in the job, she pulled in those bristles and became tolerable. Clearly a good detective, and he thanked God that she could put personalities aside for the sake of work. He didn't care what kind of hell she gave him otherwise, as long as they got this case solved before someone else's kid disappeared.

He understood what she meant about the sickening and sickened minds that became serial killers. He'd heard all the psychological theories about how they'd been abused kids, how many had suffered brain damage at some point. But any way he added it up, the world was full of people who'd been abused and brain damaged and they didn't commit crimes like this.

The idea that someone out there was enjoying all of this nearly made him want to resign from the human race.

The coffee finished brewing and he rose to get a cup. Kelly Jackson had been right: the place was decently furnished. Ready to use. He wondered if Jackson would rent it to tourists once the resort opened. People who couldn't afford the fancy hotel prices up on the mountain but might want to take a little house for a week as a base of operations.

He'd bought some sweet rolls when they stopped at the grocery for odds and ends, and as his stomach growled he brought out the package. Coffee and a cinnamon bun. It didn't get much better.

But then DeeJay showed up, rumpled in yesterday's clothes. Apparently the coffee had beat out an urge for a shower and clean togs.

"May I?" she asked.

"Help yourself. Coffee's community property. Rolls, too."

A faint smile curved one corner of her mouth. So it was possible. She didn't look pinched and disapproving, but maybe that was because she had just wakened. Give her time to ramp up, he thought, mildly amused.

She didn't say anything until she'd packed away a full mug of coffee and half a roll. Then she pushed her mussed hair back from her face and put her chin in her hands. Unlike most women, she didn't say the usual *I must look a fright*. Apparently, she didn't care.

"We didn't get a whole lot out of that file last night," she remarked.

"Unfortunately. Nothing of real predictive value, unless I missed something."

"Well, he seemed to accelerate just a little before it all stopped the first time, but these latest disappearances... He's spacing it. Unusual." Then she sighed again. "Three isn't a large enough sample set. There's some evidence of acceleration, but it's hard to be sure. If he's got that much self-control, we might have some time."

Most of these killers began to lose control of their impulses and act with increasing rapidity. So far this guy hadn't, not in any meaningful way.

"So in theory," she said, "we've got three weeks, a month, before his next move and next to nothing to go on. But we can't afford to count on that."

"I know. He could snatch and grab again this week if a victim appeals to him." And that was the devil of it. You could count on most serial killers to stick with a victim type, to stick to their ritual, whatever it was, but there was no sliding scale to accurately predict when they'd act again. Never.

DeeJay spoke again after a brief silence. "Imagine him hanging his trophies in that cargo netting in the woods. Like advertising. He had to have known they'd eventually be found."

"Maybe." He reached for another roll, then went to get the coffeepot and refilled both their mugs. "I need to know more about how many people go up into those mountains. Hikers and the like. Sooner or later someone would find it, obviously, but after a few years, how much would be left?"

"The netting would rot," she agreed. "It wasn't nylon

or plastic. If the bodies hadn't been wrapped in plastic, they wouldn't have found much as it was. Do you suppose he'd try that again in the winter?"

Cade thought about it. "He did it once before. Or maybe he kept some of his victims in cold storage until the weather got better."

"He could be doing that now." She shook her head. "He likes risks, but he's not stupid. My guess is he won't be hanging them in the woods this time."

Cade eyed her sharply. "Why?"

She shrugged one shoulder. "I bet he wasn't happy to lose his trophies."

"He must have known he was giving them up when he went away."

"Maybe, maybe not. He might have thought they'd never be found. Regardless, he knows they're gone now, and it wouldn't make him happy. He needs something more secure, and the way he hung the first ones seems to indicate a need to admire his trophies. To relive the experience."

Cade nodded. It was a common enough impulse among serial killers. That's why they kept trophies, to relive the emotional high they'd gotten. "How many serial killers have you studied who didn't accelerate?"

"None. I don't know whether the compulsion gets stronger or they start to feel invincible. I do know of some cases where they wanted to be caught and stopped. We don't know which kind we're dealing with here."

"I'm wondering because he came back. Gage is scouring the files for anyone who might have been picked up by the law five years ago and got released last spring or so. Nothing so far. But unless he was in prison, he chose to leave. That means he chose to come back here. That could be key."

"It could be." She ate another mouthful of roll and washed it down with coffee. "Thanks for these. A power bar doesn't sound good right now."

"My pleasure. We could get breakfast at the diner a little later when we go to see the sheriff. I guess search parties are going out again today, but he's not planning to be out there until this afternoon."

"They won't find anything." Her tone was almost sad. "So if he chose to come back, why? Unfinished business? Wanting to see if his trophies were still there? Thumbing his nose at the people around here? Because I'm not buying stupid."

"What kind of unfinished business?" he wondered.

Her dark eyes met his, looking almost hollow. "Who knows? But I'd wager it's personal. He's got something to settle, and he needs to settle it here. A demon's riding him."

"I'd call *him* a demon."

"No argument from me." She glanced at the digital clock on the stove front. "I guess I need to clean up to get ready for the day." She pushed back from the table, and a minute later he heard the wheels of her suitcase trundling down the hall to the bathroom.

Her eyes felt full of grit, but nights on short sleep were nothing new to DeeJay. A shower and some more coffee and she'd be fit. Plus some protein. Those rolls had been great, but she needed eggs and bacon to power up her brain.

She reached a decision in the shower, however. Cade Bankston wasn't all that bad. Maybe he hadn't wanted her as a partner for some reason, but nothing about him seemed misogynistic, at least when it came to work. They'd been cooperating like equals since last night, and she'd had enough of the other kind of relationship to appreciate it.

So okay, they could work together, which was a huge load off her shoulders.

The house seemed to have an ample hot water heater. She'd been living in a place where she'd invariably wound up rinsing the soap off in frigid water, no joke in winter Wyoming. She allowed herself an extra minute to luxuriate but, remembering that Cade might well want a shower, too, she sighed and stepped out, reaching for a folded towel from a stack on a shelf over the toilet.

Not bad for a cheap rental and a whole lot better than some of the motels her former job had put her in. Even the couch had been a satisfactory bed.

Little spots of color had been added to each room, as if the former occupant—Kelly?—had tried to inject some cheer. She figured her husband, Hank, had taken care of all that in the end.

When she finished dressing in jeans and a flannel shirt, and her combed, wet hair was tucked behind her ears, she closed her suitcase and stepped out. Men's voices reached her from the kitchen. It didn't sound like the sheriff.

Curious, she ditched her bag at the end of the couch and followed the sound. A strange man was there, and he rose to his feet instantly.

"DeeJay, this is our landlord Hank Jackson, Kelly's husband."

DeeJay shook the offered hand and smiled. "You have a nice wife."

"I think so." He smiled, a warm, unguarded expression. "But I'm the lucky one. So I was asking Cade here if you two need anything. Kelly left most stuff she used here, but you never know."

DeeJay pulled out the remaining chair and sat. Only

then did Hank sit. The way he stuck out one of his legs indicated he had some kind of old or new injury. Did all the men around here have broken bodies?

"I was just thinking," DeeJay said, "that this place has a great hot water heater. I was tempted to indulge."

Hank's smile widened. "I like my hot showers. I figured other folks would, too. It's a big tank."

"Then I'll enjoy the next one longer."

Cade spoke. "Hank was just saying that they're running another search party today. He's got to leave shortly."

"That's so sad about the boy," DeeJay said. What else could she say?

"This creep better hope I don't get to him first." Hank's face hardened. "Preying on the weak...I have no tolerance for it. None."

DeeJay could sympathize, but given that they were officers of the law... She glanced at Cade, wondering whether to let it pass. Before she could speak, however, he did it.

"You know, you've got a pregnant wife," Cade said.

"I know." Hank's face relaxed. "I won't turn into a vigilante. But sometimes you wish..."

"Yeah," DeeJay agreed. "Sometimes you do." And they were supposed to be travel writers, so she steered the conversation. "Are you planning to rent this place to people who come here to ski?"

"I might. Still need to do some work if I go that way. I rented it most of the summer to a couple who came out here to work on the resort. They're supposed to be back in the spring." He paused. "You going to write about this kidnapping in your article?"

DeeJay shook her head. "I'm sure it will all be solved. No, we're here to get to know the town a bit and pump up how this could be a great resort."

"Good," said Hank, pushing back from the table. "This

place has suffered enough since the semiconductor plant closed. We need more jobs and a better economy." Then he flashed a smile. "We're friendly folk here. Usually."

DeeJay smiled. "I'll try to keep that in mind. That Mavis at the diner is something else."

"Wait till you meet her mother, Maude. Mavis is still batting in the farm team."

They left the house a short while later with tablet computers in cases that also allowed them to carry small paper notebooks, pens and business cards. Handy little designs, suggesting they were serious writers. Also serious cops, but image was everything.

"The diner," said Cade. "I'll call Gage from there and find out when he can see us."

DeeJay climbed into her side of the car. She closed the door and waited until he had the engine running. "I hate being unarmed," she remarked.

He glanced at her. "Are you going to tell me you couldn't turn almost anything into a weapon?"

"Can you?"

"I've had to get inventive a few times."

"Me, too," she admitted. "But it still feels odd to be on the job without my service piece."

"Yeah." He pulled away from the curb and started down a street that was finally beginning to show some pavement. "Must be warming up. So if you don't mind me asking…?"

"Depends," she answered shortly.

Here came the bristles again. He decided to ignore them. "Why Wyoming? I hear you were with some big MP unit in investigations. Most of the kinds of cases we get out here will probably bore you to tears."

"I'm not bored right now," she pointed out. "And I'm

not an adrenaline junky. What about you? Are you bored? Why didn't you stay in Denver? At least I heard it was Denver."

She had turned it right back on him. She was as quick as she was evasive. Part of him was amused, and part of him argued that they had to find some trust to stand on if they were going to get through this. Trust in one's partner was essential.

Time to take the bull by the horns. "Look, we've got to work together. That means we have to be able to trust each other. You don't have to like me. I don't have to like you, but damn it, DeeJay, we've got to find some ground to meet on apart from the case. You have to believe I have your back and vice versa."

"Do you?"

Her answer made Cade angry. So that's how it was going to be. Wouldn't help anything, but they'd have to work around it. Then, just as they parked in front of the diner, she spoke again.

"My last commanding officer screwed me out of my career."

He froze. "Why?"

"Because I insisted on pushing a sensitive rape investigation. My performance report reflected my inability to follow orders. By the time he got done, I was lucky to resign honorably." Then she climbed out of the car and marched into the diner.

A half minute passed before Cade followed. Well, that explained a whole hell of a lot. And he heard more behind it. He would have bet the farm that the CO had simply been the final straw.

The place was crowded when he stepped inside, mostly younger men who were talking about the day's search party. DeeJay had somehow claimed a booth by the window, and he slid in across from her. The place was jumping, filled with voices, clattering crockery. He heard worry in the voices, but he heard anger, too. These men were ready to take the law into their own hands.

He looked across the table at DeeJay and saw her knuckles were almost white as she gripped the menu. She felt it, too, and was wondering what they could possibly do to help tone it down. Nothing. Not a thing. He could see her reach the same conclusion. He pulled out his cell phone and called the sheriff. He got the dispatcher, a crusty old crone with a froggy voice. "Tell Gage the writers are at the diner, but it might be wise for him to show up here pretty quick."

DeeJay surprised him. "Good call," she said.

The place was a cauldron, and it was getting ready to bubble over. Mavis swung by, dumping two cups and filling them with coffee before hurrying on. Breakfast was apt to take a while.

Then it happened. A male voice, right at the end of their booth, loud and challenging. "You those writers? You going to make yourselves famous on our problems?"

DeeJay barely looked up. He gave her credit for that. "We don't write that kind of stuff."

"No?" The guy leaned in. "Then what kind of crap do you write?"

In one smooth movement, DeeJay slid out of the booth and faced the guy. She was almost as tall as he was, and in that instant Cade glimpsed the MP, someone who could walk into a rowdy bar and take control.

"No," DeeJay said firmly, loud enough to be heard in much of the suddenly quieting diner. "We want to make your town look good. As long as you don't give me a reason to feel otherwise. Now we're both real sorry about the missing boy. But we're travel writers."

Cade enjoyed the show. It wasn't her words—it was her tone of voice and the way she stood. If that was command presence, she had it in spades.

The guy who had challenged her seemed to change his mind. "Sorry for disturbing your coffee, ma'am. We're all just real upset."

"I can understand that. You're good neighbors." Then she slid back into the booth.

Cade wondered if he'd get his head bitten off if he complimented her. He was still trying to decide when she said something surprising.

"Thanks for letting me handle that," she said.

"You did great. Never doubted it."

She shook her head a little. "Much as I hate to admit it, sometimes a woman has an advantage. Men don't usually want to hit me first. But you're a big guy. If you'd stood up, he would have felt challenged."

"You're right." He didn't tell her he'd have handled it without standing up at all. He was absolutely sure if he did, she'd take it wrong. Maybe he was learning a little about how to handle the prickly pear. Regardless, she'd done well and he was impressed.

Just then a piercing whistle cut through the room. Cade swiveled his head and saw that Dalton stood just inside the door, in full uniform, his jacket open so that the pistol on his hip was both visible and easy to reach.

"Searchers," he said, his raspy voice allowing no disagreement, "outside now. We need to get this day started. And while we're at it, I don't want to see any weapons."

"But…" someone said.

Gage shook his head. "Listen, Bob, we're all mad and upset, but I don't want to be carrying one of you to the morgue today. Or worse, some innocent ranch hand or hiker. We catch this guy fair and square or we're just murderers. Now get out there."

The men trailed out after him, leaving only a few very elderly types behind. Suddenly, Mavis asked what they wanted for breakfast. They both ordered large meals, then watched through the window as Gage handed out some further orders. Soon trucks were pulling away.

"He's good," DeeJay remarked.

"He's respected."

"I hope they listen about the guns."

"They'll be reminded at the staging areas, I'm sure."

Gage joined them just as they were being served large platters of bacon, eggs and toast. He pulled a chair from one of the tables, and Mavis promptly gave him a mug of coffee.

"You want a full breakfast or rolls?" she asked.

"Just rolls, Mavis. Thanks. My stomach's so knotted these days I'm in danger of losing my love handles." Mavis laughed, a deep, harsh sound, and wandered back to the kitchen.

"Thanks for calling me," Gage said to Cade. "I'm starting to feel like I'm sitting on a powder keg."

"You are," DeeJay answered. "They're looking for a way to burn off adrenaline."

"Well, the cold and hiking today ought to help with that. I hope."

Mavis delivered Gage's rolls, refilled coffee cups all around the diner, then vanished into the back. Quiet conversation resumed among the old men in their little corner.

"So," Gage said quietly, "I didn't bring over the vic photos. Obviously. I'll have Sarah Ironheart, one of my deputies, bring them over to the house later. I think you met her once, Gage."

"A long time ago, I believe."

"Well, you were never here very long. I doubt anyone remembers you."

"I sure as hell hope not."

"I was looking over them again this morning, along with the autopsy reports. Sarah will bring them, as well. But something struck me."

He looked at DeeJay a long moment, then at Cade. "These vics not only resemble each other—I guess that's not unusual for this kind of thing."

"Not at all," Cade agreed. "A lot of them seem to have a particular type they're after."

"In this case, dark-haired boys about five feet tall and lean. Small. But something struck me." Again his gaze trailed to DeeJay.

"What?" she asked.

"If you were ten inches shorter and a boy, you'd fit the victim profile." He pushed back from the table, carrying a roll with him and draining his mug as soon as he stood. "I've got to go ride herd at the staging areas. Talk to you later." He paused and looked again at DeeJay. "You be really careful, hear?"

Five minutes passed before either of them spoke again. They continued eating as if everything were perfectly normal. But Cade knew it wasn't, and since DeeJay had the same kind of training in these cases, he was sure she knew, as well.

But apparently she wasn't going to let it ruin her appetite, and it wasn't enough to make him lose his. They couldn't discuss it here anyway. Mavis was moving around again, clearing up dishes, and as much as the place had quieted down she could probably tune in on any conversation she wanted to.

Cade called out to Mavis. "Is it possible to get up any-where near the ski resort right now?"

She turned, frowned, then shook her head. "Might be a day or two. Work was called off during the storm and that's a lot of road to clear. The construction office is in the phone book. Look for Masters General Contracting."

"Thanks, Mavis."

"God," mumbled DeeJay as Mavis disappeared with another load of dishes, "a world where people still use the phone book."

Cade had to laugh. "I know. How about I just plug it into my phone or tablet."

He saw the smile flicker over her face. The woman was thawing a bit. Thank God.

"I wonder how long we'll have to wait for this deputy."

"Not long," Cade judged. "Gage wants something out of us as soon as possible. He's going to grease the skids as much as he can."

She nodded and at last pushed her plate to one side. "I'm going to need to work out twice a day for a month if I keep eating here. But it's good."

"And filling," he agreed. "We can hit the grocery later and find some healthier stuff. When we're out making like travel writers."

"Pretending to be travel writers still seems ridiculous. We have to ask the kinds of questions that have nothing to do with the case."

"On the other hand, everyone seems more than will-ing to talk about it with us. Natural interest will give us the chance to ask questions."

"I hope so."

Mavis returned, and they paid their bill, then once again headed back toward the house. As they drove, Cade mentioned Gage's warning. "Do you think that was over-the-top? I mean, you're a heck of a lot taller than the victims, plus you're female."

"I'm not going to worry about it," she said. "I'm not a victim. I can take care of myself. Can't blame the guy for being hypercautious right now."

"I guess not," Cade answered, winding them along streets that in places looked like they ought to be on a Christmas card. She might brush it aside, but Cade couldn't quite. The history of serial killers was filled with people who broke out of their supposed patterns at times. For example, the guy who killed only teenage girls until he killed his mother. But those things usually involved a long relationship fraught with emotional problems.

So, while it wasn't likely the killer would even notice DeeJay, he resolved to keep a sharp eye out. "Just don't get cocky," he said.

He should have known she would bridle. "I don't get cocky, Cade. I know what I'm capable of."

Maybe she did. He still knew next to nothing about her. But then, he wasn't exactly sharing himself, either.

It bothered him, too, that they were stuck in this partnership, because despite all her thorns and prickliness, she attracted him sexually, almost mercilessly. He kept finding himself wondering if she reciprocated. Then he'd yank his thoughts back into line and remind himself: job first. Besides, if they ever broke those barriers, he was certain it would be a flaming mess.

"You know," she said as they neared their house, "this kind of work is ever so much easier when we can just step in and help the team. We're at a fits and starts position because we can't cozy up to the local law too much. That's slowing everything down."

"I know." He couldn't argue with that. "But like I said, I think Gage is greasing skids as much as he can. Probably putting it around that we check out okay so folks won't be worried about us, but it remains…"

"I know," she agreed. "We don't want to scare the guy off."

He pulled the car to a stop in front of the house and cocked an eye at her. "Are you of the rush-in-and-bash-heads school?"

"Only when necessary."

Which probably said a whole lot about her, he decided. She could operate in multiple modes. Now that was useful.

She looked at him. "You?"

"Only when necessary."

She gave a brisk nod and climbed out. Damn, he thought, this woman didn't give an inch. A spine of steel and a ramrod with it. Of course, just that little bit she'd said about her CO ruining her career was enough, and he somehow figured that was just the tip of the iceberg. Something had made this woman tough, and even a bit difficult to deal with.

He hoped he'd find out eventually what her story was. He also hoped that wouldn't involve sharing his own.

They'd barely had time to start another pot of coffee—Cade was in favor of bottomless coffee, and Dee-Jay seemed to share his liking—when someone knocked at the door.

This time, aware of her apparent sensitivities to dominating men, he let DeeJay get it.

She came back inside with a woman in civvies. Long inky hair dashed by a few streaks of silver and pulled back in a ponytail. Sarah Ironheart, the deputy Gage had promised. Native American was stamped even more clearly on her face than DeeJay's. A striking woman.

"Brought the photos and autopsy reports," she said,

tossing a thick envelope on the table. "All the gruesome glory." She took a seat at the table as easily as if she'd been there before and nodded affirmatively in answer to Cade's question about coffee. "It fuels the world, and any excuse I can get not to drink Velma's, I'll take."

"Who is Velma?" DeeJay asked.

"One of our dispatchers. Her coffee is enough to put a hole in your stomach but she's so much of a fixture no one dares tell her. It's rumored she's going to die right at the dispatch desk."

"Sounds like a character," Cade remarked.

"She's been around as long as the mountains." Sarah sipped coffee, then regarded the two of them over the rim. "What else are you hoping for, after you review the autopsies?"

"Any information at all. The file is kind of sketchy, what we've seen so far."

Sarah nodded. "The whole thing is sketchy. We had five boys disappear over nearly two years the last time. Now there's lots of ways to go missing around here, and we couldn't find a clue. We had search parties out, like now, and never found a thing. Kids run away from home, even here. You know that. They also wander off into the mountains and sometimes we don't find them. Could have been a lot of things until we started to realize they were all the same physical type. Different in age, but physically similar." She sighed. "That doesn't hit you at first."

"It wouldn't," DeeJay agreed. "Not at first."

"Just after it really sank in what we were dealing with, and that it was happening faster, it all stopped. Then nobody was sure it wasn't all runaways and accidents until a surveyor for the new resort stumbled on the trophy stash the spring before last."

"Then you knew," DeeJay said quietly.

"Then we knew," Sarah agreed. "What we never expected was that it would start up again after all this time. We figured he'd moved on, or gone to jail on some other offense elsewhere. He wraps his victims in plastic to protect them, so we know we found our missing boys. Now this. People want blood. Be careful."

Cade spoke. "Gage has been good about trying to establish us."

"He's working on it," Sarah agreed. "But folks are still angry and there's no telling how they might lash out. Of course, I don't need to tell you that." She rose and went to get more coffee, a woman who would be familiar anywhere.

When she returned to the table, she leaned back in the chair and crossed her legs. "I assume you guys have some training in profiling?"

"For what it's worth," DeeJay answered.

Cade watched a smile walk slowly across Sarah Ironheart's face. "Yeah, for what it's worth. Not much to go on at first."

"Not really," Cade answered. "Not until we've got some evidence. The thing about the training is that it makes you alert to things that others might overlook. It's not like we can walk in and hand you a sketch and description of our perp."

"Anybody did that, and I'd question his know-how," she answered. "Okay then. Only two of us in the department apart from Gage know who you really are. The other is Micah Parish. You'll know him when you see him. Huge guy with Cherokee written all over his face. Former Special Ops. He may be getting up there, but he's still damn good. Beyond that, nobody knows."

She paused. "Gage may also tell the former sheriff, Nate Tate. Nobody sneezes in this county without him hearing about it. But right now, I don't know if Gage will bring him in. He's an invaluable source about the people around here, though."

"Then I hope Gage tells him," DeeJay said.

"Another good source if you have any need to delve into local history is Gage's wife, Emmaline Dalton. Miss Emma, everyone calls her. Anyway, she's the librarian and she's got roots here back to the earliest days, plus she's made gathering local history and lore her avocation. I'm not sure how she could be of use, but you never know."

She drained her coffee and stood. "Oh, and if you need horses, my husband raises and trains them. Gideon. I'm sure he could spare a couple of good mounts if you want to go wandering off the roads."

She left directly, telling them that she'd probably be the one to bring them any additional information they uncovered. "Less suspicious than the sheriff. Gideon has a business in trail rides I could claim to be trying to promote." Indeed, she left them with Gideon's business card. "He always knows how to find me."

Then she was gone, and the house filled with silence. Neither Cade nor DeeJay moved for a minute, as they both absorbed everything they'd just been told.

"Masters General Contracting," Cade said presently, and pulled out his notebook. "I hope there's Wi-Fi around here somewhere."

"You could always call directory information."

He cocked a brow at her. "What, go back to the old days?" Then he shook his head. "Might as well. Maybe I can find out how to get us a decent internet connection while I'm tiptoeing through the Yellow Pages."

A laugh actually escaped DeeJay. "You do that. Meanwhile I'm going to take a look at this file."

He reached for the wall phone just as she bent the

prongs on the envelope and opened it. One way or another, it wasn't going to be a pleasant day.

Wyoming was a big state, not heavily populated. The state police often relied on satellite radio because there were so many places, especially in the mountains, with cellular dead zones. It was virtually impossible at times to maintain an internet connection. Things were changing, but the change was far from complete.

By two that afternoon, they were hooked into the local police's Wi-Fi and able to map out the town and surrounding county. They both saved the maps to files on their computers.

The envelope contents were another matter altogether. Report after report of horror, accompanied by eight photos of boys who were at once strikingly similar and strikingly different. All had dark hair, all weighed less than a hundred pounds, all were short in stature—a definite type. The heartache arose not only for the terror they must have endured, but from the youth staring back at them from those photos. Lives had been stolen and many other lives had been torn apart.

"Slow asphyxiation," Cade read from the last report. He made a sound of angry disgust and swept everything from the table back into the envelope.

DeeJay simply stared back at him. There were no words for this. None. Her stomach churned, and all the toughness she had donned over the years provided no protection against what she had just read.

She got up from the table, trying to pace off the anger and horror she felt. "It's not like anything else," she said, not sure what she meant, not expecting an answer.

"No, it's not," Cade agreed. "Damn, I need some fresh

air. Do you want to walk to the market? It's only thirteen degrees out there."

"I need the walk but I also need my nose. And I don't want to stiffen up from the cold." Delayed reaction time could be dangerous, even when you thought you were safe.

"Agreed. We'll drive. Damn, there's no hole in hell hot enough or deep enough for this guy."

She didn't answer. It seemed pointless. After looking at all those young faces, this had become personal. It was no longer an intellectual detective exercise. "Dangerous," she remarked a few minutes later as they climbed into their car. "Getting involved."

"I know. I'll work it off."

"I feel the same way."

He looked at her as he turned over the ignition. At least the car didn't decide it was too cold to run. He needed to remember to plug the damn block heater in tonight. "You, too."

"Of course, me, too," she said hotly. "I'm not made of ice."

"Didn't think you were."

"Then what the hell did you mean?"

"Just trying to make conversation. You're like a brick wall, Dawkins. Pleasant to strangers when it suits you, but you act like I'm a cow patty you'd like to brush off."

"You weren't exactly glad to have me for a partner," she retorted.

He didn't deny it, and she sat with her arms tightly folded as he drove them to the store. When they found a place to park between two snowdrifts, Cade set the brake but left the car running. The defroster began to lose the battle against their breath.

"Look," he said finally, "my reaction had nothing to do with you. It had to do with something from my past.

Probably the same as your reaction to me. So how about we call a truce at least until we catch this animal."

"That gives animals a bad name."

"True."

He waited, and she knew she was going to have to answer. She didn't have to explain, she realized. No heart-to-heart about what life had been like as a female cop. He probably didn't want to share whatever his problem was, either. So if they could just take all the junk off the table, at least until they finished this job, they'd get by. "Some things matter more than others," she finally said. This job mattered more than her feelings, certainly. "Truce."

"Good enough," he said. "Now let's go squabble about what we want to make for dinner. The diner's steak sandwiches and fries are great, but too many of them and I'll be rolling down the street like a beach ball."

She laughed because she had to. A similar thought had occurred to her. "Are you aware that bicyclists who ride in races can be slowed down by as little three kilograms of added weight?"

"Interesting. Well, the two of us could be slowed down by the fat. I think I feel my arteries hardening."

The tension had seeped away, and they both climbed out of the car, walking through the cutting wind toward the grocery entrance.

"What kind of cook are you?" she asked.

"Passable. I'd starve otherwise. You?"

"Not so good. Too many chow hall meals. Lately I've been trying my hand at it. How brave are you?"

He laughed. "I'll cook. As long as you don't expect high cuisine."

Chapter 4

Fifty miles away, on his remote ranch, Calvin sat at the plank table that was as old as everything else here and tried to battle down his need to act. Every time he thought he'd won, it would steadily rise again.

He wondered if this was like some kind of acid trip. Colors became brighter, things almost seemed outlined in light. Except he hadn't taken any acid, so it must be the power flowing through him, the power he had gleaned from the lives of all those young boys. The power he had taken, the power over life and death. The blazing purity he had given them.

Regardless, it was bugging him much too soon. He absolutely had to be patient. He was certain they'd already figured out he was active in the area again. Three boys would be enough to tell them he'd returned. Caution had to be the order of the day, and he couldn't afford to take another boy so soon.

There were plenty of books out there about people like

him, and while he was away he'd read some of them. It had seemed important to discover where they had gone wrong, what had brought them to an end. Some had just disappeared, but some had been caught. In the case of Bundy, caught more than once.

It wouldn't do to get cocky. It wouldn't do to let the impulse and urge control *him*, because almost without fail, that's where others like him had made their big mistakes. Not all, but enough to act as a warning.

Maybe what he needed to do was break his routine. Find a different type of victim. It wouldn't be as satisfying, but he wondered how long he'd be able to hold out against the need that made his nerves burn like fire. Maybe he could quench it temporarily with a killing that would confuse them.

He pushed that to the back burner for now and clenched and unclenched his fists. Confusing the trail would be good, but it might not quiet his need.

"You're a bad boy, Calvin."

He jerked, then realized he was still alone. He often heard his mother's voice in his head, reminding him that he should be punished. She'd punished him quite freely and quite often. His approaching puberty had seemed to set her off. She thought he was dirty and needed cleansing. Maybe so. He admitted he'd had naughty thoughts and had done naughty things, and when she caught him she punished him.

Those boys he took were undoubtedly guilty of the same naughtiness. They were all about the age. So he was saving them from the filth his mother had never quite managed to expunge from him.

He was keeping them pure.

A sense of righteousness visited him, easing the need

to hunt, at least a little. He was continuing the good work. Taking a different kind of victim would not serve that goal.

But it might be useful.

At last the familiar aura receded and the world returned to its normal dull colors. He was powerful enough to control it. Strength seemed to infuse him.

He glanced at the clock and saw that it was nearly time for him to head to work at the crisis center. More good work to do until he found his next opportunity for a cleansing.

Dory was a good woman, and friendly when time allowed. He enjoyed her company, and had decided to forgive her for never guessing the humiliation and pain his mother had inflicted on him. Why blame her when everyone else had been just as blind?

But thoughts of taking a woman again, as he had twice before, danced around the edges of his thoughts. Finally, he made a silent agreement with himself. If he saw a woman and she brightened as if she glowed, he would know that she was chosen. If that happened, he'd find a way to take her.

"A snorkel hood would be best for this weather," DeeJay remarked to Cade as they walked down the main street of town in the late afternoon.

"Undoubtedly," he answered. "You willing to sacrifice that much peripheral vision?"

"Never."

He chuckled. "Time for a ski mask. Then all we can freeze is our eyeballs."

He pointed out the mercantile and they wandered inside. Still pretending to be travel writers. A middle-aged woman came up to them and asked if she could help.

"Ski masks," Cade said. "I swear the temperature has dropped twenty degrees since noon."

"You wouldn't be wrong," the woman answered. "Are you the travel writers?"

"The same," DeeJay answered, looking around. Only another cop would recognize how she was casing the place, not simply staring with pleasure. "I love your store. How old is it? Oh, by the way, I'm DeeJay and this is my husband, Cade."

"Mary Carliss," the woman answered, smiling. "This is a fun place to rummage around in. It's nearly as old as the town. We have a little bit of everything, although that's probably going to change when the resort opens."

DeeJay immediately became sympathetic. "Why should it change? I'm a visitor and I love it. I think stores like this were gone about the time I was born. Wooden floors! That alone is a charm worth saving."

Mary evidently agreed, warming to her. "I get that things have to change. The resort will be good for a lot of people. But it would be a shame to sacrifice our whole way of life to it. And this place is a landmark around here."

"I can certainly see why," Cade remarked. "If it's not available here, it doesn't exist."

Mary laughed. "Not quite. But we have what our customers need. I suppose people who come to ski will need something else altogether."

"They'll probably have ski shops and things like that at the resort, won't they? Did they say they were going to change the town?"

Mary shook her head. "Not exactly. I hear we're going to get brick sidewalks and new streetlights. A face-lift is what they're saying, but they claim they don't want to change the character of the town." She lowered her voice a bit. "I don't quite believe it. I've been to a couple of ski towns."

DeeJay nodded. "So have I. But some of them were built just for skiers, weren't they? This place has a real history. Maybe they can find a way to take advantage of it without making you all miserable."

Mary brightened a hair. "Well, if you say good things about us the way we are, I'm sure that'll help."

Cade felt pretty bad just then about their deception. But it was necessary, he reminded himself, and they had a killer to find.

"Let me take you to the ski masks," Mary said. "Then you can wander around and if you have any questions, just ask." She hesitated. "You're not writing about those boys who disappeared, are you?"

"Purely travel," DeeJay answered. "I know everyone's worried, but surely they'll solve this soon."

"They didn't solve it last time," Mary said darkly. "I can't believe it started up again. Everyone's angry and a whole lot are afraid. People with kids are terrified. Can't blame them."

"But you have a good sheriff," Cade said.

"Good enough. But it seems to some of us like he ought to bring the old sheriff in on this. When that man was in office, we had things happen like any place else, but nothing like this."

DeeJay spoke quietly. "You can hardly blame the sheriff for what a crazy man does."

Mary seemed almost to shake herself. "No, of course not. Just upset that they haven't solved this."

Left to their own devices in front of stacks of knitted watch caps and ski masks, they each selected one of both. Anything that blocked vision or hearing was off the table, so they skipped the earmuffs even though Cade thought

DeeJay eyed them with longing. Then she did something that made absolutely no sense to him.

She bought a touristy bright blue hoodie with the outline of mountains stamped on it and the words Where The Mountains Never End on the back.

He didn't say a word, though, until they'd paid and were outside.

"A hoodie? What good will that do you?" he asked while he pawed in his bag for the ski mask he'd just bought. Mary had been kind enough to clip the tags off.

"That house gets drafty," she answered. "Besides, Mary was nice and I wanted to make her feel as if we enjoyed the visit to the store."

"Didn't we?"

"Not by half," she said, pulling her own ski mask on and tugging her jacket hood up. "So people are bad-mouthing Gage Dalton."

"Don't they always when the cops haven't solved the crime yet?"

"Do they? Probably. Maybe they just never said it to my face."

"A lot of people wouldn't want to say anything critical to your face," he remarked with amusement. He was sure he hadn't been the only one treated to her thorns.

She faced him. "You got something to say to me, Bankston?"

He sighed. His breath came out in a white cloud. "I was joshing." Partly. But damned if he was going to argue with her on the street. "I thought we had a truce. Remind me that one of the terms of armistice is to tiptoe."

She looked away from him for a moment, then said, "Sorry. This whole situation is…well, it's not what I'm used to. I seem to need a whole new set of coping skills."

"You're not the only one," he admitted. "I've never dealt

with a serial killer before. Wyoming doesn't seem to be the most popular destination for them."

"Given this cold? I wonder anyone comes here."

"You want to look around more or head back? If you're getting hungry, then we should head back. Baking potatoes takes a while."

She turned in a slow circle, surveying the storefronts, the sheriff's office just down the darkened street, the courthouse, the church even farther down. The town appeared dead. "Things like this shouldn't happen in a place like this. And if you tell anyone I said something that stupid, you'll pay."

Truth was, though, he kind of knew what she meant. "Big cities, sprawling suburbs," he agreed. "Although there was that guy in Appalachia…"

"Don't remind me," she said, but sounded down.

"Time for food," he judged. "This cold sucks the energy right out."

"It just plain sucks," she said bluntly.

He laughed for the next half block until they reached their car.

The potatoes were in the oven, the steaks sitting on a platter in the fridge. He had promised to broil them rather than fry them, but DeeJay didn't know how she was going to eat a baked potato without a lot of sour cream or butter. Maybe the diner wasn't that bad at all. Sitting in one of those booths, they'd at least have had their ears to the ground.

She stared at the envelope on the table, the one that Sarah Ironheart had left with them. She ran her fingers lightly over it, wondering if she should make herself read it once more. She didn't know if she could stomach it.

She'd seen plenty of horrible stuff in the army, but kids? This was in a class of its own.

A chill snaked down her back and she went to get her new hoodie from the bag in the living room. She pulled it on as she walked back to the kitchen, where she found Cade as mesmerized by that envelope as she had been.

"Did we miss something?" he muttered as she took her seat.

"I don't know. He's got to be doing something that someone's noticed. Nobody is that good."

"But if he blends into the local scenery..." He left the thought incomplete. "Maybe we should talk to the old sheriff. You heard what Ironheart said. Nobody sneezes without him knowing."

"If he knew anything, he'd already have said so," Dee-Jay argued. "But I'm not opposed to talking with him if Dalton okays it."

"Sometimes the right line of questioning can pull out stuff people don't realize they know."

"True. When you figure out the right tack to take, let me know. I feel like I'm blindfolded here, and I don't like it."

Neither did he. "With one hand tied behind my back," he added.

"Of course. Undercover. It may make the perp feel safer, but it's not making me happy."

"He disappeared once before," Cade reminded her.

"I know. We don't want that to happen again. God knows how many kids he may have killed the last five years. We've got to stop him. A clue would be nice beyond the similarity of his victims."

"And that damn cargo netting. I give him points for originality on that one. There's all kinds of ways to keep trophies, but this one is unprecedented."

"As far as we know, but yeah." She drummed her fingers, resting her chin in her hand. "Was there anything unusual about that netting? And if he's into displaying his trophies that way, maybe we should find out if anyone around here recently purchased netting of some kind. And lots of plastic."

"I think they're already looking into that, but let me check with Gage. I'll ask him about the old sheriff, too. What's his name?"

"Tate."

Cade reached for the wall phone. Landlines were more secure. DeeJay listened to his half of the conversation and picked up most of what she needed to know. The cargo net had been sent for forensics and had revealed nothing. It had been out in the Wyoming weather for too long, plus it was a standard type of netting readily available for a lot of purposes. No sign that anyone in the area had recently purchased any kind of strong net, but that was being looked into. As for the plastic, standard paint drop cloths available at a million places around the country.

"God," she said when he hung up. "This guy read the books."

"So it seems. Gage agreed to bring Tate in on this. We'll get a call from Tate, probably this evening."

Cade proved he was better than average at cooking. The steaks were perfectly broiled, medium rare. Potatoes done to perfection. Frozen broccoli seasoned with a hint of mustard powder, softening the sharp taste.

DeeJay tried to go light on the butter, but finally gave up. She wanted to enjoy this potato, damn it, and this whole meal.

They seemed to reach a silent agreement not to discuss the case while they ate. A good thing, too, because she had been beginning to wonder if the knot in her stomach would ever go away.

The food also gave her an excuse not to look at Cade, which she realized she had begun to do more often than necessary. Not only did he have those amazing aquamarine eyes, but his face was perfectly proportioned with a strong jaw, and just enough weathering to make him appealing to her. He was an awfully attractive man, and her motor hummed a little when she looked at him and wasn't thinking about the case. Hummed more than a little. It remained, though, that he was a man and therefore couldn't fully be trusted. Sooner or later, most of them proved to be egotistical idiots. She needed to focus solely on the investigation. It would keep her safe, and, more importantly, kids' lives were at risk.

"So, generally speaking," Cade said, "what's it like being a military cop?"

"Interesting," she said, which even she realized was a conversation ender, possibly even rude. It said nothing at all. She hesitated, torn between the need to keep her distance and the need to keep this partnership working. "I started out low in the ranks pretty much like everyone else. Doing the standard stuff—guarding, traffic, that kind of thing. But then I took a test and they decided I'd make a great investigator."

"I thought you were an officer."

"It doesn't happen often, but I finished my degree in criminology. There was another test I took, and my CO at the time recommended me for officer training."

"He must have thought highly of you."

"I was a pain in the butt to him. You could say I got promoted up instead of out."

A smile danced across his face, and she allowed herself a dangerous moment to notice how appealing he was. Wrong time, wrong place, but what the hell.

"So were you routinely a pain in the patootie?"

"Mostly. But I kept solving cases so, at least for a while, I was fairly untouchable. I couldn't let things slide. I'm not the type. I'm cursed with a sense of justice."

"That's not a bad thing."

"That depends." She put her fork down and looked squarely at him. "You've been a cop for a while. You must have run up against cases that weren't politically expedient to pursue."

"Not many. I take it you ran into that a lot."

"The military is an interesting organization. Everything is about hierarchy and promotions. Not so much in the enlisted ranks, but when you get to the officer corps you learn that some people are important. They've got connections, they've got rank, they're being groomed for flag rank, whatever. Very political in a lot of ways. I stepped on those toes."

"How?"

"I insisted on investigating and pushing for charges against rapists. A lot of ranking officers wanted to sweep it under the rug. It didn't look good to admit that stuff like that was happening under their command. It looked even worse when they tried to scare the victims into not reporting the rape. When I got wind of it, I wouldn't let it go. It's kind of a good-old-boys network, and they weren't happy with me."

He nodded but didn't say anything. What could he say anyway? she wondered. She knew enough to realize that a lot of cops weren't good about investigating rape even in civilian life.

"And finally you stepped on the wrong toes?"

"They were all wrong," she admitted. "But when I

brought in an indisputable case against a young officer who'd actually committed the rape against an enlisted woman, my days were numbered. I get that being at war for long stretches can turn people into animals, but…" She shrugged and finally said, "If you don't insist on some rules, all you have is a mob. Justice."

"So why did this guy turn out to be so problematic?"

"General's son. You'd have thought I'd taken a dump on the family escutcheon. They wanted me to bury it and I wouldn't. JAG brought him up on charges. And that's when I got the killer performance report."

"One report was enough to ruin you?"

She sliced off another piece of steak. "That's all it takes. But there never would have been another good one after that. No more promotions, either. I had a reputation by then and that was it. I could either resign my commission and get out honorably or I could wait for them to find an excuse to ruin the rest of my life. And they'd have found it."

He was silent for a few seconds. "That stinks."

"Well, I'm here now, still doing the kind of work I want to do, and I'm more interested in catching this killer than worrying about my former career."

"But it left scars."

She could feel her eyes go hollow. This was an area she wasn't comfortable discussing. Emotions. They were tenuous and dangerous. "I really don't like men," she said flatly.

"I can see why."

She gave him points for not saying he was different. She'd heard that countless times, but saying it didn't make it so. A guy needed to prove it to her, and few enough had.

They were silent through the rest of the meal, leaving DeeJay entirely too much time to ponder the unhappy fact that there was one man she wanted to like and he was sitting right across from her.

Despite having been raped during her first year in uniform, despite having watched her superiors sweep it under the rug and even threaten her—and she'd been young enough then to be scared by those threats—she didn't have a hang-up about sex. Sex and rape were very different things. No, she had a hang-up about men. She lived with wanting something from a man and being afraid to even try for it. Not that it mattered. They were on a job and had to remain strictly professional. Nothing else could be allowed to muddy the waters.

Cade had cooked, so DeeJay washed the dishes. Just as she was finishing up, the wall phone rang and Cade grabbed it. Holding a dish towel, she turned around and waited. Once again in the middle of the table was the thick envelope, and added to it was the file they had brought with them. She had a feeling they'd be poring over it again before the night was over. On a case like this, the only break you could afford was for sleep and a meal. Too much hung in the balance.

"Okay, see you then," he said, and hung up. "Well, that was the old sheriff. Nate Tate will be here in about thirty minutes."

"I hope we can learn something from him."

He nodded. "What's killing me is that we can't go out and ask the kind of questions we need to. On the other hand, maybe we need to pull together a list of them for Gage and his deputies. Tell him what we need."

"We should have thought of that right off the bat," she agreed.

"Well, what can you expect? We still didn't know what if anything they already knew. Hard to make a list of questions under those circumstances. But now that we've seen everything they have…" He shrugged. "We probably should have turned this case down."

DeeJay surprised herself by laughing. "Yeah, right. You strike me as a man who could walk away from this and let someone else handle it."

His mouth framed a crooked smile. "Careful, DeeJay. I might get the idea that you like me."

She turned around to hang up the towel, ending that line of conversation. She was grateful that he didn't pursue it.

Nate Tate proved to be a fit man in his late sixties, with dark hair going gray. He had a folksy, friendly manner, but something in his dark eyes suggested to DeeJay that he could turn to steel in an instant.

"Sorry to take so long," he said. "We're babysitting grandchildren, and I had an infant falling asleep in my arms. That must not be disturbed."

"Of course not," Cade said as they shook hands. He introduced DeeJay, who shook Tate's hand, as well. "Coffee?"

"Never say no to that."

"And it's not Velma's," DeeJay tried to joke.

"Ah, you've heard about Velma's coffee. Woman doesn't even guess she's famous for that awful brew, but the department would be lost without her."

They gathered in the living room, away from the toxic files, and Tate took the easy chair, leaving the sofa for the two of them.

"So you're what the state sent us," he remarked. "Think I met you once before, Cade."

"You did, at a conference. It's good to see you again, Sheriff."

"Just Nate. There's only one sheriff in this county. All these years and Gage is still the *new* sheriff. I tease him about it, but he seems resigned."

"How long were you sheriff here?" Cade asked.

"Nigh on forty years."

"Hard for someone to step into your shoes."

"Only in some minds."

"More minds than usual right now," DeeJay said.

"I've been hearing a bit of that," Nate agreed. "Don't like it. It's not fair to Gage or the department. What's more, I've been saying for years this county is going to hell in a handbasket. Why wouldn't we eventually get a serial killer? Had damn near everything else."

He sipped his coffee, then set his mug down on the side table. "I'm not sure what I got to offer, but you name it and if I can it's yours. I've been mad enough to split a gut before, but this beats all."

DeeJay nodded. "I couldn't agree more. We hear you're tightly plugged into this county. You know everything."

"Most everything," he corrected. "If someone really wants to keep a secret, I probably wouldn't know. I've been working over things in my head. We all know the basic profile, but it's so general. Young guy, probably white, probably abused as a kid, maybe some head injury...thing is, I could point to hundred guys around here. Child abuse happens here as much as anywhere. Kids get thrown from horses or bang their heads other ways."

"What about somebody who went away for around five years and came back?" Cade asked the question and it settled in the room like a pall.

"Gage is working on that," Nate replied. "Thing is, youngsters leave looking for a better life. Then when all those jobs opened up at the ski resort last year, a whole bunch of them came back. Maybe forty or fifty. I didn't take a head count. Most of them the right age."

"So, many came back for a temporary job?" DeeJay asked. She seemed ready to leap on that.

"Not temporary," Nate said. "You need to talk to Luke Masters, the guy who's heading up the whole thing. These folks were promised they'd get trained for other work once construction is finished. According to Luke, this company prefers to hire locally because employees stay."

"Hell," said DeeJay. "That almost looked like a clue."

Nate nodded. "Crossed my mind, too. Then we got a number of others who finished sowing their wild oats and came home to work the family land. Kind of a dribble, but still there. Moving away and coming back isn't exactly unheard-of around here. Hell, I did the same thing myself back when. Did my six years for Uncle Sam, then came to stay put. You'll find a few of those around here, too. We're getting our vets back from the wars. Now, you could look for head injuries there, I suppose."

DeeJay shook her head. "I'm not going to sift that way."

"She's army," Cade said.

At that, Nate smiled faintly.

"That's not what I meant," DeeJay said sharply. "Not because they're vets, but because that's a limiting sieve for this thing. We can't afford to limit the search too much without better information. Besides, at his heart this creep is a coward. Picking on small boys. A real coward."

"Or a driven man," Nate remarked. "Either way, it doesn't strike me that he'd fit too well in a uniform. This sumbitch likes to write his own rules."

Nate reached for his mug, drinking some more coffee, clearly thinking. DeeJay let him, and Cade didn't say a word.

Then Nate asked, "You ever hear of a killer hanging his trophies like that before?"

Both DeeJay and Cade shook their heads. "Doesn't mean it never happened," DeeJay remarked. "Just that we don't know about it."

"I've been doing a lot of thinking about that cargo netting. It was made of rope, which meant it was old. Now at one time or another we can have call for stuff like that around here. So it's not a clue by itself. Anyone could have had some of that lying around in a barn or shed. It was big enough to be used to cover a flatbed for a truck, or to keep bales of hay in line for some reason. Probably a hundred other uses. But it's still an interesting choice. Why hang them on the netting? Why not line them up somewhere he could look at them from time to time?"

Cade spoke. "It's interesting that he put them outside, too. Why not a basement or something like that?"

"Because," DeeJay said, "there was someone at home who might have discovered them. He put them as far as he could to keep them out of sight, and it worked for years. But he also had to be able to reach them to enjoy them."

Cade leaned forward. "Now I'm wondering if he might have come back a few times to take a look."

"I'm sure he did when he came back for good," Dee-Jay answered.

Nate spoke. "Never would have found 'em except for the resort surveyor. Bet he didn't plan on that. You think he's still hanging them outdoors? In these temperatures they wouldn't leave an infrared signature. Too cold."

"But *he* might," said DeeJay. "If he's hanging them in the woods again." She sighed and reached for her own coffee. "I can't imagine the expense of trying to keep infrared eyes on all that territory. Then you'd have to pick out the wildlife… Hopeless."

"But what I've been thinking," Nate said, "was that using the cargo netting is so weird it must have some kind of meaning to him. Which ain't no help at all if you're not a mind reader. It might just have been the handiest way to hang the bodies in one place."

He rose, saying he had to get back to his grandchildren. "My wife loves 'em, but she's getting to a point where they can drain her fast. Me, too, come to that. Wish I had the energy of a toddler." Laughing, he zipped his jacket as he headed to the door. Then, just before he opened it, he paused.

"I'll keep thinking on it," he said. "I reckon I don't think about much else these days, except the grandkids."

Then he stepped out into the icy night. Even after the door closed, the frigid air hung in the small entry. Dee-Jay shivered again.

"He's right," she said.

"About what?"

"That cargo netting. I'd almost bet it's part of his ritual. Scene setting."

Their eyes met, and she could almost see the wheels spinning inside his head. "Damn, don't I feel like a fool," he said finally.

"Why? It was Tate who mentioned the netting, and I think he's right. We never saw the original scene—we never got to evaluate it forensically or psychologically. Everyone assumed it was just a handy way to display his trophies for his own pleasure. We've been working from files and some photos that are less than great."

She headed to get more coffee and take another look at the files. A new perspective. Cade was right behind her.

"Scene setting," he repeated. "Now if we can just figure it out."

They'd have a better insight into their perp, but it wouldn't necessarily provide any useful answers. Still.

She sat across from him. The coffeepot now resided at one end of the table. "All right, let's review it as scene setting. And frankly, I was getting hellaciously creeped out by the photos of the vics they found last time. Wrapped in plastic for preservation is one thing. Wrapping them so that their faces can be seen is another. Let's add that to the scene setting."

"You're on," he said, reaching for the forensics envelope.

Across town, Calvin Sweet was halfway through his shift on the crisis line. It was a quiet night, as many were, but some of his coworkers had warned him that as winter lengthened and the temperatures dropped even lower, that would change. Cabin fever would set in for some. They'd start getting depressed. Or domestic fights would break out.

He wished the lines would light up. He needed the distraction. His own thoughts kept pushing him toward the hunt, the next take, the next victim. It was almost as if seeing all his old trophies gone, he had a big hole to fill, and the sooner the better.

His hands tightened into fists until his knuckles whitened. Moving too soon would break the pattern, not necessarily bad, but it *would* signify a loss of control. He might make a mistake and he couldn't afford that. Everything had to be just so, and he couldn't risk some kind of sloppiness that could eventually reveal him.

But he was waging one hell of an internal battle.

"Calvin?" Dory called his name from the next phone over. "Are you all right?"

She was about the right size and build, he realized,

although a bit plump around the middle. Her gray hair stalled him, though. Gray hair had never called to him. He liked dark hair, the darker the better, preferably a little long. As the winter went on, the boys around here let their hair grow some. He liked it. But Dory wasn't the one. She didn't have the glow of a chosen one. He wondered how long he'd have to wait for the right woman to appear, now that he felt a strong urge to take one.

"I'm fine," he answered, hoping his voice didn't sound as tense as he felt. "Just bored."

"Enjoy it while it lasts," she said cheerfully. "Next month we'll be busy enough that we'll wish we had more volunteers."

"Seems like a bad thing to look forward to." Even in his current agitated state he could recognize that. He didn't want to harm the whole world. He had nothing at all against most people. Hell, he didn't even have anything against those boys he cleansed. With them it was necessary. Purity was important.

"Oh, I didn't say I was looking forward to it," Dory hastened to assure him. "Just that we'll be way too busy next month. I don't like it, though. So many of these people are my friends and neighbors. It's always sad when one of them gets into trouble."

He nodded, taking a deep breath and forcing himself to relax.

He managed to look at Dory and smile. No, not the type he needed, not even remotely. The urge subsided a bit.

"So this killer thing," Dory said, apparently deciding to save him from boredom. He tensed immediately. "Well, I don't know it's a killer but it seems so much like what happened last time. If it is, then another boy will disappear in a few weeks. Somebody told me this kind of killer speeds up. I hope folks don't drop their guard."

"Me, too," he answered untruthfully. Well, maybe not untruthfully. He was still enjoying the fear that haunted the town and surrounding ranches. It might make finding his next victim harder, but that was part of the challenge. Part of the risk. Part of what heightened the pleasure for him. Some killers like him preferred easy pickings. He'd had both easy and hard pickings, and he knew which gave him greater power and enjoyment.

He needed three more to fill his web. Then maybe he would move on again. Or maybe not. He supposed he could figure that out later. As long as he kept control of himself, he was in charge of everything.

The thought passed through him like a soothing, warm drink. *He* was in charge. Not the cops, not the locals. Just him.

He turned to Dory with a smile. "I'm going to run over to Maude's and get some coffee. You want some?"

"Oh, you are a sweet young man! Actually, I'd like some hot chocolate, if you don't mind." She reached for her purse to give him money but he waved a hand.

"My treat," he said firmly. Rising, he went to get his jacket and gloves.

"Don't freeze your nose off," Dory called cheerfully.

Actually, he half hoped he would. The bite of the cold would help nip his internal battle.

The City Diner, also known by the name of its founder and owner as Maude's, wasn't too far away even on a night where the thermometer was plunging to zero and maybe below. The brisk walk eased the pressure in his head, the need for action that crawled along his every nerve. At least the colors hadn't brightened. He hadn't yet fallen completely into the hunting mind-set.

They had a coffeepot at the call center, and he was mildly surprised Dory hadn't suggested it instead of walking to the diner. Maybe she felt it would be a good tonic for his boredom.

But boredom wasn't his real problem, and he cherished his secret. It made him feel special to know what no one else knew, that he was the man they all feared.

The diner was awfully empty tonight. Maude was still taking the week off because she'd burned her hand on the griddle. He asked Mavis, her daughter, about her and received a lukewarm smile, the best one could hope for in this place.

"Improving. Wants to get back to work. Coffee?"

"To go," he answered. "And a hot chocolate for Dory."

Mavis bustled around at the machines behind the counter. "Coffee's fresh," she remarked. "Considering nobody's buying any tonight, I'm wasting a lot by throwing it out when it gets old."

He sympathized even though he didn't give a damn, and was given two large, oversize take-out cups but charged only for regulars. There were some advantages to being pleasant. More than a few in fact.

Stepping once again into the frigid night, he noticed anew how empty the streets were. People around here didn't generally quail this much from the cold. They had warm cars to get around in and warm enough clothes to wear.

So it was fear keeping them inside. He sniffed the air, thinking he could almost smell terror. It kind of interested him that when he was only taking boys, everyone appeared to be scared. His power reached even farther than he'd thought. Power over every mind in this county. Power over their worst nightmares.

A smile came to his lips. Maybe he should break his pattern. It wouldn't be as satisfying, but it would spread a wider net of fear. It would also confuse those he was sure were even now trying to find him. They were probably just starting to think they could predict him.

Maybe it was time to show them they couldn't.

Chapter 5

DeeJay awoke in the morning feeling as if she'd spent the night in a pitched battle. Every muscle seemed to ache, and she was tangled in the blankets. Remnants of tattered nightmares followed her into the waking world. Vaguely, she remembered that at some point she had felt trapped and unable to move as some dark threat approached her.

Usually the job didn't follow her into sleep, but this case was different in so many ways. She didn't allow herself a lot of time to think about anything except the investigation, but apparently her mind had pulled out the stops in her sleep.

She had been dealing with emotions in her dreams. Her fear for those boys, her horror when she thought of the terror they must have suffered at this monster's hands. It didn't bear imagining, and she couldn't afford to let human feelings get in the way of analyzing the evidence. But for a few moments she sat on the edge of the couch and let herself do just that.

Feel.

For those boys, for their families, for their friends. For all the parents in this county who might be looking at their sons, wondering how to protect them. For all the people around here who must feel as if they were caught in a waking nightmare. She let it roll through her, searing, angry, despairing, unutterably sad.

She felt as if sheer emotion could rip her apart from the inside.

But then she pushed it aside, reminding herself that she had to keep her head clear for this job. Rising, ignoring stiff, aching muscles, she grabbed a change of clothing and headed for the bathroom.

"Coffee's ready," Cade called from the kitchen.

"Be there in a minute." She wondered if his night had been as tormented as hers. Examining those files again last night had been even worse than the first time. Seeing it all through the lens of a man who was setting a stage of some kind on which to play out his sick fantasies and compulsions only made it worse. Every choice he made was part of his imagined ritual. Satisfying dark urges in himself that nobody would probably ever understand. Not really.

But it was all about compulsion and satisfaction, and probably power, and most definitely about the small details that aided him in finding his satisfaction. They'd studied the small details last night, every one of them, because it was doubtful that any were simply accidental.

They'd applied a magnifying glass to a sick psyche, and she wasn't sure that they'd gotten anywhere. Maybe they should call in a forensic psychologist? Send the files for evaluation?

But that had been done when the first stash had been

found in the woods, and they didn't yet have much to add to what the psychologist had come up with then.

The shower eased her muscle aches. Toweling off made her skin feel fresh and clean. This wouldn't last long. The whole case was making her feel sullied somehow. She'd had disturbing cases before, but this beat any of them. She felt as if it were tainting her.

She realized she'd left her clothes on the bed instead of bringing them into the small bathroom with her. Instead of being warm from the shower steam, they'd be chilled like this whole damn house.

Sighing, she threw the door open and saw Cade. He was bent over his own suitcase and looked at her. At once the air seemed to sizzle, and she saw it in his eyes. He wanted her.

As the recognition hit her, she abruptly realized that she was standing there stark naked. Not even holding a towel. Everything froze, an instant in time that suddenly seemed outside of time, an instant of recognition so basic it defied thought. Her insides seemed to melt, and a yearning so strong filled her that she felt her legs weaken. His eyes swept over her, taking in every detail from her puckered nipples to her hips and the thatch of dark hair they cradled. Her breath froze inside of her, overwhelmed by a longing so intense that it shocked her.

It happened fast but seemed to last forever. It was only a second, but might have been a lifetime until the world began to move again. He looked away.

"Sorry," he said. "I needed something and didn't think you'd…" Apparently he thought that better left unfinished. Without looking at her again, he hurried from the bedroom, pointedly closing the door behind him.

She continued to stand frozen, waiting for her breath and strength to return. She closed her eyes a moment, gripping the door frame, and wondered how the hell they were going to handle this. Like it had never happened, she decided.

But it had.

Finally, cussing under her breath, she dressed and went out to face the music.

Except there was no music. Toast and bacon heaped on two plates at the table, two mugs of steaming coffee and Cade busy looking over the notes he had written last night. He didn't even look up as he said, "Good morning."

She mumbled her response and sat across from him. It never happened. Except that she knew she'd be unable to forget that it had. Desires buried since she'd first set eyes on him and realized he didn't want her for a partner, had broken free of their bonds, reminding her that she was a woman, and he was a damned attractive man. Basic. Simple. And oh so complicated in the present circumstances.

"How'd you sleep?" he asked casually, still not lifting his eyes from the notes he was leafing through.

"Lousy," she admitted. "Nightmares."

Finally he lifted his gaze, a brief glance. "Me, too. This case is getting at me in ways I've never had happen before. I don't know if it's the boys, the idea of this killer or what."

"Yeah." What else could she say? Biting into a strip of bacon gave her an excuse to say nothing at all.

"And these notes aren't telling me any more this morning than they did last night. The evaluation by that psychologist is empty."

"You think so, too?" She began to relax as the conversation remained work related. Male interest of any kind could easily send her into a self-defensive hyperdrive. It was one thing to feel an attraction herself; it was another to have it returned. Without fail, at those times she felt unsafe. "Generalizations. He could have been writing about almost any serial killer."

"He sure as hell didn't see any significance to the cargo netting."

"Are you changing your mind?"

He lifted his gaze once again and this time didn't look away so quickly. Control restored, she guessed. Good. "No. I think you're right. This was staged as part of his ritual. The problem is, you can't see any sense in it. Can't feel what might be behind it. But it's too elaborate to be anything else."

She reached for a couple slices of toast, loaded on the bacon and made herself a sandwich. "Dreaming about it didn't help, either. No brilliant bursts of insight from the subconscious. But when you think about it, Cade, an awful lot was involved in that staging. Getting the net strung on the trees, wrapping the bodies, getting them up there, hanging them. A hell of a lot of work, and the constant possibility of being discovered."

"Maybe not so much before the resort started work. We need to talk with the guy at Masters General Contracting."

"Should we call?"

"I already did. I got him on his phone at home, evidently."

"A workaholic?"

"Yeah, like us." Cade snorted. "We're going to get the grand tour and big sales pitch today. Put on your high boots."

"Waders might be better." When he laughed, she decided that everything was definitely okay again. A momentary aberration, left in the past.

As she rose to wash the dishes, she said, "I want a Caesar salad tonight. Grilled chicken. I can make it."

"Or I can, whichever. Getting away from fats isn't exactly working the way I intended."

It was her turn to laugh. "I'll never turn down bacon for breakfast. Or lunch or dinner. But you pay for a month's gym membership for me if we keep on doing this."

She was relieved to see him smile.

"I think that touring the resort today is going to burn off all that bacon and then some," he answered. "We'll be making like mountain goats in the cold."

"There is that." She wondered how cold it was that day, then decided it didn't matter. Since winter had deepened in Wyoming, the temperatures seemed to have become irrelevant. There was cold and colder, and no thermometer was going to change her perception of that.

"Are you from a warm climate?" he asked.

"Depends on which part of my life you want to talk about. Most recently I was in Virginia. Not exactly the Mediterranean."

"But not as cold as here."

"Not usually. I'll get used to it." Just the way she'd gotten used to most things. Adaptation was necessary for a soldier.

"You've probably seen a lot of the world."

"Travel, you mean? I've been all over, but most of what I saw were military bases."

"No time for tourism?"

She hesitated, then decided the question was simply friendly. She guessed her guard was still high after that encounter in the bedroom. Being friendly wouldn't kill her. Might even smooth troubled waters. "Most of the time when I went overseas I was on an assignment, an investigation, and I needed to deal with that. It was just a temporary duty, and it didn't give me time for sightseeing."

"That's a shame." But then he let go of questions about

her past and mentioned his own. "I'm pretty much familiar with this state and Colorado. I used to like to spend a lot of time up at Glacier National Park in Montana, though. Camping and hiking. Not so much anymore."

"What happened?"

He shrugged one shoulder. "Every time I went back, more of the glaciers had disappeared. Hardly any left now. I got to feeling like I was watching an old friend die."

She could understand that and felt a burst of sympathy for him. "I'm sorry."

"Well, cold as this winter is becoming, maybe some will start growing back." Then he snorted a laugh. "Yeah, right."

She didn't know what to say, but she liked what he'd revealed about himself. A guy who cared about nature. She wasn't exactly used to that. "So did you give up hiking and camping?"

"Hell, no. I just go places where I can't see the changes." He glanced at the clock. "Better get ready. We're supposed to meet Masters in half an hour."

It didn't take her long to pull on her hiking boots and her parka. She chose her ski mask but rolled it up so that it didn't cover her face. Cade did the same.

But the instant she stepped outside, the cold nearly stole her breath. "My God," she gasped. And they were going to walk around a mountain resort today?

"Yeah. We might have to cut our look-see short."

"I can't imagine why anyone would even want to ski in this!"

"It's not usually this bad," he assured her. "Usually just a few weeks at a time."

"I'm glad to hear that. I was beginning to think I could be an investigator someplace in the South."

He laughed again. The car started without a problem,

but it didn't warm up at all before they reached the construction trailer just west of town. Masters General Contracting sported a low-key black-and-white sign. The gravel parking lot had been mostly cleared of snow and the tires gripped it well enough.

"Why *did* you choose Wyoming?" he asked as he parked.

"Wide-open spaces, mountains, and not a whole lot of people."

"Sick of people?"

Half of them, she thought, but self-censored. "Not really. I couldn't think of a bigger change of pace, and I needed one."

"I bet you did."

They climbed out and headed for the steps leading up to the door. The trailer was skirted, and the steps weren't rickety at all. The guy had managed to bring a sense of permanence to what was probably only a stopgap.

Inside, the trailer was warm. A man in a sweatshirt and jeans sat at a desk with a computer in front of him and the inevitable stack of papers beside him. He rose immediately, smiling. "Luke Masters. You must be DeeJay and Cade Denton." He shook their hands warmly and immediately offered coffee.

DeeJay didn't even want to unzip her parka yet. "Thanks. It's cold out there. I was wondering why anyone would want to ski in this."

"Maybe not in this weather," he agreed. "Although you can cover your face up pretty well. But this isn't typical."

She couldn't help herself. "Is there any typical weather anymore?"

Luke Masters surprised her by laughing. "Shh. Don't inform my employers. We're getting lots of snow, and that's what I tell them about."

She noted he had a slight limp as he headed for the coffeepot, once again leaving her to wonder if all the men in this place were sporting injuries.

He caught her look as he brought the pot back to the desk where three mugs, sporting his business name, were already arrayed. "Took a fall last winter up on the mountain. The leg is fine, it just objects to cold weather."

They sat around the desk, and Luke began his pitch.

"I can show you plans and drawings to give you an idea where we intend to go. I have photos of the artist's renderings you can keep. I can take you up on the mountain so you can see where we're cutting the ski slopes and get a breathtaking view or two. But unfortunately I can't take you inside what we've built yet. It's very much a hard-hat area. We're using the winter to work on interiors, but they're a long way from looking anything close to finished."

DeeJay slipped into her role. "Do you really intend to be open next fall?"

"Barring anything unexpected and major, yes. We won't have fleshed out all the plans, though. We'll be starting fairly small and expanding with demand but all the basics will be there. The resort hotel, a few of the restaurants, some of the shops. And of course the main slopes. We can always add a few more later if we need them. And once the weather improves in the spring, we'll give the town a face-lift."

"I was hearing some concern about that."

He nodded. "We don't want to change the place. It has its own character—it's a working town, not a place created as a tourist venue. We think that'll give it its own charm. People who want only the ski village experience can stay up on the mountain for that."

"Good thinking," DeeJay said approvingly. "Of course,

that may be a bias of mine. Too much plastic loses the real charm."

"Well, people who come up here to ski can go down there and meet actual cowboys and so on. See what a real Western town is like."

Cade stirred. "What about corollary construction? Condos, houses and so on?"

"We're not looking toward much of that. Part of our charm is that we're pretty much surrounded by protected land, state and federal. So we won't develop any unnecessary sprawl."

"Unless it happens down below."

"That'll be up to local zoning boards. Up here, we're shooting for pristine. Surrounded by wilderness."

A few minutes later, they zipped up again and piled into the crew cab of Luke Masters's truck. He assured them their sporty little number couldn't make it. "We have construction roads, but the winter's done a number on them already, mainly because they were built in a hurry. We'll need four-wheel drive."

The climb up to the site was breathtaking. DeeJay leaned against her side window and stared out as deep forest repeatedly gave way to sprawling vistas of the mountains and valley below. For all her complaints about the cold, this was the reason she had wanted to be out here: the wilderness and the beauty. Too bad it had collected some of the worst ugliness known to man.

Up at the construction site, Luke showed them around briefly, then told them to wander where they liked as long as they didn't come inside and avoided the evident obstacles of heavy equipment and mounded earth.

"The slopes will be up that way," he said, pointing to the north. "They're pretty much laid out and ready. We wanted to see how they'd hold up over a winter."

It was Cade who asked the important question. "We heard about those boys. Where were they found?"

Luke's face darkened. "You're not going to write about that."

"Hell, no," Cade answered firmly. "But from what we've been hearing in town, I'm just curious. That's all it is. But, no, that's not part of the story. We're here to say good things, and since you're only halfway through development, I don't know how we could say anything bad yet."

Luke visibly relaxed. "It's terrible what's going on. Frankly, we've got some nervous investors, too. I hope they catch the creep soon. Hurting those boys..." He shook his head. "He better not come up this way. But you can follow that cut line over there if you really want to see." He pointed. "Not much to it now, though. The cops cleaned it up pretty well. Look about halfway up the slope and to the right."

Then he went inside, waving to a man who climbed out of a truck. There were half a dozen vehicles up here, probably belonging to people hard at work inside.

Cade and DeeJay wandered around a bit, pausing to pretend to take photos of the view.

"It's breathtaking up here," DeeJay remarked.

"Fabulous. And I can't believe I just made myself out to be one of those curiosity seekers who gather at an accident or crime scene."

She felt the momentary touch of amusement. "They disgust you, too?"

"Always."

"Well, at least you know you're not one of them for real." She looked up the slope Luke had pointed out, a wide swath cut through the trees. "We're going to wish they had a ski lift installed."

"I don't doubt it. Ready?"

Since no work had been done on the slope, other than clearing it, the slog was a hard one through fairly deep snow. At least the underlying layers had hardened, but the top layers were fresh powder.

"The skiing is going to be great," Cade remarked. "And next time I get a brainstorm like this, remind me they make snowshoes."

The laughter bubbled out of her, but the higher altitude left her a little breathless and cut it off faster than her amusement died. By the time they were about a quarter of the way up, both of them were breathless. Each step was getting harder.

"I'm surprised they don't have snowmobiles up here," he said.

"We could turn around and get one from somewhere, I'm sure." It was sounding like a better idea all the time. Lifting her feet so high to take the next step was reminding her of a few muscles she hadn't used in a while.

Cade turned around and looked backward at the resort. "God, this is going to be a beautiful place to ski."

"It would be a beautiful location to do anything." She frowned faintly, the most she could do when her face felt frozen. Reaching up, she unrolled her ski mask to cover her face and tucked the end inside her jacket. "I need a few." She hated to sound weak, but she wasn't used to the altitude and the cold air. Her body felt warm, even a little too warm, but breathing was almost painful.

"It'd be a good place to make snow angels," he remarked almost absently.

She looked at him, taken again by his amazing aquamarine eyes. He, too, had rolled down his ski mask and was scanning the area with an intensity it didn't seem to deserve. They hadn't reached anywhere near the place the bodies had been stashed.

"What?" she asked finally.

"The woods," he said obscurely.

"What about them?"

"It's been bothering me from the start. Admittedly we're plowing through snow here, but consider how far we've had to come. Bringing those bodies up here was risky, yes, but it was also hard to do. Unless the guy is a mountain goat, anyway. And we're walking up a cleared slope. He didn't have that available to him five years ago."

DeeJay looked around with fresh eyes and realized he was right. "He couldn't have carried them for sure. So he must have driven them. But how?"

"ATV, I suppose. But wouldn't that need some kind of clearing anyway to get through?"

"We need to talk to someone who really knows these mountains. And we need something better than a road map. Topography. Trails."

"Agreed." He looked at her again. "Should we continue or head back?"

She looked up the slope. "My nightmare hike. I'm wondering how much we could tell from the scene after all this time."

"Maybe we found out all we need to know. I'm a hiker from way back, and I'll be honest with you, my mind didn't present a truly clear picture of the obstacles our perp faced to get those bodies up here. Even one at a time."

"Add to that that once the site was found, the cops were all over it. If there was ever an original trail, we won't be able to pick it out, especially under all this snow."

He nodded. "So what's your gut instinct? Will we learn any more up there, or should we conclude that now that we've seen the general area we can work with photos and talk to someone who knows his way around up here?"

She hesitated, but she fully appreciated that he was letting her make the decision. She really liked him right then. She sighed and tugged at her ski mask. "These things get wet from our breath. Lousy design."

He laughed quietly. "Got a better one?"

"Short of a snorkel hood, no." She turned around slowly, taking in everything, absorbing details and making judgments. "Let's get under the trees," she said presently. "I want a better feel for what he was actually up against."

"Fair enough."

They plowed across the slope to the darkened area beneath the trees. Overhead a blue sky was beginning to fade, as if thin clouds might be moving in. Soon the light would become flat, making it all more difficult.

The earthmovers that had carved out the slope had left mounds of dirt just before the woods. DeeJay wondered if they would clear that away later or leave it. Where the heck would someone put all this rock and soil anyway? Use it for filler elsewhere on the resort?

They clambered over the mounds. Beneath the trees, the snow wasn't quite as deep, giving her a better sense of the terrain and the difficulties.

"He was one determined guy," she said finally. Even on an ATV without snow, working through the trees would have been a slow process. The forest was thick, dense with undergrowth in places. "He must have had a trail."

"Well, we know where it ended. The question is where did it begin?"

"We aren't going to figure that out now." She turned, and as she did so, her boot caught on something, maybe a root and she started to fall.

Instantly, strong arms caught her and the next thing she knew she was pressed against Cade's chest. Layers of down prevented it from being in any way intimate, but when she looked up into his eyes, no amount of down could prevent the hot arc of hunger that speared through her.

A flare in his gaze seemed to answer her.

"Cade?" she said breathlessly, the question almost lost as the treetops stirred in a sudden wind. It didn't matter. She didn't know what she was asking anyway.

"Damn," he said quietly. Apparently, he knew the answer because he leaned in and kissed her. Damp wool got into the mix but DeeJay hardly noticed. His lips were cold, but his breath was warm, and she instinctively tried to open her mouth to welcome him.

A sharp pang of desire shot through her, and her gloved hands instinctively rose to try to grip his upper arms for support. An ache rolled through her, and the merest touch of his tongue against hers electrified her.

Then, as quickly as it had begun, it was over.

They pulled back quickly, at the same time. "No," she said, adrenaline surging, filling her with a flight-or-fight response. Men didn't touch her. Not anymore, not without asking first.

"Not good," he agreed, his words tripping over hers.

It might have been comic if she hadn't been left feeling hungry and bereft. It was ludicrous, she told herself as she waited for the rising tide of passion inside her to ease. Ridiculous. Bundled up like Inuit on a frigid mountainside, what could they have done anyway?

And it was wrong, so wrong, to risk their professional relationship on something like this. They had to work together, and everything else could just go hang.

"DeeJay?"

"Mmm?" Talking seemed difficult.

"Clouds moving in. I think we'd better get off this mountain."

By the time they reached the foot of the slope and

trudged toward the resort, she felt frozen to the very bone. Except for one kernel of white heat between her legs.

Nothing seemed capable of freezing that.

Luke Masters drove them down the mountain a short time later. "I see you didn't get up to the crime scene," he remarked.

"No, but we learned you've got some great snow for skiing here," Cade answered smoothly. "Hell, I'd pay to ride the lift to the top just to take in the view."

"I was hoping for that reaction. We may have to make some of our own powder at times, mainly in the early winter and spring, but mostly I think nature is going to take care of us. And it *is* beautiful up there."

"The way you angled that one slope we were looking at is amazing. It opens up the view."

"Some of that was necessitated by geology, but it worked out well. All the slopes have great views."

DeeJay decided to speak even though her lips still felt frozen despite the heat blasting inside the car. "Are you going to be open the rest of the year for hikers?"

"We're thinking about it. But we need to work things out with the forest service. Like I said, they surround us, pretty much. You might want to talk to someone there about that."

"They would have people who know those mountains like the backs of their hands?"

"Absolutely. Some of them live in them year-round. Craig Stone might be the best person to talk to. He ranges all over those woods constantly and has for years."

He dropped them at their car, excusing himself to get back to work but making sure they exchanged cards. "Any questions, call me. Oh, wait, I promised you those photos of our plans."

They were in their car, waiting for it to warm up, when

he darted back out of the trailer with something that looked like a large portfolio. "I'll need these back," he said, "but they'll give you the best idea. In the back there's an envelope of smaller photos you can keep."

"Don't I feel like a sham," Cade said as they drove back toward town.

"Yeah. I always wind up thinking of that line about how undercover cops have to lie." She slid down a bit in her seat. "He was a nice guy. I didn't like lying to him."

"I think he'll understand once we solve this case."

"Needs must. And speaking of needs, food and heat are on the top of my list right now."

"You wanted a chicken Caesar salad tonight, right?"

"That's for later. Right now I want as many calories as I can tuck in."

He laughed and headed them toward the diner. The kiss on the mountain seemed to have been put firmly in the past, an aberration.

Except to DeeJay, it didn't feel like an aberration at all. It tingled through her with an awareness that wouldn't quit, and a drumbeat of desire for more. Not good. She needed to cut it out, to be ruthless with herself as she had in the past. As ruthless as necessary. Everything else aside, her aversion for men, her own rape, none of that seemed as important as not screwing up her first partnership in her new job.

"Do you want to call this Craig Stone at the forest service?" he asked. "Or should I?"

"I'll do it." Despite being worn-out from the fruitless climb up that ski slope, the need to take action of some kind was still riding her. She hated how slow cases could move sometimes, like they were just marking time as they waited for a break. It was even more frustrating because right now they were dealing with a ticking bomb. Nobody could be certain when the killer would act again. The bomb could blow up right in their faces.

She dried to drag her thoughts back in line. "So you hadn't really thought about how hard it would be for him to get the bodies up there?"

"No," he admitted. "In retrospect that seems stupid, but I hadn't. The crime-scene photos didn't give me a real sense of the surrounding terrain, and I guess I was assuming there had to be a road nearby. A track of some kind."

"Maybe there was. This Stone guy should know."

"I hope so. There's enough mystery surrounding everything without wondering if our perp is capable of levitation."

That drew a laugh from her, and finally she let go of the tension inside. It had been just a kiss, after all. One little kiss and not a very big deal at all because of the cold and the quickness with which they had ended it. No reason to get all tied up in knots about it.

But she knew what she was really afraid of: that he might come on to her later. That he might think that was an invitation for more. That he might want to take this places she didn't want to go.

Didn't men always do that?

They decided to get takeout from the diner. The place was crowded. Either the search parties had quit for the day, or they weren't going out.

"Storm brewing," Mavis told them. "Gonna be a nasty one."

"Great," said DeeJay. Another hindrance, not that there was much they could do, storm or no storm. They didn't need to review the photos and plans for the resort at all. That left getting in touch with Craig Stone, and who knew how long it might be before they could meet.

She turned from the counter with her share of the takeout and realized a young man was staring at her. Dark haired, dark eyed, slender just shy of frail. He stared, appearing almost hypnotized, then looked quickly away. Well, it wasn't the first time some would-be stud had stared at her. She was used to it.

"Hey, Calvin," one of the men called out.

The slender man turned. "Yeah?"

"You better not stay in town tonight to work the phones or you won't be getting home."

"I heard," Calvin answered. "A good night to be by the fire."

DeeJay swore she could feel his eyes on her as she and Cade walked out.

And for some reason she remembered the sheriff's remark that in some ways she resembled the victims.

"Cade?" They were heading for the grocery now to get tonight's salad makings and some other things in case they couldn't get out tomorrow.

"Yeah?"

"Do you agree with Dalton? Do I look like the vics?"

"What brought that up?"

She wasn't about to tell him that a young man's stare had made her uneasy. It wasn't the first time and wouldn't be the last.

Sheesh, it wasn't even as if he had stared for long. "I don't know. It just popped up." She felt foolish already for her reaction to something so common, and to link it with a remark from the sheriff that had been clearly off-the cuff, the way some folks said others looked like movie stars? Or maybe the guy had known one of the victims and had, for an instant, seen the resemblance that Gage had noted. Still, she filed away his face and name in case he turned up again.

"Apart from being a woman, nearly a foot too tall and at least twenty pounds heavier?"

She thought he was going to laugh at her, but then he surprised her.

"Yeah," he said. "You do."

"Actually, thirty pounds," she said, once her heart stopped skipping nervously. "Muscle."

A laugh burst from him. "Well, then, you've got nothing to worry about. And isn't that a guy's line? It's all muscle?"

Reluctantly, she laughed, too. "Yeah. But in this case it's true."

"Then even more reason he won't look your way."

Unless he decided to change his routine for some reason. The thought plagued her all the way home.

A ticking time bomb. One who made his own rules. Time seemed terribly short.

Chapter 6

They had barely finished carrying the groceries in when their landlord, Hank Jackson, showed up. He was so bundled against the cold that it was impossible to tell how lanky he was. They invited him in for coffee, but he waved the offer away. "Figured you don't have the TV hooked up, seeing as how you're not gonna be here long, so I wanted to warn you. We've got a really bad storm moving in, maybe a foot or more of snow by morning. Best lay in supplies and plan to hunker down. If you need anything, I'll be at home."

"Did they call off the search parties?" DeeJay asked.

Hank nodded. "No point in getting somebody else lost. High winds are coming in, too, so visibility will be shot."

"That's got to be hard on that boy's family."

"No doubt," Hank answered. "But sometimes you can't fight what is." He spoke with a kind of weariness that seemed to spring from experience. "Anyway, I don't know

exactly what you folks are used to, but trust me, the locals are staying at home. It won't be long before the snow
starts flying. Call me or trot over if you need anything."

DeeJay closed the door behind him and thought of
Hank's heavily pregnant wife, Kelly. "I hope Mrs. Hank
doesn't decide to go into labor tonight."

"You know, I bet Hank could handle it if it's uncom-
plicated."

Together they put away the groceries, then sat to eat
the meals they'd bought at the diner. The foam containers
had managed to keep them somewhat warm, although the
fries were ruined. DeeJay didn't care. Soggy or not, she
devoured them, fueling the engine that kept her warm, re-
placing the calories they'd spent on their cold hike. Cade
seemed to feel pretty much the same way.

"I like this town," she announced when finally she
could slow down her eating. "Sorry, I've been eating like
a pig at a trough."

"And I haven't? What do you like about Conard City?"

"The people, mainly. Even Mavis with her attitude.
Everyone's been nice."

"Ah, but either they know we're here to help or they
think we're writing a travel piece."

She made a face at him. "Don't dash my illusions."

He flashed a grin and picked up the other half of his
sandwich. "Unfortunately, I don't know how much more
we'll be able to get done today. You call Stone, I'll call
the sheriff and see if they've learned anything new at all.
Then we're stuck in a storm."

Craig Stone turned out to be surprisingly easy to get
a hold of. "I can come over after the storm and show you
all the maps and trails you want," the forest service ranger
assured them. "Right now I'm tasked with pulling in a few

winter hikers before it's too late. At least we have a pretty good idea where they are. Tomorrow?"

Tomorrow it was.

"People choose to go hiking in this," DeeJay said after she hung up. It wasn't a question.

"Winter camping is great for the hardy," Cade responded. "Lots of solitude, pristine woods, a good excuse to sit around a big fire. I need to show you after this case is over. With cross-country skis or snowshoes, it can be refreshing and restorative. You just need the right gear."

For all her carping about the cold, DeeJay didn't really hate it. But she *felt* it and wondered if they made the proper gear for someone like her. Then she realized that Cade was talking as if they would have some kind of relationship after this case. The kind that could involve going off into the woods camping together.

She stole a sideways glance at him and decided it had just been an offhanded remark on his part, the kind of casual thing people often said. She needed to get off high alert with him, she thought. Other than that kiss on the mountain, for which she took a full share of responsibility, he'd been amazingly easy to work with—and that despite the fact that she had begun their partnership by making issues over every little thing.

Whatever objection he'd had to working with her initially, it seemed to have vanished. While they weren't exactly a smoothly oiled team yet, they were managing pretty well, and he treated her with a great deal of respect. That's all she wanted from him—his respect. The rest of it, like the snares of attraction she kept feeling, had to remain off-limits. He was far from earning her trust as anything but a professional partner. Hell, at heart he was probably like most men. She just hadn't seen it yet.

He reached for the phone. "Now for Dalton. Then we'll

figure out how to spend some time. What did you do in the army when you got slowed down?"

"Poker," she answered. "And it's not much fun with only two."

Another smile, then he dialed the phone. She could hear only his side of the conversation, but then he started talking about potential access to the crime scene on the mountain and how they were going to speak to Craig Stone tomorrow and look at maps. "Yeah, it'll help us get a handle on the type of guy our unsub is. How determined, and so on. Every little bit helps."

A pause. "Really? Yeah, that would be great. Thanks, Gage."

He hung up and looked at DeeJay. "You'll never guess. Craig Stone is law enforcement, too. Gage thinks he should be let in on who we are and why we want to know about access to the crime scene. He thinks Craig will be a whole lot more helpful if he knows what we're after."

DeeJay didn't need to think about it for long. "I agree. Why waste time talking about scenic hikes if we can come straight to the point?"

Cade nodded. "I'm with you. Gage said we should tell him as much as we choose, and he'll back us up. As for new information…none."

DeeJay leaned back in her chair, toying with a French fry, watching it flop soggily back and forth. "This guy's impossible. He accelerated five years ago, toward the end, then quit. Skipped town, whatever. Maybe he just stopped, which means it could be anyone in this county." She dropped the fry. "Then there's what appears to be his timeline this time around. He's taking victims closer together than five years ago. He accelerated, but is this acceleration controlled? Will he start moving faster again? We can't count on his spacing at all."

"I know. I hate these cases with a ticking clock, especially when I can't see the countdown timer."

She nodded, knowing exactly what he meant. The passing of each minute seemed like a minute lost, even though they were doing everything they could. "Then there's his scene setting. He hung his first trophies in the middle of nowhere so they couldn't lead back to him. I wonder if he's doing that again."

"I don't know. That depends, don't you think?"

"On what? Whether he's furious that his first batch of trophies is gone? He might be."

"In which case he'd keep them closer to home."

She closed her eyes to think, and looking at Cade for some reason wasn't helping her thought processes. She could have drowned in those eyes of his. "I keep getting hung up on that cargo netting. On the way he wrapped his victims. It's familiar in some way, but not from a criminal case. It's something else. Dang, I wish I could get at it."

"All I keep thinking of at the moment is that he's in the driver's seat, and even if he doesn't accelerate we haven't got a whole lot of time. And what if he does accelerate? He could move in a matter of days. God, I hate having my hands tied."

He sighed and went to get them more coffee. The first icy pellets rattled against the window, and the house creaked a bit as the wind hit it. "Here it comes. The only good thing I can say about this blizzard is that it will shut him down, too."

Fifty miles away on his isolated ranch not far from the foot of the mountains, the storm had indeed shut Calvin down. He spent an hour or so with his web and his trophies, but eventually at some level his preoccupation was pierced by the blizzard. He had to get back to his house before he risked getting lost out there in a whiteout, or stay here and freeze with his chosen ones.

Calvin had no desire to commit suicide, either accidentally or deliberately, so he trudged back to his house before the wind wiped out all visibility. It was going to be a bad one. Nobody had exaggerated that.

When he stepped inside and closed the door behind him, the keening wind became muffled. For an instant it felt as if he'd lost his hearing. But then the endless tick-tock of the grandfather clock reached him. He hated that sound, was goaded by it. It had marked the endless minutes of his suffering at his mother's hands. Reminded him of when the universe had devolved into pain and her measured ranting as she had cleansed him.

Sometimes he thought about throwing it outside until the elements killed it, except that the ticking sound sometimes helped carry him away to his new life of purifying others.

He felt cold to the bone from sitting out in the barn for so long, and from the long walk in the wind to get back here. The fire in the woodstove was still cranking out heat, so he went to make himself a hot drink.

It was as he was standing in the kitchen that he realized his thoughts had followed a new path while he'd been out there enjoying his boys. He'd been measuring a spot for his next one, and he realized he was looking for a larger place. To fit something bigger than his usual.

Like that woman he'd seen in the diner. It hadn't taken him long to find out who she was, some travel writer visiting the town to write about the ski resort. With her husband.

But her look had attracted him: dark, dark hair, a little long like the boys he preferred. In fact, based on that alone, she fit his profile. But she was a woman, taller than he liked, and certainly older. That should have ruled her out.

But somehow it hadn't. She looked something like his mother. As he sat near his woodstove in a chair that needed new springs, he turned her around in his mind. The more he thought about her, the more she seemed to glow in his memory. Was he imagining it, or were the Fates trying to tell him something?

Twice before he'd been guided to a woman. He hadn't got the same satisfaction from them, but it had felt essential at the time. Maybe it was part of his mission, a part he didn't fully understand yet.

But she would be more difficult. Hard to get her away from her husband. Bigger, so therefore stronger. But still a woman, which meant weaker. And fear, as he had learned, could weaken people if it was handled properly.

Once he had her, he could focus on her face and pretend she was one of his boys. He was good at that. Since she was bigger, and more of a challenge, the power that filled him as he took her life might be greater. Her resemblance to his mother at once repelled him and drew him.

He thought about where on the net he would hang her, how she would fit in, and whether he'd feel as good about her as he did about the boys.

The wind strengthened, rattling windows, as he sat thinking for a long, long time. The spider in his web with an especially large and juicy morsel.

It could work. He just had to plan it carefully.

Smiling, he rocked on and thought about that woman.

"I found a Scrabble game," Cade announced, emerging from the bedroom.

DeeJay, standing and looking out at the front window,

turned. "You can't even see across the street," she said. "Heck, I can't even see the street."

He came to stand beside her. "So we get a break. It's kind of pretty, though."

She looked out again and nodded. "I guess so. As long as there's no need to go out in it. Scrabble?"

"Yup. It's old, and I make no promises about whether it has all the tiles. Wanna give it a shot?"

She nodded. "Maybe we can limit ourselves to making words associated with the case."

He arched a brow at her. "Do you ever stop working?"

"Not when I'm on a case. Do you?" She watched his dubious look gradually melt into that engaging smile.

"Not really," he admitted. "But since we're kind of mired at the moment, and I suspect I have the files memorized well enough that I could recite them off the top of my head, I'm thinking a change of perspective might be useful."

"Like clearing the decks and then seeing where everything falls afterward." She smiled back at him. "I'm game. Maybe whatever it is at the back of my mind will get jogged loose."

"Still have that sense that there's something in that mess you should recognize?"

"I can't escape it."

They brewed another pot of the inevitable coffee, then sat at the kitchen table with the game. They disagreed briefly about whether they should find out if there were missing tiles, but it was humorous and they knew it wouldn't change anything in the end. If the tiles weren't there, it wasn't as if they could replace them somehow.

The game was from a time when the board had no guides to keep tiles in place, when the tiles were still made of wood and contained in a cloth bag. It all looked worn and well used.

DeeJay drew the highest-numbered tile and played the first word: *cereal*.

Cade laughed. "I thought we weren't sticking to the case."

An unexpected laugh escaped DeeJay. "Um…is that what you think we're looking for? A cereal killer?"

"You should see what he did to my oat bran."

"I hate to tell you that you're slightly off track."

They continued in the same vein for a while, joking lightly back and forth, in no hurry and not even keeping score. Cade proved to have a wicked talent for managing to hit triple-word scores, but as the tiles began to run out, the words became shorter. So did the distraction the game provided.

DeeJay looked toward the kitchen window and saw only swirling white. Even the neighboring Jackson house was invisible now.

She leaned back, forgetting the game, and cupped her mug with both hands. "I hate being stymied," she admitted. "I hate it when I can't do anything, when I'm missing important information, when I'm just plain stuck."

"Me, too," Cade said. Without asking, he began to gather up all the tiles and replace them in the bag. The break was over. "Unfortunately, nothing's going to happen until tomorrow."

"So we're left running over the same tired ground."

He didn't answer, but what could he say? The storm held them prisoner, but she wasn't sure it would have been any different if they'd been able to go out and about. Any information anyone had on this killer was already in their hands. Even reading it upside down wouldn't change that.

"Tell me about yourself," she suggested. "I heard what

a good investigator you are, and everybody seems to like you, but I don't know anything else about you."

"If you listen at night, you know I snore."

That drew another laugh from her.

"We could play truth or dare or whatever the kids call it," he suggested.

"About as likely as playing strip poker." As soon as the words were out, she wondered what devil had caused her to speak them. At least Cade didn't miss a beat.

"Too much chance of frostbite," he replied. "This place is drafty. Okay, about me. I was ranch raised like a lot of young people in this state. My dad was a foreman on one of the bigger spreads, up near Gillette. The place got turned into an oil field about the time I was graduating from the police academy."

"You wanted a more exciting life? And what about your parents?"

"They're gone. Dad had a heart attack about six months after he got laid off from the ranch. He didn't know how to do anything else, and he couldn't find work. I blame it on stress."

"And your mom?"

"Grief took her about a month after my dad. She just sat down in a chair after the funeral and hardly moved again."

"God, I'm sorry."

He looked up from the game box he was putting the lid on. "I was pretty sorry for me, too, but not for them. They were done. Might as well have put it on a neon sign. Their way of life and everything that gave them purpose was gone."

She nodded. She thought she could understand that. "Did your dad mind that you wanted to join the police?"

"Hell, no. I grew up hearing that he wanted me to get out just as quick as I could. Make something better of my life. I don't think he hated what he did, not at all. I think he loved it. But I think he also didn't see much of a future in it for a young man. Agribusiness was moving in, small ranchers were on the way out, oil fields were chewing up the land. I think he saw the handwriting on the wall, at least from where he was. So they were proud I decided I wanted to be a cop."

"That's good. That's really good."

There was a smile in his eyes as he pushed the game to one side and looked at her. "What about you?"

"Not very many parents are happy when their eighteen-year-old daughter announces she's enlisting in the army."

He tilted his head a little. "Big fight?"

"More like big fears. Maybe they were right to be afraid. But I'm still here, they're proud of me, and they're still living in the one-horse town I grew up in. Texas, if you want the state. I just wanted to escape to bigger and more exciting things."

"I guess we both succeeded."

She shook her head. "Nothing more exciting that sitting locked up in a snowstorm waiting for another shoe to drop."

He threw back his head and gave a deep laugh. "Okay, I can't argue against that. But at least it's temporary."

Silence fell again, except for the storm battering the outdoors and the incessant sound of the forced-air heat trying to keep up. Talk about being at loose ends. She glanced at Cade again and saw him studying her with a faint frown.

"What happened to you, DeeJay?"

She stiffened. "What the hell do you mean?"

"I don't know. I mean, I get that your CO screwed you royally, and I can't imagine that would make you very fond of men in general, but there was more, wasn't there?

What turned you into a caped crusader until you got yourself into trouble?"

"I don't know what you mean."

"I'm sure you do."

For an instant, she hated him. Really hated him. But that passed in a flash as she realized it wasn't true. "Soulbaring time?" she finally said tightly. "Maybe you wanna tell me why you didn't want to work with me. Was it just because I was new, or because I was a woman?"

He gave a low whistle. "Wow. You *do* have a thing about men."

"And you've got one about women."

"Only as partners." He hesitated. "And it's nothing to do with you. I was partnered with a woman once before. It became a heavy-duty problem. She wanted to take it beyond the professional. I wasn't interested. So she made some accusations. Lucky for me, Internal Affairs put us under a microscope without telling either of us. They dismissed her complaint as unfounded. She had to look for another job."

DeeJay looked down at her hands, lying side by side on the table. "I'm sorry," she said.

"I got through it, although for a while I was mad enough to chew iron and spit nails. I wouldn't treat a partner that way."

Remembering the quick way he had withdrawn from their kiss on the mountain, she believed him. Not good, he had said.

"I shouldn't have kissed you this morning," he went on. "And if anyone should know better than to do that, it's me."

"It just happened," she said quietly. "I'm not holding it against you. I didn't exactly stop you. So don't worry about it."

He shook his head quickly. "Actually, I'm not. I've already figured out one thing about you."

"What's that?"

"You may be a prickly pear cactus, but you're an honest one. You wouldn't lie. Hell, it keeps bugging you that we're undercover so you *have* to lie."

"It doesn't bother you?"

"It's necessary. We're trying to save lives here."

She nodded but still couldn't bring herself to look at him. She felt she owed him equal honesty but didn't know if she could force the words out.

"DeeJay?"

The words burst from her as if driven by irresistible force. "I was raped."

Silence greeted her words, followed by some quiet cussing from Cade. Then he said, "So you set about to right the world's wrongs?"

"As much as I could," she admitted, blinking to hold back unwanted and rare tears. "What really pissed me about the whole thing, though…it wasn't just the rape. It's what happened when I reported it. I heard all about the good of the unit, and damaging an excellent soldier's career, ruining my own… Oh, I heard it all."

"So it got swept under the rug?"

"So deep you're only the fourth person to hear about it."

He stood up abruptly and walked out of the kitchen. She heard him taking long heavy strides into the living room, back into the bedroom and around again. Pacing. She hated sitting there feeling so emotionally naked and wondering what he was thinking.

She should have kept her secret. Should never have admitted her deepest secret. Hell, she was a soldier, a former MP. She knew all about keeping necessary secrets.

She wished she could walk out of this house into the

storm and get her equilibrium back. She had buried the whole thing so deep herself that eventually she had decided it was a good thing she'd been talked out of pursuing the matter. It had propelled her instead to help out other victims. That was a good thing, right?

She kept men at a safe distance and hunted those who transgressed, and never again had she let any man, no matter his rank, talk her out of pursuing an investigation. Overall, she really didn't like men. At least not many of the ones she had served with. Too many of them seemed to think women owed them something, and she wasn't dishing out for any of them.

But Cade seemed different, so she couldn't dismiss his reaction, whatever it was. She guessed she'd know shortly if he was like others of his gender. God, she hoped not.

Because in some crazy way she needed him to be different.

Pacing like a caged lion wasn't helping a damn thing, Cade thought as he strode furiously in tight circles. He kept seeing DeeJay's face as she told him she'd been raped, had seen a naked vulnerability she probably shared with no one. She had trusted him with that, and instead of being in the kitchen with her, doing and saying whatever supportive things a person should be doing at such a time, he'd strode away to try to walk off his fury.

There was no walking it off. At this late date, there was nothing to do about it, either, but right then he'd have loved to get his hands on whoever had hurt her that way. All of them, including the officer or NCO who had told her she'd kill her career if she accused her rapist.

They were like bookends, he and she, he accused of misconduct he hadn't committed, she unable to get justice for real misconduct. For a crime. No wonder she'd been willing to risk her career on that sensitive case. She'd not only become a crusader, but she'd become a voice for those who might otherwise be silenced.

God, it was ugly.

He had to get a grip and go back to her. He couldn't leave her sitting there wondering what he thought, whether she repulsed him now, or if he was seeing her in a class with his old partner who had falsely accused him.

Get a grip, he told himself again and stepped down firmly on his fury before returning to DeeJay.

DeeJay heard Cade's return. She looked up almost fearfully and noted how he filled the doorway. He was tall, and his shoulders were broad, tapering to narrow hips and long legs. A perfect specimen of manhood. Despite feeling as if she'd exposed herself to huge danger by telling him the truth, she couldn't help but notice. Despite years of building calcified layers of self-protection, beneath them a woman still lived.

"Can I come in?" he asked.

"I never asked you to leave." She waved vaguely at the chair and refocused her attention on the coffee she still clutched as if it were a lifeline. What had possessed her to blurt the truth?

The chair scraped on the floor as he sat. Outside the wind howled like a banshee bringing a horrible portent of doom. Ice rattled on windows, sounding like the taps of skeletal fingers. Nature was conducting a massive assault at the moment, and even being indoors wasn't making her feel safe.

"I got angry about how you were treated," he said, keeping his voice quiet. "I figured you didn't need that. You've probably been there yourself countless times, so what can I add? Just that I hate rapists. Loathe them. And that I wish you could have gotten justice. But I'm no fool. So many rape victims don't. I am, however, really impressed by the way you turned it around to help others. Not everyone would do that."

DeeJay shrugged. "It just made me see things clearly. There's a big institutional problem in the military when it comes to rape. You know. It's been in the news."

"I know. And it's not just in the military."

She lifted her eyes then, amazed that he understood. "No, it's not."

"Anyway, I'm truly sorry that you didn't get the support you needed when you most needed it. You were violated in more than one way."

"Thank you." There seemed to be nothing more to say as she tried to stuff it all back into the dark mental box where she had kept it locked up all these years. Dragging it out didn't fix anything—it just upset her all over again, reminding her of how vulnerable she could be against someone of greater size and strength. It also reminded her that she was never safe, even with a comrade. She couldn't afford to live that way or she'd be cowering in a cave somewhere.

The important thing was not to be ruled by fear. Ever.

"I guess you're not a misogynist," she finally said.

His eyes widened. "Me? No way. Did I do something?"

"Only your reaction to having me as a partner. Now that I know why, I'm sorry I gave you such a hard time."

A slow smile split his face. "I was wondering how we were going to be able to jolt along."

"You're right. I'm a prickly pear. I probably see slights where none are really intended. But mainly I want to make sure I'm treated as an equal. I guess I can go overboard sometimes."

"I never met anybody who couldn't, if the right buttons

are pushed." He got up, emptied the dregs from the coffeepot into the sink and started to make fresh. "Part of it was what happened to me with that woman. Part of it was that I knew nothing about you. I had no idea if you'd be a help or a hindrance."

She nodded. "Have you decided?"

He faced her. "You're a damn good investigator, Dee-Jay. We can leave it there if you want. A good partner."

"Except for my carping about the cold."

He came back to the table and sat. "Secret? It's too damn cold for me, too. And I lived most of my life here. Still, there are at least a few weeks every winter when I wonder why I didn't take a job in a warmer place. So carp away."

She put her mug down at last, no longer needing to hang on to it. "I just need to adapt. I'm adaptable." She closed her eyes, trying to finish the journey from her past into the present. "Part of me still wishes we'd climbed up to the crime scene. The rest of me knows it would have been a waste of energy after all this time. Buried under snow, whatever may have been left rotted…but it feels like unfinished business."

He reached for the envelope containing the photos, opened it and spread them out across the table. He moved the game box to the floor. "They haven't changed, but maybe we missed something. It sure seems to be nagging at you."

There were so many photos that they all partially concealed others, but that was typical of crime scenes. Every angle, different light, some zooms and some from farther back. She gathered the ones that focused on the whole scene and laid them out. The net, the carefully wrapped bodies, the overall scene front, back and side.

They hadn't changed, but he was right, they were nag-

ging at her. She turned them a little, studying them, trying
to reach whatever it was they reminded her of.

"The net," she said finally, noticing something. "Was
it deliberately draped that way or had it come loose in
places?"

"I don't know." He pulled out more papers and began
sorting through them, a whole stack of reports from the
crime-scene team proper. The ones who were supposed
to go over everything with a microscope.

She kept staring at the netting, moving from view to
view, turning the photos this way and that.

After what seemed a long time, Cade looked up. "Nothing in the reports."

"Okay." She kept looking, photo after photo.

Cade picked up the phone, and she listened with only
half an ear as he spoke to Gage. No one would know, she
thought. Because no one would have thought of it. Whatever *it* was. She spoke, interrupting something Cade was
saying to Gage. "Did anybody take any overheads of the
scene?"

Cade repeated her question into the phone. "He doesn't
think so, DeeJay."

"Okay." She took one of the photos and turned it so
that she was looking at it almost end on. Then she saw it
and her heart slammed.

"My God!"

"Wait one," Cade said into the phone. Then he turned
to her. "What?"

"He looked at his vics from above. Were there any deer
stands up there? Did anyone look for any sign that someone had been up in the trees?"

Cade spoke into the mouthpiece again and, a moment
later, answered her. "They assumed the signs of climbing

were a result of hanging the net. Evidence of some deer stands, but there was nothing and the signs were old."

As they would be, years after he'd moved on. She nodded. "Maybe. Maybe." But the more she looked at the photos from the end, and nearly upside down, the more convinced she became. Her heart was hammering. Useless information, probably. But then again.

"Call you back," Cade said and hung up. "Tell me, DeeJay."

"See how I'm holding these?" She pushed some his way. "You try it. He may sometimes have viewed his trophies from below but I think most of the time he liked to look at them from above. Do you see it? That's one big spiderweb."

Night settled in. They'd closed the curtains against the stormy world, not that there was anything to see out there. Night or not, the blowing snow caught any available light, fracturing and reflecting it until the darkness seemed almost bright. Cade took over the task of making dinner, broiling some chicken breasts to add to the precut greens they'd bought, tossing in some ripe olives, slicing red onions.

A spiderweb. She was right. Whether they'd be able to do anything with that, he didn't know. She was still absorbing the photos, but now that he'd looked at them from her perspective, he couldn't see it any other way.

A damn spiderweb. What did that mean about their killer? He ran in mental circles, trying to find something.

"He wrapped the bodies the way a spider does," DeeJay said from the table. "Plastic in lieu of silk. But now this damn display makes sense. Does this guy think he's some kind of spider?"

"I'm asking myself the same question. Do you like grated Parmesan in your salad?"

"I like anything in my salad."

He was stumped, as stumped as he'd ever been. "What could the connection be? Nobody knows how a spider thinks. If it thinks. For Pete's sake, *what* is he thinking?" And that was what they needed to get to.

"I don't know." She fell quiet for a while.

He checked the chicken breasts, and turned them. Good smells had begun to fill the room, making the blizzard outside seem a little farther away.

"If he's doing the same thing now," she said after a bit, "then he needs to be doing it somewhere he can look down on them. That means a big building, unless he's back in the woods."

"Plenty of big barns out there, some of them big enough to have even a third floor. We can't check them all."

"Of course not. I'm thinking out loud."

"Even if he's not back in the woods, it doesn't have to be a barn. There are some old silos out there to this day. Hell, he could do it inside a house somehow."

"I know."

He pulled the chicken out of the oven and turned off the broiler. They needed to cool down some before he cut them and tossed them in with the rest of the salad, so he rejoined her at the table.

"I wonder," he said, "if looking at them from above makes him feel more powerful somehow."

She lifted her gaze from the photos. "Power? You think that's behind this?"

"At least to some extent. Power, madness, and some kind of ritual I can't begin to imagine yet. But then I can't imagine him thinking of himself as a spider."

"I think I can. Not exactly, of course. But maybe he

sees himself as casting a web, taking whatever comes to him. Snaring it."

"But his last one certainly wasn't just a target of opportunity. He had to puncture the dad's tire."

"So we think. But how did he know that kid was going to be waiting for a ride?"

He froze for a moment. "Everyone assumes...you're right. No one knows, everyone is assuming. The two things seem linked, but maybe they're not."

"Coincidences happen." She ran her fingers through her black hair, tousling it even more. He hoped she didn't realize that right now she had a bad case of bed head. He thought it was cute.

Quickly he yanked himself back from that cliff.

"He's clearly organized," he said, forcing himself back to the task at hand. "He leaves no traces. No trail. Organized killers usually stalk their victims. Hunt them until the moment comes."

"And not every serial killer is all one but not the other. He's a risk taker. We agreed on that much. Coming back here after five years and resuming his pattern was a huge risk. One he didn't have to take. We've got a few dozen serial killers running around the country right now. If they keep moving, we don't catch them."

"So why come back?" Cade answered his own question. "Because there's business of some kind here for him. Something he needs to finish, to take care of, something that's eating at him about this place."

"Maybe," she agreed. "Or it may be a huge act of stupidity. Hanging those bodies in the woods could be read as risk taking, because somebody could have stumbled on them, or him when he was there, or it could have been stupidity driven by his compulsion."

"God," he said, "give me an ordinary murder any day." Rising, he went to dice the chicken. The knife fell on the cutting board with more force than necessary. "Can I be frank?"

"Please do."

He caught movement out of the corner of his eye and saw she had come to refill her coffee.

"Want some?" she asked.

Apparently they'd gotten past the point of worrying about whether it was sexist to pour coffee. He let a moment of amusement pass through him, but it didn't do much to lift his mood.

"Frank?" she reminded him.

"This is the kind of case I never wanted to work. I've seen awful, terrible crimes in my day, but one like this? No clues, having to try to get into some sick head and become proactive...not my thing."

"I'm there with you," she replied. "What's Gage's number?"

"Hit the redial button. We haven't called anyone else."

But then she didn't call. "Bad time. What's he gonna do about it, anyway? He's sure as hell not going to call the grieving father in the middle of a blizzard to ask him questions on the phone. I wouldn't."

"Neither would I." He scraped the diced chicken into the salad bowl and used a couple of big spoons to toss it. "It won't make any difference to wait."

"No."

He figured they both knew the missing kid was already dead. None of the earlier victims had been tortured for long periods. Whatever this guy needed, he didn't need it to go on for lengthy periods. So the boy was already gone, and a day wouldn't make any difference to him. And the killer was as pinned by this storm as anyone, so even if he wanted to accelerate his crimes, he couldn't right now.

For now everyone, living or dead, was safe beneath a deepening blanket of snow.

Chapter 7

As the evening deepened, the storm continued unabated, weakening not even a little bit. From time to time, one of them would go to a window to peer out but could see almost nothing. DeeJay settled on one end of the sofa, wrapping herself in a blanket against the drafts, breaths of the storm reaching inside, sinuously twisting around despite the laboring heat.

"Times I wish I had a TV," Cade remarked. "I'd like some info on the storm. How cold it is, how long it's going to last."

"We could ask Gage."

"Sure, ask the sheriff to be the local weatherman for me." She laughed quietly. "Bet he wouldn't mind."

"Better if I could get a connection on my cell phone."

She couldn't, either. Either the snow was blocking the signal or the tower had gone down in the wind. Either way, they were snow locked and dependent on a landline.

She picked up her tablet again, but that hadn't changed, either. No wireless connection since late afternoon.

"Bad," she said, stating the obvious.

"I'll call Gage," Cade decided. "He's probably busy as hell with people who have real problems, though. Maybe Dispatch can tell me something."

She watched him head toward the kitchen but felt very little interest in what the storm was doing. The night shut them down as much as the storm had. Their predator was in his cave, wherever that was, and thus not doing anything that might leave a clue for them.

Not that they were doing so well with clues. The spiderweb idea haunted her, though, and even as she tried to think of something else it kept stalking the edges of her mind. Some kind of information or message lay there, but she couldn't pick it out. Couldn't imagine how it revealed anything about their killer's psyche.

These killers almost always took trophies of some kind. Usually smaller ones, but the idea was the same: they could relive the experience, refresh it in their minds, enjoy once again whatever it was they got from their kills. Like a photographic memento, but apparently much stronger.

So what was with the spider connection? Did he feel like a spider? Or did he admire spiders? Why imitate one? She kept feeling that was a key, possibly a key that would help them either pinpoint this guy or figure out a way to draw him out.

As profilers, they were supposed to be proactive, thinking one step ahead of their subject, finding ways to get him to screw up or ways to locate him. Right now looking for spiderwebs was useless.

And that assumed she was even right about what she thought she saw in the netting and the way he wrapped his victims.

Dang, she wished she could let it rest, but she had a

stubborn mind, and once it got onto something, it didn't want to let go.

Cade returned. "Cell comms are down in most of the county. Police wireless is down. Roads are blocked in every direction, and with all this blowing, the plows aren't making a dent. Even satellite communications are spotty, Velma said. The whole damn place is in lockdown."

"I guess so."

He sat across from her, resting his elbows on his jean-clad knees and clasping his hands. "I can almost smell the burning rubber. You're still thinking."

"Yeah. And I'm beginning to wonder if I saw something that wasn't there. I may be going down a blind alley and wasting time."

"The problem isn't a blind alley. We'll go down lots of those. It's inevitable. The problem is that we don't know what it tells us about our killer. He built an unusual display. Everyone's pretty much agreed on that. I think your description of a spiderweb is the best, but it's not telling us anything except that he may prefer to view his victims from above when he can. And what does that say?"

"Not a damn thing."

"Yet." The correction was quiet. "Stick with it. I am. It's the best explanation I've heard yet for a guy who is breaking some of the usual paradigms for his sort."

"Well, we assume he is. This is just too weird."

"This acceleration thing. He's accelerated hugely compared to five years ago. Maybe it's not just the result of a pent-up need. What if he's been hunting elsewhere all this time? There's nothing in the file to indicate one way or another. I assumed it was because there were no similar crimes, but maybe…"

Their eyes locked, and for once when they did she noticed something besides how amazing his eyes were.

"Hell," he said, and rose, striding back to the kitchen. After a moment she followed him. She didn't have to hear much before she realized he was talking to the FBI at Quantico. Tugging the blanket tight around her shoulders, she forced herself to wait while he described what they had to someone on the other end.

Lew, he mouthed to her as he listened.

She remembered Lew Boulard. He'd been one of her teachers at Quantico, and she'd always thought him amazingly levelheaded. Nor was he overrun by ego, which she thought too many profilers were. He didn't let anything get in the way of clear thinking.

"Thanks, Lew," Cade said finally. "Let me know. Yeah, this is the best number right now. A snowstorm has shut down everything that isn't hardwired."

He hung up. "Lew was working late. He's gonna start a database search for us. Victim type, missing persons reports, et cetera. He said it'll take a while, maybe until morning."

"I wish we could fax him the photos."

"Maybe tomorrow if he needs them."

DeeJay looked down, her mind still racing in circles. Then something popped out. "Spiders don't all hunt, do they? I mean, I know some do, but most rely on a web and patience. Victims come to them."

She looked up and found Cade staring at her. "Holy hell," he said. "They come to him."

"But how?"

He threw up a hand. "Think about it, DeeJay. You were right when you said we were assuming the flat tire was linked to that last boy's disappearance. That was a leap we shouldn't have made. Like you said, coincidences happen. How, you asked, could the killer know that boy was going to be waiting for a ride? But if a spider weaves a web, the food comes to him, gets stuck and can't escape."

Her heart started hammering. She let the blanket slide from her shoulders and rose to start pacing. "So he could be luring them somehow. Just like a spider. Then when they get too close, he's got them. It's possible. There sure as hell is no one left to talk about it."

"Exactly. So assume for argument's sake that he gains their confidence. I'm sure kids around here are given the same stranger warnings they get everywhere else. Besides, he was in this county once before, so he may not be a stranger. That's been a question from the outset. A stranger would stick out around here."

"Right," she agreed. "So they either know him or meet him under circumstances that create trust of some kind. The kind of trust that might get them into a vehicle with him or to his house, wherever that is. So he flattens a tire, tells the last boy that his dad is broken down and he's going to give him a ride instead."

"And the kid isn't afraid of him. Doesn't even find it strange. Ergo, our victims know him from somewhere."

"That was a possibility from the outset," she reminded him as she extended her pacing from the small kitchen to the living room. Soon Cade was pacing right along with her.

"Of course it was. We discussed it. It's been a premise all along—that it had to be someone local. But the spider thing… It's not a snatch and grab, DeeJay. That's why no one ever sees anything. These kids are going willingly."

She nodded, halting midstride. Cade bumped into her.

"Sorry," he said.

She hardly heard him. "This kid must have mentioned to him that his dad was driving him home that afternoon.

How else would our spider know to be there, and to flatten the dad's tire? So the boy had a relationship with him."

Sickened by the images filling her head, images of a human spider preying on weaker victims, she pivoted sharply and found herself chest to chest with Cade.

Instantly all the air seemed to vanish from the room. She looked into his aquamarine eyes and felt her heart flip. Someone struck a match to her very center, filling her with all the heat of a raging fire.

Where the hell had that come from? She wanted to step back, ignore it, pretend it wasn't happening, but she remained frozen, imprisoned by the sudden, overwhelming bonds of passion. Wrong time, wrong place, wrong situation. My God, they were working an important case and there was no room for this. Was she losing her mind?

But he didn't move, either. For an instant he looked startled. He waited a moment, and she was sure he could read her mind. Or her face. Or her entire body.

"DeeJay?" His voice had gown husky, quiet.

She couldn't have made a sound to save her life. In the airless, heat-filled universe she had just entered, she was trapped by her own needs. Needs denied for far too long.

"I won't touch you," he whispered. "Not unless you ask. Won't go there…"

She understood. His last female partner. But not even understanding could make her back away and release him. Maybe he was uneasy because she had been raped.

But all of that barely bounced across her brain as deeper, more primal impulses held her in thrall. Any question about whether she could turn off her obsession had just been answered by another obsession.

She still couldn't speak so she raised her arms and pulled him in for a kiss. That, too, had been running around in the back of her mind all day, much as she had tried to ignore it.

And this instant she did it, she knew it was so very right.

Cade had a million reasons to back away. From the outset he'd successfully ignored his attraction to her. She was prickly and difficult and, mostly, she was female. Danger, as he'd learned in Denver. Except DeeJay didn't play games like that. He'd already figured it out. If anything, she was too damn honest.

All of that ceased to matter in an instant. Everything he'd been trying to ignore and pretend he wasn't feeling suddenly burst the bonds he'd placed on himself and exploded into a maelstrom of passion. It was as if banking the fire and ignoring it had made it erupt violently.

He clamped his mouth over hers and kissed her as if he could fuse them in the heat into one being. Then her head tipped back, welcoming him more deeply, as hungry as he for what was to come.

Finesse flew out the door. He would never after remember how they had stripped, only that four hands had worked wildly at pulling away layers of clothing as if they were in a race against time.

Naked, his mouth still clinging to hers, breaking only for gasps of breath, he lifted her into his arms and carried her back to the bed.

Rough, ready and impatient. He might regret it later, but every movement she made encouraged him. Her hands grasped him, pulled him ever closer, found his stiff member and squeezed a groan out of him.

Dimly he remembered a condom, but just in the nick of time. Together they fumbled it on him, then he dove into her depths, warm and welcoming and delightfully tight. Her legs wound around his hips, pulling him in all the way.

His heartbeat hammered in his ears, and his breath came in ragged gasps. He found enough presence of mind to rise on his elbows and look down at the woman beneath him.

Her face had softened into new contours; her breaths were nearly quick moans. She was already on the way to the moon. To hell with it, he thought, and pumped harder.

A cry escaped her and moments later he jetted into her, an explosion of satisfaction that wiped out the rest of the world.

He collapsed on her, hot and sweaty, and at some level realized they had rutted with less grace than animals in a barnyard.

And he didn't feel even a tiny bit bad about it.

The wind still keened. Ice rattled against windows. Cade managed to move enough to cover them with blankets and draw DeeJay into his arms. "Sorry that was so rough and abrupt," he murmured. His nose was pressed to her hair, and he liked its scent and silkiness.

A small, quiet laugh escaped her. "I needed it," she said bluntly. "So much. No apologies."

"Next time—"

But she cut him off. "Shh. I said no apologies."

So he held her close, wondering at his own behavior, wondering where this would take him and if it would be the biggest mistake possible.

But she didn't seem in any hurry to roll away. Her fingertips traced his back gently, reawakening urges he thought he'd just satisfied. It had all happened so fast he couldn't believe it. He'd never made love like that before, had never expected to. Yet she seemed content.

"Sometimes," she murmured, "when you're in a foxhole you have to move fast and without thinking."

"So this was some kind of instinctive thing?"

"Wasn't it?"

He supposed it was. Lines they couldn't cross had needed crossing to get here, and he guessed the immediacy and explosiveness had carried them past a whole lot of things that had been inhibiting their desires. Bam! No more lines now, unless they redrew them. He didn't want to do that.

"No apologies, no regrets," she said. "Promise."

He could promise that, he decided. "Agreed."

"Good."

She pushed his shoulder until he rolled onto his back, then straddled him, with the blanket hanging from her shoulders. There was almost no light, but he could still make out her breasts hanging over him like an invitation. He waited, though, wanting to see what she would do. Passion had begun to thrum in him again, surprisingly soon. The woman had a hell of an effect on him.

Leaning on one hand, she reached for his and drew it downward, cupping it over her dewy cleft. "Here," she whispered. "Touch me here."

So he complied, stroking her lips, finding the moist nub of nerves with a touch that made her arch. The blanket slipped lower. He liked that she was telling him what she wanted.

"Don't stop," she said thickly.

No way would he stop. He was enjoying this too much even as his groin began to swell with new needs of his own. Hard, driving needs.

She lowered her head, brushing a kiss on his lips, then, supporting herself with one arm, she reached down and enclosed his erection with her hand. He nearly jerked as electricity jolted through him.

"Oh, my…" The rest of his exclamation stopped behind clenched teeth. "You wicked, diabolical woman!"

She gave him a hazy smile as she pressed herself into his hand. "I'm a control freak sometimes."

"Have at it."

He was loving it. A sorceress held him in her grip, enthralling him with pleasures beyond imagining. He bucked a little at her touches, and smiles flitted across her face. Their eyes locked, his so blue-green, hers so black, and he felt as if he were being sucked into a fantastic, incredible black hole.

Enslaved to her, he wanted nothing more than to be enslaved forever. She ground herself against his hand, encouraging him to deepen his touches. He complied readily, sliding one finger into her while he rotated his thumb over the swollen knot of nerves.

Her smiles faded. Her breathing accelerated. She rocked. He rocked. Not quite coming together but not needing to. He reached out with his free hand to cup one of her breasts, feeling the hard pebble of her nipple in his palm.

She groaned and suddenly her head arched back. Her movements against his hand sped up, her stroking of his member keeping pace.

They were climbing this mountain with frightening ease, higher and higher until they soared over the pinnacle in an explosion of shuddering bodies, then drifted weakly back down.

When he found strength, he wrapped his arms around her again and held her to his chest.

She continually surprised him. In every way.

Later, clothed again, they made their way to the kitchen and the inevitable fresh pot of coffee. The atmosphere in the house had changed dramatically, however. The tension that had been between them, alternating from subtle to not so subtle, had vanished. In its place had come a kind of relaxed familiarity. A sense of promises half-made rather than potential declarations of war.

The files and photos still lay on the table. DeeJay gathered them up and tucked them away, out of sight for now. Cade brought them coffee and a couple of sinful slices of Danish.

"What?" she asked. "No doughnut for the cop?"

"This cop deserves more than a doughnut."

The joke was so old she was almost embarrassed to have made it. But then they were facing each other across the table again, and their jobs were returning to the forefront. Driving away memories of pleasure in worries about the future.

"So was it hard being a woman in the army? Or were there good guys, too?" he asked.

The question was so far from her train of thought that it took her a moment or two to corral her mind and answer. "That depended."

"A lot of misogynists?"

"Well…" She hesitated. "Some were, of course. With some guys it was just youthful testosterone, you know? I don't think they were really aware of it. Most kept in line the way they would with their sisters or I wouldn't have stayed in for so long. Occasionally, I had to prove I had brass cojones, or that I could outfight them. I learned a lot."

"I hope some of them did, too."

She laughed. "You bet they did." She lifted an arm as if flexing his biceps. "Like I said, it's mostly muscle. But there was a lot of quick thinking involved, too. If I could defuse a situation, I would. I didn't have anything to prove, really. Except to a few idiots, anyway."

He nodded, sipping coffee and leaning back with a contented sigh. "At first when we got together, you seemed loaded for bear. I was wondering how we'd get along."

"I was awful and I know it. But you seemed so reluctant to work with me I thought you might fall in the classification of misogynist. So I was protecting my turf in advance, I guess you could say."

"Your point was taken. But the truth is, I'm not a misogynist. Never was. My mother would have kicked me from one end of the barnyard to the other. Or my dad would have. Funny story."

She leaned toward him eagerly. "Yes?"

"When I was about nine or so I was all full of being a guy. Hanging out with the guys around the ranch, picking up a lot of bad habits. Anyway, one night my mom wasn't feeling well and my dad told me to do the dishes. Macho idiot that I was, I announced that was woman's work."

"Ooh." She couldn't help smiling.

"My dad read me the riot act and made me do the dishes for the next month. One thing he said really stuck— There's no men's work, there's no women's work, there's only *honest* work."

"I wish I could have met him."

He half smiled. "He'd have liked you. He wanted to hire a woman to help with the horses, but the ranch owner wouldn't hear of it. Dad fumed for days. A man ahead of his times, I guess."

"He raised a good son."

"Time will tell. Okay, then, do we work or play?"

She thought longingly of climbing back into the bed with him, accompanied by discomfort as she realized how close she had let him come. But apart from that, the inescapable reason for their presence here wouldn't let her go. Somehow they had to get ahead of this killer. Find some key, some way, to get at him.

"Are you asking me what I want or what I think we should do?" she finally said.

He sighed and straightened in his chair. "That was my answer." He reached for the files and pulled them back to the middle of the table. "You found one clue we missed, that web thing. Let's see if either of us can find another."

"I wish I could get online. I'd be studying the habits of spiders."

"I think you already gave us a lot. I agree, he knows these kids. They trust him. That last boy had probably confided that his dad was going to pick him up after school. For most kids, that would be a special event, rather than taking the bus. Maybe they even planned to stop somewhere and get a treat. Whatever it was, our killer knew about it. I think you're a hundred percent right about that."

She looked down at the papers beneath her fingertips. "It could be a cop." She hated to say the words, but the possibility couldn't be ignored.

"Of course it could. That's why Gage has told so few people who we are. He's not just worried about gossip. Right now he's worried about a lot of people who work for him."

"Thank God I'm not him."

But while speaking of Gage, and finding his position unenvious, another unpleasantness was creeping through her: she'd broken her major rule not to become involved with a coworker, however casually. A beer after work was one thing. Tumbling into the sack was another, and she'd gone and done it. Broken the rule. And she didn't know what had caused her to cross that hard-and-fast line. So much for her bold comment about no regrets.

She moved papers around her, keeping her gaze fixed on them as if they were all that held her attention, but now that the glow had worn off, reality was crashing in on her.

She'd acted, reacted, without thinking it through, without weighing the dangers, without even pausing to stop for one clear minute of consideration. That was unlike her, and scary all by itself. Strict rules of conduct, whether her own or the army's, had gotten her through a lot of tough spots, had kept her out of messy situations, and now this. God, had her brains gotten scrambled?

She'd known attractive men before. She'd had flings and relationships before, however truncated, and they always followed the basic rule: never with a coworker.

She'd acted like a woman possessed, without a single rational reason for busting the rules wide-open. There'd be a price to pay for this, she was sure. Cade seemed willing to put things back on a professional footing, but she didn't think that was going to work now.

How could it? They'd just had amazing sex. She wanted to do it again, and she was almost positive he did, as well. Hadn't he just given her a choice between work and play?

How was she going to handle this? She didn't want to make him feel rejected, but she had to get back to the professional distance that had been her creed for so long. Work and pleasure shouldn't mix, and when they did, trouble brewed too often. She hadn't created this rule for herself out of thin air.

"DeeJay?" Cade reached out and touched the back of her hand. "You're...nervous."

She lifted her gaze glumly and decided she needed to be truthful, even if it meant admitting her own shortcomings. "We shouldn't have had sex. It was wrong. We're colleagues. That's always messy."

His fantastic eyes narrowed a hair. He drew his hand back and studied her. "Sex is always messy," he said finally. "But I'm not going to wish it away. So the question is, Agent Dawkins, are you capable of separating the professional from the personal? Because I am. I made love with you and it was wonderful, and I'm not going to act like it never happened. I want to make love with you again. But I think *I'm* capable of focusing on the case and working with you without letting that become a major problem."

It was a challenge. She couldn't mistake the tone of his voice. "Are you sure?" she asked finally.

"Hell, yeah. I don't know how you factor all these things, but I know myself. I can work with you and save everything else for appropriate times. Or not at all, if that's what you want. I'm sure as hell not going to force myself on you."

That stung a bit, but she took it in and made herself think about it. He was willing to agree not to have sex with her again if that's what she wanted. Not words she liked hearing, silly as it seemed to her. She wanted him to want her. Just that simple. She even kind of needed it.

But he was saying he could turn it all off if she preferred. While that didn't make her feel very good, it also made her feel safer.

"I'm confused," she said finally. "Sorry."

"It's confusing only if we let it be. I can draw a line between business and personal. Can you?"

A fair question. "Since I've never done this before, I guess I'm going to find out." The bald admission should have embarrassed her but it didn't. "I wasn't thinking about other things," she admitted. "Just about...you. Us."

She half feared she might anger him, but he surprised her with a laugh.

"Well, thank God for that," he said. "I'd hate to think our lovemaking was a cold, calculated decision."

He had a point, she realized, and then surprised herself by laughing, too. "Am I making a mountain out of a molehill?"

"It's no molehill," he said firmly, "but it's also not a mountain. Don't ever call what we enjoyed a molehill. But I can multitask. Can you?"

She nodded slowly and let go of her concerns, glad she'd talked about them. He'd made her feel better, as if she hadn't just committed a crime of her own. And he'd given her permission to enjoy what had happened instead of carrying a whopping load of guilt and self-recrimination.

Now she just needed to give herself the same permission. That might be harder. It usually was. But at least they'd talked it out like two adults who knew where the lines still lay. A good thing, right?

"Relax," he said. He reached out once again and this time clasped her hand. "We're grown-ups. We can do this." Then he paused. "I guess the military made you used to living with rules, huh?"

"It kept things cleaner and clearer sometimes."

He nodded. "Nothing in life is clean and clear, Dee-Jay. I think you already know that. Whatever rule we just broke, it doesn't have to keep us from being good partners on this case. That's up to us." He squeezed her hand, then released it.

"Back to work?" he asked.

She wanted to sigh, because truthfully she wanted to make love with him again. But the case lay spread out before them and someone's life was on the line. Sooner or later this guy would strike again, probably sooner, and if there was any way humanly possible, they had to find him first. Or find a way to draw him out. Before someone else died.

Calvin hated the storm. It kept him from going out to look at his boys, which always made him feel better, and without them the nagging urge to act was growing stronger…just when he couldn't do a damn thing about it.

He paced the small ranch house, seeking the control that was so important to him. Control was everything. Control of his victims, control of their lives and, yes, control of himself.

He couldn't become a slave to his desire to cleanse and purify or he'd become a useless tool, one that got itself caught. No spider would be stupid enough to get caught in its own web.

His thoughts kept drifting back to that travel writer, though. He should just dismiss her, but for some reason he couldn't. She somehow drew him as much as any of his boys.

Trying to rationalize the urge, he decided she'd make a great red herring. If he broke his pattern with her, it might be possible for him to stay longer in this county before the law sniffing around caused him to head elsewhere.

And she vaguely reminded him of his mother. He pushed that aside quickly. He didn't like the confusion that overtook him when he thought of a potential victim that way. Love, anger and hate warred in him when he thought of his mother, muddying the straightforward mission she had left him with: purification.

His purifications in other cities had never been as satisfying. Working here was his great need, to teach the people of this county something they'd never forget. They'd turned a blind eye to what was happening to him, and now he was teaching them a lesson about fear. About loss, about anguish. And at the same time he was purifying those boys, saving them from the sins they'd inevitably commit. It was a noble purpose.

But the urge crawled through him, like a million bugs under his skin until he scratched himself hard enough to bleed. The sight of his own blood didn't repel him. It relieved him. It was a sign of his own purity. He'd learned that very young.

But the urge to go hunting again was apt to drive him insane. Since the beginning it had been trying to egg him on to take more, take them faster, but he was smart enough to hold back until he felt safe in his power. Just as his mother had been smarter. If she'd beaten him carelessly even the dullards in this county would have taken notice eventually.

But maybe he could take that woman.

He stopped in the back bedroom, which he never used, and turned on the lights. A spider was still laboring to build a web in the corner. Pickings were slimmer in the winter, so the spider just kept building. Walking close, he studied the gleaming web and a new realization struck him.

The spider wasn't particular about what it caught. It didn't limit its meals to flies or small beetles—it ate whatever tumbled into its web. He wished he had an offering for it, but the best he could do was leave some rotting food in the corner. Maggots grew on it, and eventually they became winged and fed themselves to the spider.

Some were tiny little fruit flies. Some were as big as deerflies. The spider had even caught a couple of moths.

No, it wasn't so particular. Maybe he didn't need to be, either.

So he left the room, turning out the light, and paced the house some more. Rubbing at his skin to assuage the crawling sensation helped until he realized he was bleeding again. So he went to the sink and washed and put on a bandage.

The woman. Maybe she really was his type after all. A life was a life, after all. He suspected she was long past purification but…it *was* purification. No reason it could only be achieved by the young.

Finally, focusing at last, he sat again and thought about her. How he might be able to get her.

Like the spider, he vastly preferred to have his prey come to him. Now he just had to figure out how to get her to come. First, he had to meet her. That was essential to drawing her in.

He'd find a way. After all, he'd gotten through the first three boys and he still didn't see a bunch of FBI agents wandering around town. Stupid sheriff thought he could find Calvin all on his own.

Well, Calvin was about to surprise him.

Chapter 8

The storm continued to blow throughout the night. When fatigue finally caught up with DeeJay and Cade, it somehow seemed natural that they went to bed together. Stupid, now, for her to sleep on the couch.

But they didn't make love. Almost by silent agreement, they snuggled in, out of the cold, and offered the kind of comfort only closeness could.

Things were almost back to normal, DeeJay thought as she drifted off to sleep. Normal...

She awoke from a nightmare. The wind still howled outside, though less violently, and the darkness blanketed everything. Breathing rapidly, her heart racing, she slipped out of bed and pulled on her slippers and fleece bathrobe. After a quick trip to the bathroom, she went back out into the kitchen and defiantly turned on lights and started coffee.

She'd had nightmares before, but this one was directly

related to the case. She'd been struggling against bindings, trapped in a stickiness she couldn't escape, watching in horror as a giant spider began to move toward her.

Just a nightmare, she told herself, reaching for calm. If ever a case was designed to give her horrific dreams, this one was it.

She was standing at the coffeepot, watching it brew, when Cade's voice startled her.

"Something wrong?" he asked.

She whipped around to see him standing there in jeans he hadn't yet buttoned, his feet bare, a sweatshirt in his hand.

"Just a bad dream."

"Must have been more than bad." He raised his arms to pull on the sweatshirt, and even in her disturbed state she registered the smooth ripple of muscles over his torso.

"I still feel as if someone walked over my grave," she admitted, then turned to face the coffeepot again. Awareness of Cade's sexiness wasn't going to help anything at all.

But then his arms closed around her from behind. "This entire case is a nightmare. I'm not surprised it's getting into your sleep."

"I was trapped," she confessed. "In a big spiderweb and it was coming for me."

She felt him kiss the back of her head. "Ugh."

That about covered it, she thought. The coffeepot finished brewing, and Cade reached around her, bringing out two fresh cups. Still standing behind her like a bulwark, he filled them.

"You ready to sit?" he asked.

"You can go back to bed," she said. She was used to dealing with things by herself and feared the closeness growing between them.

"Yeah, right," he said.

They moved to the living room. He turned on all the lights as if to drive back the remnants of her dream and sat beside her on the couch. He didn't say anything, giving her the space to just think or to talk as she chose.

"I wish," she said slowly, "that I thought it was just all this thinking I've been doing about spiders."

"But?"

"You heard what Gage said. I look like this guy's type. I guess that got to me more than I thought at the time."

Cade frowned down at his legs for a few seconds. "I dismissed it, too. Really. You're a woman, and you're taller. Not his profile."

She heard something in his tone, however. Her heart skipped uncomfortably. "But? There's a but in there."

"Sometimes these guys break their own profile. I don't have to tell you that. I don't blame you for being uneasy, even if it's only coming out in your dreams."

She looked at him, searching his face, then stared across the room as the truth of his words sank home. "Yeah. Sometimes they do."

He slipped his arm around her shoulder, offering her comfort. "What do you want to do?" he asked finally. "We still have time before he should act again unless he's accelerating. If you want, we can get you out of here and bring in someone else."

"No!" The word erupted from her with force. She turned to face him again.

He spread his hand. "Okay, okay. I just want you to know that you have options here. You wouldn't be the first person who couldn't work a serial killer case."

"I'm not going to let a nightmare scare me off. Or some stupid remark that probably means nothing..."

Then her voice trailed off as another thought struck her.

"DeeJay?"

She bit her lip so hard she feared she would break the skin. "What if Gage is right? I know it seemed to come out of nowhere when he said it, I know there's no reason to think it was anything but a stray thought. But it remains—sometimes stray thoughts pop up for a reason."

He thought it over. "Maybe. It's possible."

"I thought of the spiderweb thing, and we're thinking that I'm right. Where the hell did that come from? Something niggled at me. Maybe something niggled at Gage, as well. No way to know."

His arm tightened a bit around her shoulders. "Say he picked up on something. No way to be sure, as you said, but you're never going to be alone."

She shook her head as a sudden resolve poured through her. "We have to be proactive."

"DeeJay—"

She interrupted without apology. "No, Cade. If there's even a small chance that Gage sensed something important, we have to take it before a new boy disappears. I need to make myself available. I need to take the risk."

"No. I can't allow that. Even on the slim possibility that Gage picked up on something, it's too dangerous."

"Not really. Our perp is used to charming kids. He's never dealt with an army MP before."

She waited for him to argue, but he didn't. A long time later he said heavily, "No, he hasn't. But if you're going to try this, we're going to plan it very carefully. I don't want any slipups if he moves against you."

"I'll be his biggest slipup if he does," she said firmly. She'd dealt with nearly every kind of creep, some of them at the end of her fists. She knew she could take care of herself. She knew it in her bones.

But that didn't make it any easier to think about. This

guy was truly unhinged in ways she could scarcely imagine, and that made him dangerous in a whole different way.

Silence fell inside the house while the storm howled its fury outside. Chilly drafts crept through the place like unseen ghosts wafting here and there.

"I've got to think about this," Cade said finally. "Really think about it. And we need to talk it over with Gage. He's the boss, we're just here to assist."

"Fair enough," she agreed. But her stomach had turned into a hard lump, and her fists clenched tight. Maybe she was losing her mind at last. It was always possible. The link between her and this killer was virtually nonexistent, other than that one man thought she resembled the victims. It would probably be a waste of time, she told herself. She was the wrong sex, the wrong height for this guy.

But that didn't mean squat. Like it or not, these types sometimes changed their patterns, breaking their own molds.

"One thing," she said finally.

"Yeah?"

"Whatever we decide to do about my suggestion, we have to keep looking at everything else. I don't want to waste time because I have a feeling."

"Of course not. We'll keep on looking for the needle in this huge haystack by every means." He caught her chin in his hand and urged her to look straight at him. "Whether you agree or not, Gage has the final word."

"I can take orders," she answered stiffly, staring into aquamarine eyes in which she could have cheerfully drowned at another time.

He sighed. "Yeah, you can take orders. Like you took the order not to pursue your last investigation in the army. Sure, I'm counting on that."

His response shook her out of the cloud of doom that

had been hovering around her since she woke from the nightmare. She jerked her chin free of his gentle grip and shoved his arm lightly. "Don't be an ass, Cade. I said Gage had the final word."

He just shook his head. "I want one promise."

She hesitated. "If I can."

"That you won't try to do something on your own if you don't agree with Gage or me. At least for the love of heaven, let us know."

"If time allows."

"If time allows?" He shook his head almost fiercely. "I don't know what's going on in that head of yours, but I swear, DeeJay, you're going to drive me nuts. Totally bonkers. Rule number one—never keep your partner in the dark. Hear?"

"I hear. And I'm not planning anything crazy. Mainly I want to see if I get approached in some way that doesn't seem exactly right. I'm not looking to wind up in the spider's web."

He closed his eyes. "Famous last words."

They turned out to be the last words for a while. She had no idea what drove him, but he scooped her up as if she weighed nothing at all and carried her back to the bed.

It was a good thing she didn't feel like sleeping, because he showed her he could do as much with his tongue as he could with his hands.

Startled, transported by a new experience, she felt worshipped. He started at her feet, first rubbing them gently until she couldn't help relaxing. Then he bent and ran his tongue along the arch of each foot. He might as well have plugged her into an electric socket. She felt the zap of desire from her feet to her head and arched helplessly.

Then he dragged his tongue up the insides of her legs, pausing at times to just kiss her. By the time he reached the insides of her knees, she knew she had never felt so cherished.

Higher he moved, parting her legs gently, approaching but not quite reaching their apex. The desires he woke in her felt like a spell. She couldn't have stopped him to save her life, couldn't have resisted even a little bit.

Just as she thought he would at last kiss her very center, he moved up and began to trail his tongue from her neck down to her breasts. Helplessly, she clutched at his shoulders, torn between a need to have him hurry and a need for him to take forever. She never wanted this to stop.

Sheer torment and sheer delight met head-on in her as he found her breasts and sucked them as gently as he had licked and kissed her elsewhere. She grabbed his shoulders, trying to bring him closer, but he resisted. Clearly this was going to happen his way.

She groaned as his mouth left her breasts and worked its way down over her belly, causing muscles to ripple helplessly. "Cade…" His name was the only coherent word that escaped her. She was capable of nothing else.

Then, at long last, he closed his mouth over the sensitive nub of nerves between her legs, a sensation so intense that at once it hurt and felt so good she almost couldn't bear it.

But he offered her no quarter, lashing her with his tongue, nipping gently with his teeth, carrying her to a mindless place where nothing existed except sensation. Colors exploded behind her eyelids, as if fireworks and rainbows were the only way she could process what was happening to her.

The explosion that tore through her made the entire world vanish. She might have fainted—she didn't know and didn't have time to wonder, because then he slid up over her and entered her, pumping into her until she began to fly all over again.

She knew the moment he found his own explosion of pleasure, but she followed him so swiftly it seemed simultaneous.

For a long time, she was aware of nothing except his weight on her.

She had no idea how much time passed. It seemed not to matter. He stirred first, rolling off her and pulling her close. They'd visited a realm she had never known existed. Visited worlds beyond her imaginings. She wished she dared to let him know how she felt.

She hoped he felt the same. And then she cursed her own weakness. For the first time it occurred to her that she might be seriously messed up.

A long, long time later, he sighed. "Did I make my point?" he asked.

"Mmm?" She still had hardly enough energy to speak.

"Take care of yourself. You matter to me."

His concern warmed her almost as much as his way of showing it.

Reality, however, wouldn't go away. The case insisted on creeping back into her mind—what they needed to do, the uncertain time frame before another youngster disappeared.

"You're tensing again," he remarked. "Okay. You hit the shower, I'll make more coffee. It must be almost late enough to call Gage."

She emerged into the kitchen wrapped again in her robe with a towel around her head. Fresh coffee was waiting, and she smelled toast.

"Grab a seat," Cade said. "I'll be calling Gage shortly."

"How's the weather?"

"It might have calmed a bit, but only a suicidal idiot or a plow driver would attempt to move out there."

Instead of sitting, she went over to him and wrapped her arms around his waist, giving him a hug. "Thank you."

He returned her hug, giving her a squeeze, as well. "I should thank you." He dropped a kiss on her forehead, then said, "Now sit. Neither of us has had enough sleep, and I don't want to burn the toast because you're a major distraction."

A silly smile twitched the corners of her mouth as she took a seat at the table. Maybe she wasn't as messed up as she sometimes thought.

The table, where the files still sat stacked like a reminder, although it seemed to her that Cade might have been looking through them again this morning. "Find anything?" she asked.

He glanced over his shoulder. "In the files? No, and that started me thinking. Give me a minute to finish the toast."

A short time later he put a huge stack of toast on the table along with their coffee. Two jars of jam and butter followed. She reached for a slice, picked up her knife and began to spread it with butter.

He set a mug of coffee in front of her, then sat in his own place. His hair was still mussed from bed, but he looked good enough to eat in a blue sweatshirt and jeans. Damn, she had to get her mind back on track.

"Okay," he said, spreading his own toast with raspberry jam, "the thing that struck me was how little I found in the autopsy reports. Something is missing."

She froze with the toast halfway to her mouth. "Missing?"

"Missing. You read them. Slow asphyxiation, proximate cause the plastic wrapping. No signs of strangulation, and minimal signs of a struggle against bindings."

She nodded slowly. "But these were just terrified kids. They might not have been able to fight hard. Maybe they were too scared to fight."

"To a point, that's possible. Asphyxiation inside a bag takes a long time, though, and usually induces a hell of a fight. But did you see a tox screen in there? For any of them?"

Her head jerked a little. "No. Fill me in."

"It's speculation, but think about it. They go with him willingly. Maybe he even turns his little plastic handcuffs into some kind of game so they don't fight too hard. Maybe they don't fight at all. At least not until they realize something bad is happening. But apparently that didn't last too long. Abrasions were actually minor, given the circumstances. I'd have expected raw skin from a violent struggle, especially once their faces were covered with plastic. Some evidence of a blow or two. But it's not there. Just like the toxicology isn't there."

She was beginning to see it but wanted to hear his scenario. "Tell me."

"Okay, our perp establishes himself with the kid. Friendly. Nice. Someone they can talk to, whatever. Regardless, he gains their confidence. At some point they go off with him. He creates a game for them that gets them to acquiesce to the cuffs. With a kid that age it wouldn't be hard. Maybe part of the game is wrapping them in plastic up to a point."

"I can't imagine a game like this."

"We don't really need to, although I have some ideas. Just keep in mind the age of the victims. God knows how he got them to go as far as they did, but it's apparent from the autopsies that there was very little violence or struggle.

So just accept the premise for a moment. All these kids were reaching toward adolescence, becoming sexually aware and maybe even active to a point. He could have promised them the best sexual experience of their lives. I don't know. Just stick with the point—he got them bound before they knew they were in trouble."

"Okay." She nodded. She tried to take a bite of toast, but finally put it down. "You've mentioned toxicology twice."

"Because it's missing. My scenario is that he gets these kids to cooperate until nearly the last minute. Then, like your spider, he stings them."

Everything inside her froze. She stared blindly, absorbing what he was saying. "Oh. My. God."

"A paralytic maybe, so he can finish wrapping them and watch them suffocate. I'd like to think he knocked them out, but…" He shook his head. "Not likely. He had to get something out of this. Your spider analogy really got me to thinking. Spiders paralyze their prey before they wrap them. And there's not one tox screen in the bunch. The cause of death seemed obvious, so why look any further? Hell, nobody would have thought to look for a minute needle puncture, especially with bodies that old, however well preserved. Decomposition would probably have made it all but impossible, and I doubt anyone even considered it. They thought they had all the pieces."

A nauseating feeling washed over her in waves, and she put her head in her hands. She'd forgotten the towel wrapped around her head, but as it started to tumble, Cade moved swiftly to catch it. She was vaguely aware that he tossed it over the back of a chair.

"DeeJay?"

"Give me a minute," she said, her voice muffled. "I'm not feeling well."

"I don't blame you."

What he said made perfect sense, but the imagery horrified her. A few minutes passed before her stomach stopped rolling over. Finally, she reluctantly reached for the toast as a way to settle the rest of her nausea. Maybe some jam would help it go down. She scooped some onto it.

"Adolescence," she said. "That's probably a key point."

"It seems obvious now."

"I was thinking small, easy to take and handle, but what you just said..."

"Boys that age would be easy to get that way. They're a bundle of walking, raging hormones. Adventurous, too. Think of all the autoerotic strangulations."

"I'd rather not."

He paused. "You've dealt with it?"

"Unfortunately. One case. It didn't require a whole lot of investigation. The file was closed almost immediately, but I'm sure the hell continued for his parents."

"Yeah, it would. DeeJay, eat. You haven't slept, now you're not eating. I need a partner."

She bit into the toast. Not even the jam could keep it from tasting like dry cardboard. The hell of it was, she could see the ugly logic in what he was suggesting. All of it. However twisted it might be, there was always some kind of purpose behind what a serial killer did. Some kind of play or scenario in their own heads that they acted out at the expense of others. Whether they felt empowered by their actions or got some kind of sexual thrill, there was always a reason for their rituals.

"Now we have to figure out how to use this," she said. "How to get proactive and draw him out, because there sure isn't enough here to point us to him."

"Well, that's always the problem, isn't it? Understanding what he's doing isn't necessarily a way to get to him. Assuming I'm even right."

She looked at him from gritty eyes, the lack of sleep beginning to catch up with her. "I think you're right. Unfortunately we can't bank on it."

"No. But we certainly need to think it through to see if we can wring any ideas out of it."

She nodded, then reached for more toast. Anger was beginning to build in her, and it was driving her appetite. She couldn't afford to let her feelings get in the way of clear thinking, but she could indulge for a little while.

Being in the army had exposed her to some of the very best in human nature, people willing to give and risk everything for an ideal. But her job in the army had unfortunately given her too much exposure to the dregs, people who polluted the uniform simply by wearing it.

She was no wide-eyed naïf—she'd seen plenty of violence—but this guy was so low she had discovered she could still be shocked. He shocked her. Horrified her. Sickened her in ways she'd never felt before.

The mere fact that he was still drawing breath infuriated her. Out there somewhere, sitting in his hideous web, probably already planning his next abduction. Maybe already making the contact with some boy.

Seldom had she felt the urge to commit cold-blooded violence with her own hands, but she did right then.

That shocked her, too. She knew she wasn't that kind of person. She could do plenty with provocation. Her history was littered with it. Being an MP wasn't always a nonviolent job. But never without direct provocation, and only to the extent necessary to bring a situation under control.

This was different.

"DeeJay?"

Cade's voice seemed faraway. She shook herself and answered, "I'm having some unholy thoughts."

"So am I."

She met his gaze at last and saw a cold anger there for the first time. Apparently, his calm explanation of his theory had belied his feelings about it. Bad enough to think of these youths being kidnapped and killed. Worse to plumb the insanity and depravity behind it.

The phone rang, jarring DeeJay so much that she almost jumped. Her mind had been far away from the mundane, looking into one of the pits of hell.

Cade twisted and grabbed the receiver. A moment later, she heard him say, "Lew. Good to hear from you. How'd it go?"

She glanced at the clock, registering Cade's noncommittal responses. Shortly after six here, but eight in the morning at Quantico. Lew must have just hit his desk and found something. She waited impatiently, but Cade's end of the conversation revealed nothing. When he grabbed for a nearby pad and began scribbling things down, she knew only that Lew's digging had yielded some kind of treasure.

Get a grip, she told herself. Stop thinking about what those boys must have endured and think about how good it would feel to catch their murderer. About how much they still had to do, how they needed to turn slender threads of information into ropes they could use against this guy. About how important it was not to waste any precious minutes. Some kid could already be in the killer's sights.

At long last, Cade hung up the phone.

"Well?" she demanded.

"We'll have to thank our sheriff. He apparently put all the information from five years ago into the national database, so Lew even had photos to work with. I can tell you for sure our guy hasn't been in prison for the last five years."

She closed her eyes, nodding slowly. "So there have been other victims."

"Minneapolis, Chicago, Houston and Boston."

"Timing?"

"Closer together there than here. Bigger cities so I guess he felt he had more cover. Lew's emailing everything he has, so whenever we get the wireless backup, we can take a look at all the fine details."

"But he's sure?"

"MO is the same. Victims the same age and description. Only two possibles that don't exactly fit."

Her eyes snapped open. Her heart began to thunder. "Tell me."

Cade looked down at his pad, then straight at her. "Two were women. Died the same way. Fit the general description, but not exactly."

"God," she whispered. "You know…"

Cade nodded. "You're probably thinking exactly what Lew suggested. Our guy could be going for boys who remind him of himself at that age. But the women…"

She drew a deep breath. "The women could have been stand-ins for his mother. There'd be a resemblance."

"That's Lew's thinking exactly. This guy has a grudge against mama."

Her mind began spinning at top speed. She rose from the table and began pacing. "It's fitting," she said finally. "It's coming together. Mother mistreated him. He hated her. He couldn't get back at her, maybe because he was too young or too afraid, or maybe because she was his mother and he loved her anyway. And somewhere in that tangled mess, he's doing to these boys what she did to him. He's carrying out the same torture, following whatever reason she gave him for the mistreatment he suffered, essentially doing what she would have done. Reenacting, fulfilling her stated purpose, whatever. It could even be some kind of sick tribute to her. But every so often, he acts out his rage against her. It's not logical, but it freaking fits."

"If you start looking for logic in the mind of a serial killer, you'd need to be a pretzel," he said heavily. "One other thing that was omitted from the autopsies here, but was picked up on some of the others—genital bruising."

"Perimortem?"

"Definitely. And only on the boys."

She swore and sank slowly back into her chair. "I could write his history now."

"So could I. Now we need to turn it into action. That's where Gage comes in."

She looked him straight in the eye. "That's where I come in. If I look enough like those boys that Gage noticed it, then I may well look like his mother. I need to see photos of the women."

"Lew's sending them," he said grimly. "They're definitely coming."

The storm had bollixed everything up. Gage said he'd be over as soon as he could, but he didn't want to come in his official vehicle. He joked about hitching a ride on one of the plows.

Looking out the window, DeeJay could well believe that might be necessary. Craig Stone from the forest service called and said it would probably be afternoon before he could make it. Everything was still on hold, and the snow was still falling.

DeeJay turned from the window to Cade. "I have to keep telling myself that we have a little time, that the timer on this bomb isn't set to four minutes or something."

"I hear you. But considering the stakes, it might as well be."

They'd both been doing a lot of pacing, but she could

tell he was also doing as much ruminating as she was. Neither of them had apparently yet come up with something they thought worth sharing. At a stand. She hated it.

She heard him swear and he faced her. "This isn't doing a damn bit of good. I mean, I'd wade out there right now, but everything's closed. I couldn't even get into a decent conversation about this with someone without barging into a living room."

The image made her smile faintly. "The questions we'd ask would only raise more. We might even get committed."

Some of the tension seeped out of him. "You're right. So how about a nap? If we can. Right here on the couch. We'll hear if anyone knocks."

She *was* feeling weary from lack of sleep. "Worth a try," she agreed.

They settled on the couch with a couple of blankets. She curled up, and he stretched his legs out across the floor, sliding down until the back of his head rested against the couch.

"I wonder," he said, "if our guy is feeling as bottled up as we are right now."

"I hope not. I don't want him taking any action at the very first opportunity."

"Yeah." He closed his eyes. "I just like the idea of him being miserable."

She couldn't argue with that. The wireless was still down, so she laid her tablet on the end table and wiggled around beneath her blanket until she felt reasonably comfortable and warm.

Sleep was not usually a problem for her. Time spent in the military pretty much taught everyone to grab a nap at any opportunity. You never knew how long it might be before you slept again.

But exhausted though she was, sleep eluded her. There

was far too much rolling around in her mind, none of it pleasant. She tried to replace thoughts of the killer with thoughts of making love with Cade, but even they couldn't take over. She lay there growing tenser by the minute and arguing with herself over whether she should just get up and go to the kitchen. If she lay there much longer, she feared she would start wiggling and keep him awake. He needed sleep every bit as much as she did.

But then he astonished her. She felt his weight as he leaned over and rested against her.

"If you curl up any tighter," he murmured, "you'll turn into a black hole."

"Sorry."

"Shh. Am I making you uncomfortable?"

"No." It actually felt good to have him pressed against her like this. At some level she knew that was danger-ous, that she shouldn't indulge in this. After all, this was an ephemeral thing, whatever was happening between them, and they'd need to work together for years. But she couldn't make herself resist, not when he made her feel so good.

Little by little, her muscles relaxed. Finally, she dozed off, carried away from the nightmares of reality.

Chapter 9

A little before noon, she awoke. She felt Cade stir and sit up, leaving her to feel amazingly bereft. Never would she have imagined that a man leaning on her that way could have been so comforting and relaxing.

Reluctantly, she returned to the world, sitting up and stretching. Cade rose from the couch, saying nothing, and returned a few minutes later with mugs of coffee. He handed her one.

"Good morning," he said. His voice sounded rusty.

"I guess it's here again," she agreed. "Thanks for the coffee." And for the comfort. She didn't say it, aware that there were some places it wasn't safe to go.

He wandered to the window, pulling back the curtain and looking out. "The blizzard has settled down. Just a little gently falling snow, but you can't actually tell where the street is."

"I guess Gage and Craig might not even show today."

"It's possible." He dropped the curtain and came back to sit on the other end of the couch. "Just enjoy your coffee. No need to jump right back in with both feet. I think we've earned a little slack time."

As if there was anything else they could do right now. But she simply nodded and tried to let her mind wander over things that had nothing to do with the case. Blind alleys were most likely to develop when you couldn't put something aside for a little while, when you focused too hard. Letting the mind drift could not only be refreshing, but it might allow new avenues to suddenly appear all on their own.

"I've always liked this town," he remarked. "Not that I was ever here for very long, and it's been quite a while."

"What did you come for before?"

"Mainly just to bring information or pick some up. Passing through. Didn't even stay the night or meet anyone except the sheriff really. Usually the locals can handle their own problems, but sometimes they spill out of the county, so we exchange information."

"So you're not worried anyone would recognize you?"

"Not likely. It's been quite a while and I didn't exactly hang out. But I still liked this place."

"I like most of what I've seen of it so far. I'm wondering about the ski resort, though."

He turned on the couch, raising one denim-covered leg a little so it rested, bent, on the cushion. "Exactly. I've seen what oil did to places, and I've seen what tourism can do. I realize you can't fight change, but the idea that this town won't change if it becomes a big ski destination... well, I'm not buying it."

"It bothers you?"

"I don't want to see it become plastic, like you said. But they need the boost to their economy. Only time will tell what it does to the area. They've been through changes before, though. A big semiconductor plant was here for a few years. Lots of jobs, kids didn't leave as often, new people came in. It created some tension. Then the place shut down and everyone paid in some way. But they did finally get a community college." He smiled, then sipped his coffee.

"You think the same thing might happen with the resort?"

"They talk about hiring locally. I think Masters believes it, too. But if it grows…" He shrugged. "Time will tell."

She peered at him. "Are you getting nostalgic?"

"Why not? This was like a place out of time for so long. The modern world impinges every so often, chipping away at the rural life. Inevitable. I've watched it happen all over the state. No point in making a judgment about it. It just is."

She nodded, thinking about it. "That one-horse town where I grew up?"

"In Texas. Yeah?"

"It's still a one-horse town. It'll probably never change because it's planted in the middle of ranch- and farmland, and there's no reason anyone would want to build anything in the middle of nowhere. Not there. So my mom and pop run a small pharmacy. Would you believe it still has a lunch counter? That's how little the place has changed."

"But you moved on?"

"Obviously. I couldn't find what I needed there. A lot of kids move on, like you were saying about this place. Some make it to college, others enlist, taking the fastest bus out of town. Very little opportunity, unless you want to be someone's hired hand. If the distances weren't so huge, the place would probably have dried up and blown away, but it's easier for most of the ranchers and farmers to head to our town for some things. The co-op is booming, for example. Plenty of feed, seed and fertilizer to sell. The equipment companies do a decent business. And nobody's going to drive to Amarillo or Lubbock to get a prescription filled or to go to church. So it hangs on. But it's a little like watching sunset in slow motion."

"You make it sound sad."

She shrugged one shoulder. "Once upon a time it seemed that way to me."

"Now?"

"I'm glad Mom and Pop are still doing well."

"You look Native American."

She smiled. "My great-grandmother was Comanche. I'm told I look a lot like her."

He laughed quietly. "I hear the Comanche were great warriors. I guess the blood runs true."

She blinked, surprised, then laughed. "Maybe so." She felt complimented by his remark, even though he was probably only referring to her decision to join the army. She hadn't been unique in that. It *was* the fastest bus ticket out of town.

"You ever think about going back to take over that pharmacy?"

She shook her head. "I came here because I like the rural life, but only to an extent. I'd die spending my days behind a counter." She needed more action than that. So far, her new job in Wyoming seemed to be doing that and more.

"That bother your parents?"

She shook her head. "Maybe at first, but they adjusted. They've hired a young couple to help out, and they'll probably buy the place when my parents retire." All neat and tidy. At least her parents didn't resent her for not taking over the family business. That would have disturbed her, but instead they seemed more than willing to accept she had different needs.

Her hometown was so far away from where she was now in space and time. She felt a twinge of longing for her family and familiar sights but knew she could never go back for more than a visit. Whatever it was about her, she had been driven to take a different path through life.

Rising, she went into the kitchen and made toasted scrambled-egg sandwiches for both of them. Cade joined her just as she was finishing up, remarking that he couldn't ignore the good smells.

"About the limits of my cooking," she told him wryly. "It's not my thing, anyway."

"Don't enjoy it?"

"Never have."

"I guess it's a good thing I do," he answered casually enough. Her heart skipped a little, wondering if he meant anything more, then she dismissed it. Sometimes she just needed to turn off the investigator inside of her and take things at face value.

He complimented her scrambled eggs as they sat at the table. But sitting at the table had an inescapable effect: the files stacked at one end drove DeeJay's thoughts back to the case. She sensed by Cade's silence that he was also thinking about the case again. Well, it had been a nice break.

They didn't talk about it, however, not even as they washed the dishes and made more of the inevitable coffee. DeeJay checked her tablet and found the police wireless was still down. Same for the cell phones. They hadn't heard a plow yet, and DeeJay finally looked out front to take in a world that had become almost formless under a deep blanket of snow. Oh, she could see the houses across the way, but drifted snow rode up onto porches and covered roofs thickly. Even the trees that lined the street looked as if they had donned heavy white coats.

Cade came to stand beside her. "Hard to say how much of that is snow that fell during the storm and how much is snow that was blown until it found a relatively wind-less place to land."

"Does it make any difference?" she asked.

"Only when it starts to melt over large areas. Ten inches would only cause light flooding. Even two feet over a large enough area could swamp some places if it melts fast enough. But for now the problems are the same, ten inches or ten feet, we're snowed in."

"I'm honestly surprised we didn't lose power."

"Me, too. We lost just about everything else, though."

Including email. She was impatient to see what Lew had sent them, but there was no way to get to it. She wanted to talk to Gage, and to Craig Stone, but she couldn't imag-ine that either of them had a magic carpet to bring them here. They were definitely on hold.

She wondered if she should go through the files again, then decided against it. Cade's nearness at once aroused and troubled her. She felt relief when he left her side to return to the couch, a relief that was tinged with disap-pointment. Caution lights flared in her brain, but the rest of her didn't seem to want to listen.

Maybe she was having some kind of reaction to all the years she'd refused to dip her toes into a possible re-lationship. She'd buried a part of herself because it just wouldn't fit safely in her career. Oh, some managed it, but she hadn't even been willing to try. Nothing more miser-able than having to see a guy every single day when you'd just broken up. It could create other kinds of problems, too.

She *had* dated, well outside her unit, but had always

broken it off because she was wary and uneasy. She couldn't say exactly why, unless maybe it was that rape so long ago, but she found it hard to trust that any relationship would endure. Especially when life had sent her all over the world.

Now she'd gone and done the very worst thing: she'd had sex with her partner. Great sex. The kind she would call lovemaking. But where did that leave them now? Confined to a house together, with a difficult, haunting case to work on, and trying to ignore the fact that they'd crossed the lines?

Cade seemed to be fairly comfortable but how would she know? Neither of them mentioned last night. It might as well have been erased.

Except that she couldn't erase the memory, or her tingling awareness of him. Couldn't wipe away a hunger to tumble back into bed with him. The only way to live with that was to pretend it didn't exist even as the memories dogged her. Maybe that's what he was doing. Or maybe it had been utterly meaningless to him.

She half hoped it had been, because it would be easier to pretend she felt nothing if he was unaffected. All they had done, really, was scratch an itch. Now they could move on.

She wished like hell she believed that.

All of a sudden, movement caught her eye. Leaning forward, she saw a man coming down the street, skimming along the top of the snow on cross-country skis. He was covered from head to toe in winter gear and seemed to be wearing a backpack.

"Well, will you look at that," she said.

Cade rose and joined her. She felt his laugh before it reached his lips. "Doggone, talk about prepared."

"It never would have occurred to me!"

"If I'd been home, it would have crossed my mind, but they didn't issue us skis for this job."

DeeJay started to smile as she watched the man glide down the street. He was using the traditional Nordic style, long strides that were much like walking except for the glide that carried him forward even farther.

"I prefer that stride," Cade remarked. "The stuff athletes do these days that looks more like speed skating? Not a fun way to ski cross-country."

"This looks like something you could do almost all day long."

"Exactly."

Much to her surprise, the skier paused before their house, then began to glide toward their porch. "What the…?"

When he reached the porch, he bent to release his bindings and leaned his poles against the rail. Clearly, he had meant to come here.

"I'll get it," Cade said. "If you don't mind."

She didn't mind, but she followed him anyway, curious.

Cade opened the door to the icy day, and DeeJay peered around to see a tall man with gray eyes smiling at them. "Craig Stone," he said. "Special delivery."

They gathered at the kitchen table after Craig dumped most of his outerwear. He brought the backpack with him and answered DeeJay's question.

"Well, two things brought me this way. I got back into town late yesterday afternoon and I got a curious call from Gage Dalton. It left me feeling like I needed to get these maps to you as soon as possible. Then my wife, Sky, got to craving some chocolate. She's pregnant and from what I can tell these cravings are pretty strong. I found out the convenience store over this way is sort of open, but of course she didn't want me to come out just to get her chocolate. So when I told her Gage wanted me to see you two as soon as possible..." His eyes danced. "Two birds with one stone. Me."

DeeJay and Cade both laughed. Charming man, Dee-Jay thought. She brought him coffee, which he accepted gratefully, and asked if he was hungry. She was sure she could find something easy enough for him to cover her lack of skill.

"Not at all hungry," he answered. "I'll probably pig out on chocolate along with Sky when I get home, though. So you wanted to see trail maps and contour maps." He leaned over and pulled a stack of folded printed maps from his backpack and laid them on the table. "Anything special?" His gaze was curious. "I'm thinking you're not just looking for touristy reasons, not if Gage thought it was important."

Cade and DeeJay shared a look and reached agreement silently. Both stuck their hands into their hip pockets and pulled out their badge cases. They opened them on the table in front of Craig.

"This is about the boys, isn't it?" he asked.

"Yes," Cade answered. "Gage said you're law enforcement."

"In the forest, anyway. Also a biologist. I can tell you which hat I prefer." He leaned back, lifted his coffee, sipped and then sighed. "All right then. How can I help?"

DeeJay leaned forward. "We need to know how the perp got to the site where he hung the bodies last time. It's not in the reports, and you know the country."

"About as well as anyone," he agreed. "Nobody asked me that before. Curious. Or maybe not. They found the scene so long after it all happened." He straightened, put down his cup and began to sort through maps. "We've been looking for the boys, you know. None of us can get what happened last time out of our heads, so we're looking to see if he's stashing bodies in the forest again. Nothing so far."

He pulled out one map, moved the stack to the side and unfolded the one he'd chosen.

"Did you get all your hikers safely out yesterday?" DeeJay asked.

He looked up from the map and smiled faintly. "We did. Those that wanted to ride it out are hunkered down in cabins we have here and there. Weren't that many. Great skiing now, though, not to mention avalanche risk. I guess we just have to hope they aren't too foolhardy."

He pulled a mechanical pencil out of his breast pocket and pointed to a spot on the map. "This is where the guy hung the kids last time. Pretty dense forest, lots of rocks, lots of undergrowth. Not the kind of place some hiker might come on casually." He looked up, meeting their gazes. "Not an easy place to get to with a body."

"ATV?" Cade asked.

"Possible, but it wouldn't be a straight line. What are you hoping for?"

"A direction he might have come from."

Craig nodded and looked down at the map. "Considering we allow ATVs only on designated trails, he'd have been running a real risk coming that way."

"He's a risk taker," DeeJay said. "He wouldn't be operating here again otherwise."

"I figured that. Well, I'll be honest. There's no real trail in that area, not close by anyway. And these maps don't say much about what's growing there, where the boulders are and so on. You're going to be relying a lot on my memory here, unless you want me to go out there and ride over it. And if he came up over the property that the resort just brought…well, that's private and never been my headache. After all they've done out there to put in the slopes and build roads, it would be pretty much impossible to tell anything now."

Cade leaned closer. "So he could have come across the private property, then into the forest land?"

Craig nodded. "It would be my guess he did exactly that. Less chance of running into me or one of the other rangers, who'd have given him hell for driving off a designated trail. Nobody would think twice about him doing that on basically abandoned private property."

DeeJay looked at the map. She was reasonably good at reading them—it had been part of her early training—but as a military cop she hadn't often needed to rely on terrain maps. "There was a way to get up there on the private property?"

"Most likely." He drew a finger down the map south of the forest boundary. "Lots of people have bought that land and sold it over the years, all of them with ideas for some kind of resort. None of them ever came to fruition until this last group. Luke Masters could probably tell you better than anyone what kind of access there was before the build started. I'm sure there was some. Maybe enough to get a pickup truck at least part of the way. Then an ATV? I don't know. It's pretty rugged out that way, but you'd either have to hoof it or use an ATV to get up that far. I'd bet on it."

He pulled out a different map. As he spread it, DeeJay could clearly see it was a road map. "Here's another part of your problem. At the bottom of the resort property, you have a couple of county roads spreading out, as well as the one that goes directly to town. I don't think you're going to get much help from direction, not unless there's some evidence somewhere that he came from a different direction and came through the forest. I sure haven't heard it."

"Neither have we," said Cade. "For whatever reason, the age of the site, or just not thinking about it, nobody seemed to show any official interest in how he might have gotten there."

"Probably the age of the site," DeeJay said, looking at Cade.

He nodded. "Yeah. Three years after the last boy disappeared means a lot of rain, a lot of winter, a lot of new growth and probably a million ways his tracks wouldn't be clear."

Craig left them with some maps, promising to keep thinking about access to the scene. DeeJay watched him ski off down the street. She thought she might have heard the rumble of a heavy engine, but if so it was faraway. A plow probably wouldn't reach them soon. She figured this storm had taxed the county hard.

"Dead end," she heard Cade say.

She turned to him. "So it seems."

He arched his brow. "You don't agree?"

"I'm not sure." She returned her gaze to the snow-buried world outside. It seemed safer than looking at Cade right now. Crossing the line last night had been bad enough, but now every time she looked at him she felt a jolt of sexual awareness that bordered on serious arousal. One night wasn't going to be enough. She wished she knew if he felt the same. If she had any wiles, she'd long since forgotten them, so she had no idea how to find out.

"Oh, well," she said, forcing herself to turn from the window and face all the messes from the killer to blurred professional lines. "We knew when we went out there that we were looking at a Herculean task to get those bodies up there. Nothing's really changed. I hate to think Craig came out in this just to tell us that we're not going to find a Day-Glo arrow to the killer's point of origin."

"We have to try everything. You know that. Anyway, he was clearly looking for a good excuse to get his wife chocolate."

She had to laugh. "That was cute."

"And probably true." He paused, then said, "If I don't get some exercise, I'm apt to start climbing walls. Care to join me in some shoveling?"

She hesitated. "What about the phone? And do we have a shovel?"

"I'll call Gage and tell him we'll be outside. He won't get here soon anyway. There's a storage shed just back of the house. Maybe there are some shovels in there."

"I'll shovel with my hands if I need to. Better than chewing nails."

Apparently a lot of other people had the same idea. An hour later the neighborhood had become a kind of beehive of shared work. Those with snowblowers were cheerfully clearing all the sidewalks. Other residents helped each other with porches and buried cars. DeeJay and Cade met a lot of people in a short time, and everyone wanted to know their impressions of the locality.

It was kind of like meeting a friendly PR committee. When they took breaks, it was an excuse to cluster and chat, and coffee and tea were coming out of all the houses in a stream. Share and share alike. DeeJay approved of this neighborhood.

At some point everyone seemed to decide that DeeJay and Cade weren't there to do a hatchet job on the town, and conversation turned to the missing boys.

"It was bad enough that we went through this once and

never caught the creep," said a woman about DeeJay's age. She held a cup of tea beneath her face, and every time she spoke a cloud of steam emerged. Small, she seemed almost pixielike. "I've got a boy myself and I won't let him out alone anymore. I've had to become a guard dog, and that's not good for either of us. Lots of parents are feeling the same way. And the families whose boys have disappeared…" She looked away and just shook her head. "I'd go out of my mind."

DeeJay nodded her agreement, staring down the street, which looked a bit odd at the moment with so much of the sidewalks, driveway, porches and cars cleared while the street between remained buried in snow.

She'd been resolved from the outset, but her resolve was hardening. If she could turn herself into bait, she would. The only problem was figuring out how, and she needed to see photos of the female victims to know if she resembled them at all. If she did…

Well, that was the problem, wasn't it?

The distant rumbling she'd been hearing for a while suddenly became loud. Heads swung around to see a big yellow plow turn onto the street.

"About time," someone said. The party mood had vanished the instant the subject of the missing boys had come up. Apparently, fear and horror didn't leave these people alone for long.

"Might as well get inside and warm up," a man said. "We're going to have a lot more shoveling to do when he gets done."

Nods and goodbyes were passed around, then DeeJay and Cade joined the exodus, heading back into their house.

The phone rang just as they were shedding their outerwear. DeeJay answered to hear Gage.

"Had to move heaven and earth, but your street should be clear soon."

"It's getting done right now."

"Give me about twenty, then. I'll come over."

He had fixated on the woman. Calvin knew it and quit making excuses. He ran the plow attached to the front of his pickup up and down his drive, even though the county plows probably wouldn't reach his road until tomorrow. He'd grown up here and didn't expect the impossible to happen.

But clearing his long drive gave him an excuse to clear a route to the barn, if anyone happened to notice, not that anyone was out and about. An excess of caution. Besides, from time to time he heard the helicopter for the emergency rescue team fly by. Not exactly overhead, but he didn't want to stand out in anyone's mind.

The woman. DeeJay, someone at the diner had said when he'd asked who she was. Odd name for a woman. It sounded more like a man.

But he wasn't really thinking about her name. He was thinking about her, about the way she seemed to glow in his mind's eye. He recognized that aura and knew what it meant. He'd settled on her. He had to take her.

Back inside for a break, drinking hot cocoa made with the instant mix—his mother would not have approved, but the small act of defiance pleased him in some way— he looked at his mother's photo. It sat in a small frame along with other family photos, on a piece of furniture his mother had called a lowboy. To him it was just a table with drawers.

He picked up the photo, staring at it, wondering if her eyes had really been as dark as they appeared in the photo. He couldn't recall them now, except flashes from the moments when she had been cleansing him, and then they had indeed appeared black as night.

A thin woman, with a severe face and a will of iron. Sometimes when he thought about her, he could understand why his dad had killed himself. Other times, he thought his dad was a rat for abandoning his wife and child.

But the woman, DeeJay, had those dark eyes. Short hair, like his mother, who had called hair a vanity and often took her shears to both of them. Kate Sweet had been tall, too, like DeeJay, as if life had stretched her out in some way, making her all lean angles. She had towered over him for most of his life. He hadn't equaled her in height until he was almost eighteen.

Taking a woman would change his pattern, cover himself, but it didn't quite answer the questions that loomed in his mind each time this happened. Maybe it was like the time he had finally turned on his mother and whipped her with his belt until she left him alone. Maybe he hadn't felt his mother was pure enough to be cleansing him. It was possible. Certainly the two other women he'd fixated on hadn't been pure, had probably been past purification.

He set down the photo and told himself to stop wondering. He was the person she had made him to be, a man with a mission. Whatever went on inside him that he occasionally needed to take a woman like her—well, she had made him. Maybe this was part of what she wanted, too.

But satisfying a dead woman was the least of it. The urges that goaded him came from deep within him, like an ebbing and flowing tide he could only ride. The tide was flowing strong in him again, and he had to find a way to meet this DeeJay.

Dreaming about it, he set out for the barn. He was stuck because of the snow, and the urges were riding him hard.

Maybe spending some time with his boys would help. Especially if he climbed all the way up so he could look down on them.

Looking down always made him feel more powerful. It juiced him, to use a term he'd learned on city streets, although he meant it differently. It zapped through him like an electrical surge, making him feel big. Huge. Important.

Like a man with a mission.

Gage arrived in the late afternoon. Surprisingly, he walked through the door with a bag of takeout from the diner and began putting foam cartons on the table. "Emma's making pizza for the boys. I'm tired of the sound of video games, and she's been wearing headphones and listening to music to avoid it. I just decided to escape." He was half smiling, though, and appeared to be enjoying himself.

"How are things otherwise?"

"What you'd expect after a storm like this," he answered. "Some outlying ranches without any power, a couple of women who decided now would be a good time to have a baby, some injuries from falls, a few heart attacks from shoveling…" He trailed off. "Thank God we've got a great emergency response team. They've been flying those helicopters since the wind died down enough. So what's up? Was Craig any help?"

"Maybe you'd better explain," Cade said to DeeJay. "I wish we could get to Lew's email. It would make everything clearer."

Gage spoke as he opened containers. He'd brought disposable utensils and napkins, so all they had to add was mugs of coffee. "Lew who?"

"Lew Boulard. An FBI profiler. We had him do a little

research. He called this morning, and promised to send an email with the information."

Gage shook his head. "Might be tomorrow before we have the wireless back. They're working on it—it's a top priority, they tell me—but it's tough out there. Getting to the repeaters, climbing towers in all that snow and ice…nobody wants a broken neck. Wonder why?" After he swallowed his bite of steak sandwich, he said, "Okay, what's up?"

So they explained what DeeJay had noted about the guy's method of displaying his trophies. For her, the worst of it was that what had sounded so brilliant when she first conceived of it now sounded stupid the second time around.

But Gage didn't react that way. Instead, he asked to see the pictures, turned them the way she had and nodded. "I can see it. Now where did that take you?"

"That he lures his victims. He's not snatching them, he's getting to know them well enough that they don't think twice about getting in a vehicle with him."

Gage stopped eating, his gaze growing distant. "Makes sense," he said after a moment. "They had to know him. It's been kind of worrying me from the start. But the web?"

DeeJay let it slide. The web had been a key to her thought processes, but it wasn't essential. Instead, she moved on to the other ugliness, including the part about him using a paralyzing drug on the victims. Now Gage put his sandwich down. He was looking more disturbed by the minute. "There's more, isn't there."

"Well, that remark you made about me resembling the victims. It wouldn't leave me alone."

He shook his head slightly. "The resemblance is slight. It bothered me for a minute there. But—"

DeeJay interrupted him. "Lew, the FBI profiler, found what appear to be two female victims of the same killer. He's been traveling the country, and he left a trail. But the women interested me. Serial killers often have a problem with their mothers. I'm going to go out on a limb here and say he's continuing what was done to him by his mother with these boys. He internalized whatever she was using as a reason. But every so often he goes after his mother. Not surprising the female vics would resemble her if he does. And I resemble his known victims."

Gage gave up on eating. DeeJay hadn't even started, and Cade was making only minor inroads on his food.

"I can leap to conclusions," Gage said finally. "Are you proposing to dangle yourself out there? I don't know if I can agree to that. This guy is clearly dangerous. He might not be as easy on you as the boys because you're a bigger threat. Besides, we've got a little time before this guy strikes again, right?"

Cade spoke at last. "These types accelerate. From what Lew said, he did some accelerating while he was away from here. You had five boys over nearly two years the first time. After he left, he started averaging five a year, and the last year in Boston, he really sped up, finally reaching once every couple of weeks. And since he came back, while three isn't a great sampling, he's taking them closer than he did here before. There's no guarantee we have any time at all."

Gage closed his eyes and remained still for a few minutes. "I don't like this. What are you planning?"

"No plan yet," DeeJay admitted. "I'm just hoping that I'll get an approach that seems a little out of line. Someone trying to lure me in some way. At least then we'll have a direction to look."

After a few minutes, Gage started eating again. Dee-

Jay finally started her own sandwich but discovered her coffee was cooling. She went to get the pot and bring it to the table.

"I need to think about this," Gage said. "We should hash it out. You *do* somewhat resemble his preferred type, and you may be right about this thing with his mother. Little surprises me anymore. But we have to do this in a way that keeps you safe."

"I'm not getting in a truck with anyone," DeeJay protested.

"No," said Gage, "but what if he hits you with this paralytic you theorize before you can stop him? There's being bait and there's being a fool."

DeeJay's stomach knotted, and she once again put down her sandwich. "You're right. But this is about the boys, isn't it? All about them."

"No," said Gage, "it's about stopping a killer before he hurts someone else. *Anyone* else. I'd like you to keep that in mind."

Chapter 10

Two days later, the county was back to near normal, with everyone talking about the severity of the winter storm. And the boys. They had begun to surface frequently in conversations with DeeJay and Cade, as if people were beginning to trust them.

"I'm getting an itch," DeeJay said. They'd finally received all the data and photos from Lew and had devoured them, then read them again. At the same time, she was acutely aware that Cade hadn't tried to make love to her again. Disappointment seared her, and she wondered if she was that bad in bed. Or if he was waiting for her to make a move. How the hell would she know?

"What kind of itch?" he asked. Another morning spent worrying over puzzle pieces that didn't exactly fit into a finished picture.

"You read how he accelerated when he was away from here. I'm not sure he can leash himself for much longer.

Something's going to happen and I am so freaking angry that we've got so little to go on."

"I hear you."

She looked at him, finally. She'd been trying to avoid that since he had stopped expressing personal interest in her. Maybe that was the real problem between them. Or maybe it was a problem with her. Every time she looked at him, longing blossomed deep within her. Under other circumstances she might have tumbled into bed with him and not emerged for a week. Assuming he wanted her.

She told herself to cut it out. They had to be professional. They had a job to do, and everything else needed to be safely on a back burner, most especially her feelings about Cade, feelings she was afraid to deal with.

"We should wander around separately today," she announced.

"Gage won't like it. He doesn't like this whole idea."

"He can stuff it. I get that he has to be worried about everybody, but catching this guy before he kills another boy is the most important thing. It could happen anytime now. Sooner or later he's going to speed up again."

She noticed he didn't argue with her. Mainly because she was right. Lew's file had shown that he'd taken some of his victims only two weeks apart in the past.

She continued, "Just because he seems to have sense enough to realize that moving too fast in such an underpopulated place might somehow give him away doesn't mean he'll be able to maintain that control indefinitely. These guys tend to get full of themselves. You know that. With every kill they get a little bolder. Feel a bit more invincible."

Again, he didn't argue with her, and she knew he couldn't. One of the scariest things about these killers was the way they seemed to grow in confidence, the way their compulsions drove them harder, possibly escaping any ability to control them.

"I look something like those women," she said, not for the first time that morning. "They were even tall like me. And don't tell me you don't see it."

"I see it," he said heavily.

"Tell me what else we're supposed to do. We have every bit of information we can get. And none of it points to any particular person. No one has seen anything or suspected anything. Not one whisper. In a town this size, if he'd done something weird, it would have come out."

"Maybe."

She sighed. "I figure he's the ultimate normal as far as most people are concerned. Nice, attractive, pleasant, friendly. He'd be among the last people who would be suspected. He's back in town, but nobody finds that unusual, so he has roots here. Nobody noticed him five years ago, after all. He must do a really good job of blending. People like him. Maybe they instinctively trust him or have a reason to. They don't imagine him capable of anything approaching these acts."

"Obviously."

"All right, I'm beating a dead horse. But the fact is, we're supposed to find a way to be proactive. Definition of the job. Sitting on our hands is a long way from proactive, and we can't hope he's just going to turn himself in. I have to get out there, Cade. Make myself available. Since I know what we're looking for, I might even be able to point us in a direction before he does anything at all. It's a slim hope, but it's the only one we have right now. If he tries to cozy up to me in any way, I'll smell it in an instant. Trust me."

He'd been almost like carved stone until that moment, but now his voice took on an edge. "I trust you, DeeJay. I believe you're capable of looking after yourself. I figure the army taught you lots of useful defensive and martial skills, and you've probably used them often enough to know what you're capable of when it comes to protecting yourself or taking some creep down."

"But?"

"But I don't want anything to happen to you. If I could find a better way…"

She knew she had him then. There was no better way. None, not yet. And until it turned up, she had to at least attempt this.

"I'll take us into town," he said finally, reluctantly. "We'll head in different directions, pop into shops, chat up people. But don't you dare leave the downtown no matter what. Let's see if this works first."

She'd won. Why, then, did her mouth taste like ashes?

By six that evening, she figured her first stab at this was turning into a bust. Not one person had seemed the least untoward, no one had tried to be more than ordinarily friendly. She was supposed to meet Cade at the diner soon, and it was beginning to sound really good. Going into various stores and bars had been like taking saunas followed by cold plunges all day. When she was inside, she perspired even though she unzipped her jacket. Back outside, the cold found that dampness and froze her.

When she got back to the city center, near the courthouse square, she faced the sheriff's office. Too bad she couldn't go in there and chat. Or maybe she could.

On approach, she saw Gage Dalton emerge, zipping his jacket. He caught sight of her and stopped. She crossed the street to him while he waited. The traffic light had turned to blinking red for the night.

"Let me guess," he said when he reached her.

"You'd guess right."

He shook his head. "You don't listen well."

"Not when it's important."

From a storefront just up the street, facing the square and just behind the sheriff's office, she saw a man peer out from a window. She hadn't been up there yet. Keeping up the pretense, she waved. He didn't wave back.

Gage turned to look. "That's our crisis hotline office," he said.

"I wouldn't have expected to find one here. Part of your department?"

"We started it when the semiconductor plant came. A lot of new people, and the move wasn't easy for them. Then it turned out to be more useful than we could have thought. Grants keep it going, and, yes, the staff are under my purview, but the hotline has its own director. I mostly stay out of the way."

She hesitated. "I don't suppose I have a legitimate reason to go in there."

"They keep the doors locked. When you're dealing with a family dispute, there's plenty of reason to fear backlash, even later. But I can give you an excuse. Come on."

She noted again his limp, but it didn't seem to slow him down much. They covered the distance quickly, and he knocked on the door, then stood back so they could see through the window. The only window in town that had bars on the inside.

The door opened, and a middle-aged woman with graying hair looked out, smiling. "Sheriff. What can we do for you?"

"Hi, Dory. I was just bragging to Ms. Denton here about you all, and I thought I could show you off. You're high point in this town."

"Well, that's nice to hear. We're quiet tonight, so it's okay to bring Ms. Denton in."

"Just call me DeeJay." DeeJay smiled, pulling off one glove to offer her hand. "I promise not to keep you long."

Calvin watched from his console, headset firmly in place. When he'd looked out the window earlier and seen DeeJay, he'd immediately started wondering if he should hurry out for coffee in the hopes of running into her.

Now he could stay put and meet her anyway. As she entered, he saw the brilliant light around her, the light that meant she was chosen. His mouth grew a little dry from excitement.

Dory introduced her with a smile. "The sheriff is bragging about us, Calvin. Maybe you can get your picture in a magazine."

DeeJay spread her hands, one with a glove on and one off. "Sorry, didn't bring a camera. We're going to be limited mostly to scenic pictures, though, so don't take offense. I've seen you before, haven't I? At the diner?"

"I think so. Everyone meets there." He had risen to his feet, as a gentleman should, and smiled at her, trying to contain his rising excitement. She had come to him. They always came to him. He could almost feel the Fates pushing them together.

He shook her hand and noticed its warmth. It wouldn't be warm for long, he thought. Soon she'd be as icy as his boys, and as pure. Well, as pure as he could make her.

Dory laid a hand on his shoulder. While he usually hated to be touched, Dory was different somehow. In no way did she remind him of his mother, and she was always nice to him.

"These folks do a tough job," the sheriff was saying. "They do it well."

DeeJay was smiling. "It must be a hard one. I can't imagine all the grief and despair you must deal with."

"Actually," said Calvin, "it makes me feel good to help people."

Her dark eyes, so like his mother's, settled on him. "Then you're a remarkable person, Mr. Sweet."

"Calvin, please. We're not too busy tonight. Would you like me to show you around?"

She agreed. Of course she did. She was drawn to him the way most people were. In his role as savior and saint, he ushered her around the small office, explaining that the phones were manned around the clock, but they tended to get busiest at night and when the winter deepened. "Cabin fever isn't a great thing for people who are alone or who are in so-so marriages."

"I wouldn't think so," she agreed. "Did the storm we just had cause any problems?"

"I can't say," he admitted honestly. "We were sent home and the calls were transferred to the sheriff's department."

"Purely for safety reasons," Gage said from his position by the door. "No point in having people camp out in this office when we were going to be working anyway."

Calvin smiled at him. "Of course not."

"So did you grow up here?" DeeJay asked him as they returned to his console. The computer screen remained blank as no calls were happening right now.

"I did," Calvin said. "Born and bred. I have a small ranch outside of town, but I don't work it. I was away for a while, and my mother died. I came back as soon as I could, and I still haven't decided what I want to do with it."

DeeJay nodded, listening to him. "It would be a hard decision," she said. "I come from a town even smaller than this."

He looked at her, wondering about her. But it didn't

matter. She was still glowing, still drawing him. "Why'd you leave?"

"Too small for me." She gave a little laugh. "I wanted more travel and excitement. How about you?"

"I had this crazy idea I'd like the big city better."

He noticed the way her gaze suddenly focused on him. "Which city?"

"Oh, a few of them." For some reason he felt reluctant to name them. "But I did this kind of work there and I loved it. I'm glad I could do it when I came home."

She nodded, her gaze drifting away. "That was a great break. I recently lived in Houston," she added. "You been there?"

"On a visit," he said vaguely. "I lived in Boston for a brief while."

She nodded, but he could tell he was losing her. That offended him somehow. He sought a way to get her attention back. "If you're after scenic pictures, you should come to my ranch. Fantastic view of the mountains."

She returned those dark eyes to him, and he felt soothed. She was interested. He could see it. "I'd like that. We usually send a photographer out, though. A pro. But I could take some pictures to give him ideas."

"Cool! Not all your photos should be from the top of the mountains."

Just then the phone line rang. He cursed it because it was for him and he was next on the rotation. But he couldn't let her see that he didn't want to answer, that she had become more important.

Another friendly smile. "Excuse me." He touched his headset and walked toward the console. "Crisis hotline, this is Calvin. What can I help you with tonight?"

DeeJay moved toward the door, spoke a few words with Dory, then turned to wave at him. He had her, he thought as he waved back and continued to listen to the woman sobbing on the line. DeeJay would come to the ranch. He just had to make sure she didn't bring the guy with her. Of course, if necessary he could deal with the man, too. In fact, it might make things cleaner. Folks would just think they had finished their job and left, rather than have her husband raise a ruckus. Yeah, that would work better.

Gage opened the door, letting her exit ahead of him, and Dory locked it behind them.

Later, when he was done with his call and they were waiting for the next, Dory remarked, "That was odd."

His attention pricked. "Why?"

"I just can't imagine why a travel writer would be interested in us."

He could. She had been summoned. But even as he thought that, a warning sounded in the back of his head. Maybe she had another motive. Maybe he should watch her carefully before he made his move. Spiders, after all, waited until their prey was truly tangled and even tired before they approached to sting it.

Spiders were so smart, but he was smarter.

"I want everything you've got on Calvin Sweet," Dee-Jay told Gage when they reached the corner and were about to part ways.

"Why? Houston and Boston?"

"That and an invitation to his ranch."

Gage shook his head a little. "There's probably not much. He's never been in trouble with the law, but I'll see what I can get, starting with his job application. Really, do you think a serial killer would be working at a crisis hotline?"

"Ted Bundy did. By all accounts, he was good at it, too."

She took some satisfaction from seeing his eyes widen. "Hell," he muttered.

"It's a long shot, but right now it's the only one we have. And I'm late meeting Cade at the diner. By now he's probably wondering if I got myself abducted."

She was turning away when he touched her arm. "Good job of questioning," he said.

"It was only one remark. Wish I'd had time for more." Then she marched down the street, remembering the young man with the dark hair and eyes. He seemed so nice. So inoffensive. Almost eager to please.

He was at least worth looking into.

"I was starting to wonder," Cade said when she slid into the booth he'd staked out.

"I ran into Gage, and he showed me the hotline center. We'll talk about it when we get out of here."

She looked at him and saw that he had raised one brow. "Takeout or dine in?" he asked.

"Takeout," she said immediately. "I've scratched the itch for now."

He smiled crookedly. "I got another one to scratch."

She could still blush, something she hadn't realized. She thought she'd left that in her distant past, but there was no mistaking the heat in her cheeks. There was also no way to mistake the way his smile widened.

They skipped the steak sandwiches this time and ordered grilled chicken breasts, broccoli and baked potatoes. A meeting of minds, DeeJay thought wryly.

Excitement dogged her all the way home, even though she warned herself not to make too much of it. Cade let her be until they were back at their own kitchen table, a table that was steadily disappearing beneath papers and notes.

She pushed everything to one side while Cade apparently decided they were going to eat like civilized people. He brought out plates and cutlery and started another pot of coffee.

DeeJay went to get her tablet, and while he put the food on their plates, she started a search for Calvin Sweet in Houston and Boston. If she could find anything, she'd expand it.

Of course he didn't pop up at the top of any list. There seemed to be a lot of Calvin Sweets in the world. She tapped her way through page after page, while she ate with one hand. Next she intended to switch to state databases.

"Going to fill me in?" Cade finally asked.

She looked up from the computer, suddenly realizing she'd broken yet another rule of partnership: sharing information. "Sorry."

"Don't be sorry. But something's got you going. I'd like to hear it."

"It's probably nothing," she said truthfully. "But I met a young man tonight at the crisis center. Probably in his early thirties. We had a casual conversation, and I questioned him about where he lived. Houston and Boston came up."

He grew still. "Amazing," he murmured.

"Too amazing, probably. But he grew up here and left for the city lights, I gather. Came back after his mother died. And he invited me out to his ranch because he has a great view of the mountains. Like I said, too amazing. Slim to unlikely. But Gage is going to look into his background. He doesn't expect to find much because this guy's never been in trouble with the law. But then, there's his job application. It might reveal more."

All of a sudden Cade was smiling broadly. "Great job, DeeJay! Great job."

"Or maybe a waste of time and resources," she admitted honestly. "I'm trying not to get too excited."

"Doesn't look like you're quite succeeding."

She pushed the tablet to one side and forced herself to pay attention to dinner, and to him. "Houston and Boston are big cities," she said. "You could probably find a dozen people in this town alone who've been there, or even lived there. And he said he only visited Houston."

"Did he give you any kind of vibe?"

She shook her head. "Friendly, courteous, warm. Exactly the kind of guy who would take that job. I don't doubt for a minute he was sincere about liking to help people."

He nodded, his gaze growing distant for a few seconds. "Liking to help people doesn't mean you can't also like to kill them. In fact, you might even see some murders as a form of helping."

"Too true. Anyway, a call came in before I could learn anymore. I'd have given anything to find a spiderweb in that office and have time to carry on about it."

He surprised her with a chuckle. "That would have been a sight to behold."

She pursed her lips at him. "I can pretend to be a weak, scared female when necessary. I don't like it, but I can do it."

"I hope I get to see the show sometime." But his eyes were still smiling at her. "Not much scares you, does it?"

"I've faced most of my fears, but that doesn't mean I don't have any left." Like fear of letting a man close enough to hurt her again.

He ate some more chicken, pointing to her plate as if to remind her to eat, as well. She needed to, she realized. The army had taught her not only to sleep at any opportunity, but to never pass up a meal when you were in the field. All the cold walking around town had caused her energy to ebb. She was running on excitement now. Sooner or later, the crash would come.

"So which databases do you want me to search? No point in duplicating your efforts, or Gage's."

She swallowed a mouthful of chicken and quickly sipped some coffee to wash it down. "That diner may make killer steak sandwiches, but the chicken is dry."

"Maybe it's something new they added and they're just learning how. Or maybe Mavis was annoyed at how much room I took up while I waited for you. They were fairly busy."

She laughed at that.

"Databases," he reminded her. "What do you want to know?"

She thought he could probably work it out on his own, but it was nice of him to ask. "I was thinking DMV. If he moved away for a while, we should be able to find out when he canceled his Wyoming license and when he got it back. In short, the period of his absence. If the dates come close…"

He nodded. "Anything else?"

"I'd like to look at his birth registry. Once we know who his mother was, maybe we can find out what she looked like."

"I can check local obituaries, too. In case." He paused, a broccoli floret on his fork. "I hate to say this, because I'm truly worried about you, but your idea could work."

She felt flattered. She was more used to hearing about how she wasn't getting it, that she didn't understand what she was doing—at least when it came to those rape cases. She gave Cade high marks for saying it when he'd been so opposed to her taking the risk.

But Cade was different, she admitted when she had finished eating, cleared away her dishes and gone to get more coffee. At every turn he treated her like an equal. Her first impression of him couldn't have been more wrong. Clearly, he wasn't part of the men's club that she'd come to know all too well that thought women were not as good as they were.

Cade cleared his own dishes. She had a feeling they were going to wait a while before washing.

Then he stole her breath. "So, do you want to work or do you want to make love?"

Speechless, she watched him standing there, leaning back against the counter. A faint smile danced over his lips. Wonderful lips, as she had discovered.

She knew what she *should* answer, but it was too late. His words had stoked desire in her instantly, pushing it from the back burner right to the front, and it was set to a high flame.

"This is insane," she heard herself mumble.

"Maybe." But instead of dropping the subject, he came toward her and held out his hand.

Now that they'd crossed the first line, she could no longer pretend to herself that he wasn't a fabulous figure of a man. Broad shouldered, narrow hipped, his chiseled face softened with a small smile.

But it was more than that that drew her to him. Despite their rocky start—and she had to admit she'd set out to be difficult because she had misinterpreted him—he had remained on an even, respectful keel. Not once had he attempted to diminish her mind or her skills. Truly a new experience for her. The few men she had dated—mistakes!—had always eventually tried to find some way to reduce her. When the power plays and the criticisms had begun, she'd invariably taken a hike.

But she'd been in close quarters with Cade for days

now, and not in the least little way had he tried to de-
value her.

That made him unique in her experience.

He was still holding his hand out to her, and she reached
for it. Whether they were burning bridges or building
them, she had no idea. She just knew she couldn't pass
this up.

Cade was past arguing with himself. The bug had bit.
He wanted this woman again, craved her. He couldn't exactly put his finger on what was so special about her, but
she *was* special. Attractive, yes. Smart, certainly. A good
detective, among the best. She consistently impressed him,
and without her thorns he'd dropped his caution.

Maybe that had been a mistake, but the mistake had already been made. She might never want to see him again
after this case, might even have good reason, but at least
they could steal a few blazing moments of pure delight in
between rounds of shadowboxing with this killer.

At that point he was past caring whether she'd learned
something important that day or if they were headed to
another dead end. Events would unfold one way or another,
but right now he wanted to bury himself in her.

One thing for sure, reality wasn't going away. Hell,
maybe what was happening between them was real, too.
Maybe it wasn't just a fleeting attraction and a need for
brief escape from the ugliness they were forced to deal
with.

He liked her, he wanted her, and he decided to put his
head on hold for a while and just enjoy the next hours with
her. Little enough to ask when they'd been thrown into
the vile maelstrom of a serial killer.

The bedroom was still dark, the curtains drawn. Some
light seeped in around them, enough to guide them as they

faced each other and undressed. The air became pregnant with expectation and the enticing scent of growing arousal. Even before he had shucked his jeans, he was throbbing so hard he thought he'd burst. His entire being seemed to exist between his legs, everything becoming irrelevant except the woman who faced him, steadily revealing her exquisite charms.

And they were exquisite. Keeping herself in shape had kept her shape perfect. Life had endowed her with just enough womanly charm—full but not overlarge breasts with brown, engorged nipples, a small waist and flaring hips. Height had given her long, graceful legs and gently tapering lines, the sight of which made his mouth grow dry.

He filled himself with the sight of her, and then she startled him with a small laugh.

"Cade," she said, "I'm cold again."

He could deal with that. He swept the blankets back on the bed and carried her down, wiggling just enough to pull the covers back up over them before he lay atop her, cradling her face in his big hands.

"Warming up?" he asked as he watched her eyelids grow heavy and passion relax her face.

"Like a house on fire," she murmured. Her hips pushed up against him. "Don't dawdle. Please…"

He took her at her word. A pause to roll on a condom, a pause that he cursed because it let the cool air beneath the blankets, then he lowered himself swiftly and filled her with his entire length. She drew a deep breath, eyes widening.

"Feels so good," she mumbled.

Then he was lost. Her hips rose again, and he plunged even more deeply. It was going to be a hurried, wild ride, but apparently that was okay with her, too.

The explosion came fast, furiously, deafening him like a thunderclap. He knew instant pleasure when he felt her peak with him, heard the moan escape her.

When he collapsed on her, her arms wound around him as if she were afraid she might fall.

It took Cade a long time to return to earth. Longer than it had taken to claim DeeJay. He lay beside her, stroking her from shoulder to hip beneath the blankets, wondering at himself. That was surely the most graceless coupling of his life. Like a bull rutting in a pasture. No foreplay, nothing. Just a taking.

How did she bring him to that point? He'd never gotten that way before.

"You okay?" he asked finally, his voice rusty. He half feared what he might hear.

"Mmm." She rolled toward him and slipped an arm across his chest. "I liked that."

"I'm feeling like I shortchanged you."

A little shudder, like a silent laugh, moved through her. "Trust me, I don't feel like it."

He hoped not, then decided to take her word for it. Only she could know. Now he ran his hand down the silky skin of her back and rump, loving the way she felt. "I could get addicted," he admitted.

"I think I already have."

Their eyes met, and suddenly they were laughing and hugging like a couple of silly kids. He wondered if he'd ever felt this comfortable with a woman right after sex. He doubted it. Something about DeeJay made him more honest. Damned if he knew why.

Maybe because she lacked any pretenses. Except, he suspected, for her aura of toughness. Somewhere inside she must have been wounded by her rape and by needing to resign her commission. There had to be scars, but she carried on like a soldier.

No pun intended, he told himself. He brushed her short hair back from her face and smiled into her dark eyes. "You are one hell of a woman," he said.

"You're one hell of a man," she replied.

"No, I mean it. You amaze me."

"I meant it, too. You're the first guy I ever worked with who has made me feel fully equal. And you don't seem to be struggling with it."

"I'm not. You're at least as good as anyone I've ever worked with, and probably a whole lot better."

She smiled, a beautiful smile, and moved her head closer to kiss him.

"Well, if that's how you thank me for compliments," he said a breathless minute later, "I'll be sure to hand them out like candy."

She laughed and touched his nose with her fingertip. "Don't ruin it."

She cupped his cheek and kissed him again. Then she rolled back a little and sighed.

He knew what she was thinking: time to get back to work.

She was right, but that didn't mean he had to like it. "I wish that shower was bigger," he remarked, holding off the inevitable moment.

"You take one first. I'll go make some more coffee. I think we're going to need it."

"Someday I'd like to get off the hyped-up-on-caffeine train. Just for a few days."

She laughed again and rolled out of bed, stretching before she reached for her clothes. He could have watched her do that forever. "Do you really think," she asked, "that you'd be happy sitting on a beach with nothing to do?"

"Hell, yeah, for a few days."

But she was right and he knew it. He watched her pull on her robe, jam her feet into slippers and head for the kitchen. They were both action junkies. It would make for an interesting relationship.

If they had one.

Because there was one little thing about DeeJay that had begun to niggle at him. No matter how close they got, he felt as if she were maintaining a distance. This close and no closer. He'd left her alone the past few days, much as he wanted her, because he hoped she'd open up in some way. But she hadn't approached him. Hadn't asked him.

DeeJay, he realized, was keeping all her walls up, and she hadn't really begun to lower the drawbridge. He was beginning to feel like a handy roll in the hay.

Chapter 11

Night had settled over the world with an almost surreal quietness. If anyone was out and about, the snow effectively muffled any sounds they might have made. Dee-Jay made coffee and hunted up the coffee cake Cade had bought before the storm and put it out. If they were going to be up for a while, they needed some energy.

Not that they seemed to have lacked any in bed. She smiled to herself as she puttered, realizing that she had liked the way they had rushed. It had been exciting to be so unconstrained, to just give in to the most basic needs. She felt amazingly relaxed and sated now. Maybe it would get her through a few more hours of dealing with this case before she got tightly wound again.

But now that she knew for certain that Cade still wanted her, she felt she had something to look forward to, instead of just dreading what might happen next.

When he entered the kitchen to join her, he was wearing jeans, socks and a green flannel shirt that hung open. He brought his own coffee to the table and sat facing her.

She was already beginning to work with her tablet, but he startled her by reaching out and running his fingertip over the back of her hand. She looked up.

"Before we take the plunge again, I wanted to tell you how wonderful that was."

She felt her cheeks heat faintly and returned his smile. "It was every bit of that."

"We'll do it again soon. Maybe with more finesse, though."

She had to laugh, and he joined her quietly. But her gaze was drawn back to the tablet, and a moment later he withdrew his touch, reaching for his own computer.

"I can't help it," she said after a moment.

"Help what?"

"I can't stand an unsolved case. It won't leave me alone, not for anything."

He reached out and this time covered her hand with his. "It's okay. It's who we are. It's what we do. We'd be lousy investigators if we acted like it was just a regular day job."

She smiled, feeling a bit better that she'd explained herself. She wasn't trying to ignore him, not at all, but this case gnawed at her, and the gnawing hadn't eased one bit with the appearance of a possible suspect.

Probably the wrong guy, given how most things went, but she was willing to chase it all the way to the end. Nothing, absolutely nothing, could be overlooked.

Twenty minutes later, her hopes faded. The DMV database showed that Calvin Sweet had never let his license lapse.

She looked up. "Don't we have an integrated DMV in this country?"

"They're working toward it. Slowly. Forty-six states

share information about major infractions. Minor infractions can vary. But as for general information…not yet. So unless this guy committed an offense bigger than a parking ticket, or in many cases a speeding infraction, you're not going to find out where else he might have had a license without a warrant."

"DMV just shows his license is up-to-date, last renewed six years ago. Nothing else at all. So if he lived elsewhere, he either never got an in-state license there or he never turned in his Wyoming license."

"It's not all that uncommon," he said. "Especially the part about turning in your old license. Unless the state requires it, most people don't bother. They just get a new one. And sometimes the new states don't even ask you to turn in your old one. And then there are folks that never get a new license."

"True." She sat back, rubbing her eyes briefly. "Dead end. I sure as hell don't have probable cause for a warrant to get information on his residency in the other states."

"We're not done yet."

Of course they weren't. She stood up and went to get some more coffee, turning everything around in her mind. Maybe she'd been too quick to leap on Calvin Sweet. Just because he'd said he'd visited Houston and lived in Boston didn't mean he had anything to do with this horror.

Cade had asked her if she'd had any kind of vibe, and she'd answered that she hadn't. Didn't mean anything one way or another. It wasn't as if evil radiated off someone. In fact, in her experience evil seemed to have a benign face all too often, like that guy who had raped her, like so many others she had investigated.

At least not unless you were psychic, a thought that twisted her mouth wryly. She'd never claimed such a thing and didn't really believe in it. Some people were just better at intuition than others. If you looked really hard, you could probably find a reason for what seemed like a supernatural insight.

Which had been Cade's essential question. Did anything about Calvin Sweet bother her at any level? She'd been so focused on her responses to what he'd said about where he'd been that she might have missed something.

Mug in hand, she began pacing through the house, avoiding the kitchen so she wouldn't disturb Cade's research. In her mind, she tried to replay every single second of her time with Sweet. It had been brief enough, and she had a very good memory for details. Being observant had been trained into her. She even remembered every detail about the time he had looked at her in the diner.

She needed to look past the conversation, though. Yes, she'd gotten those nuggets about Houston and Boston, but that really wasn't enough. Something in his manner, his tone of voice… Like a video camera, her brain replayed the entire encounter, once, twice, then again.

All of a sudden she straightened and hurried back to the kitchen.

"He wanted me to come out to his ranch," she said to Cade. "He said he had a beautiful view and I should take pictures from someplace besides the top of the mountain."

He looked up, regarding her thoughtfully. "That bothered you?"

She slid into the chair across from him. "Actually, it did. Most people have been worried we'd say something about the missing boys and make their town look bad. He slid right past that as if it weren't going on and wanted me to come out to his place. Who else has suggested that?"

"No one," he admitted. "And you're right, damn near everyone has been concerned we might do a hatchet job because of the missing boys."

"Exactly. Totally protective of their town. Not Calvin. No, he wants to show off a ranch he isn't even working."

"He could have just taken an interest in you. Men do that." He winked, but in no way did it suggest that he was making light of what had passed between them.

She waggled her ring finger at him, reminding him that they appeared to be married.

He smiled faintly.

"Okay," she said. "He wants me to come out to the ranch. Now in the context of our meeting, Gage said nothing about why I was in town. Dory, his coworker, mentioned he might get his photo in a magazine, but that didn't interest him at all. Not even a bit. That's rare."

"Intensely private people…" He paused. "Yeah. Okay, it's rare, and intensely private people include our killer type. On the other hand, mention of a photo in a magazine might have been enough to make him want you to see the view from his ranch. Maybe he's proud of it."

"Could be." She put her chin in her hand, pondering. "It's also interesting that he didn't ask Dory what she meant. The whole thing indicates that he knows why we're here, or at least our cover story. And he wasn't worried we might say something bad about the place. That's entirely possible, I guess. I'm sure not everyone around here is bursting with local pride."

"But it's still bothering you."

She focused at him again. Looking at him was rapidly becoming one of her favorite things in life. "Yeah. You asked if I got any vibes, and I said no. But the more I think about it… Cade, something was off. I guess I can't quite put my finger on it. Again."

"Then let it go for a while. Gage is doing what he can, and neither of us is getting anywhere online… Hell, I even went to the NCIC. Nada. The guy is a shadow who leaves few traces, at least in the databases we can get to. Short of a warrant, we're at a standstill."

He rose and brought the coffee cake over to the table along with knives, forks and plates. "Let it rest. Something will pop out of that amazing subconscious of yours. Or maybe even mine."

She arched a brow as he began to slice the cake. "What makes you think your subconscious isn't as good as mine?"

"Did I say that?" His eyes twinkled at her. "Maybe we should arrange to pay this guy a visit at his ranch."

"You weren't invited."

"And you go alone over my dead body." He paused, then said, "How about we change the subject? The subconscious works better when we're not beating on it. Something will emerge from somewhere."

Neither of them mentioned the invisible countdown clock.

They settled in the living room with their cake and coffee but weren't especially interested in eating. Outside, the wind seemed to have picked up and occasionally keened a bit.

"We're going to be shoveling again," Cade remarked.

"Are we getting more snow?"

"No, but it's blowing around. One of the things you need to get used to in these parts is shoveling the same damn snow again and again."

She laughed, but the sound was cut short as he reached out a strong arm and urged her to come sit beside him. She didn't even hesitate. It felt so good to curl up against him, and the weight of his arm around her shoulders was nice. Funny how she'd never really taken the time before to notice such things.

Then he asked about her rape. She tensed immediately

but forced herself to relax. She'd told him about it, sort of, and naturally he'd wonder.

"It was a long time ago," she said. "I was nineteen, young and stupid."

"Hold your horses. That doesn't excuse a rape."

"I didn't say it did." She rested her head in the hollow of his shoulder and tried not to let memory take over. Best to keep it clean and brief like a report. "I *did* learn not to go places with a guy where there was no one else around."

"But you came here with me."

"I've learned a lot. I've learned how to take care of myself for one thing. Anyway, I felt like I was raped a second time when I reported it and faced those people telling me I'd better put up and shut up or I'd ruin *my* future with the army, as well as his. I let myself be intimidated. I never allowed that again."

"I can believe it. You're very strong and determined. But how do you deal with something like that?"

"You find a civilian psychologist who doesn't give a damn about the military and you work through it as best you can. I won't say I'm totally over it, but it seems a long time ago now. Scars yes, open wounds no."

"And then you became a crusader."

"That took a little longer," she admitted. "First I had to get somewhere beyond being a gate guard." Which she had, filling her nights with courses at local colleges or by correspondence. "I made up my mind I was going to have some influence, and eventually I got there. Of course, I had my moments. Like I said, I'm not entirely sure that I didn't get promoted up instead of out. But I went to OTS and gained my commission."

"That's officer training, right?" He chuckled. "I bet you turned into a big surprise."

She was able to laugh. "That I did." And she'd never let

herself be intimidated again. When at last she had looked reality in the eye, after her final case, and realized that while it might take them several years, they were going to force her out, she made up her mind to resign and find another job. She hadn't even given them that satisfaction.

"Are you angry with the army?"

"I'm angry with some of the institutional bias and blindness, but not with the whole army. Most of them are good people. It's like anywhere else."

"You've taught me a lesson, you know. Not to judge my partners by one partner in the past."

"Well, you're lucky I came along…" Feeling surprisingly lighthearted all of a sudden, she wiggled around and straightened until she could look at him.

He smiled and gave her a quick kiss. "I'm glad I didn't pursue that option."

So was she. She assumed he'd had a number of relationships. At his age, he'd have had to be a monk to avoid them. Even she had had a few of her own, however brief.

"I dated before," she told him. "But never military people. You'd be surprised how small that community really is. And I'm breaking every rule I ever wrote for myself with you."

"I'm breaking them, too." He lifted his hand and drew his fingertips along her jawline. "Swore I'd never do this, then this cute prickly pear comes along and…" He smiled almost ruefully. "I was engaged once."

His admission caused her heart to skip. She was certain this wasn't a happy story, and she wondered if it would give him another reason to want to terminate their relationship when they were done with this case. "Yes?" she finally managed to ask.

"About five years ago," he said. "Her name was Dawn, and what started out as exciting ended up with both of us disagreeing about nearly everything. Sex isn't enough. It may get the ball rolling, but there's no guarantee it'll keep rolling when you get to the day-to-day nitty-gritty."

"I suppose not." She wondered if that was the first in a long line of reasons she was going to hear once this case wound down. But first they had to solve the case.

In the meantime…well, in the meantime she decided she was going to savor every intimate moment between them. She'd never dated a man like him, had never known the kind of lovemaking he showed her. Or maybe it was just that something about him made her hotter than a fire-cracker.

Either way, he was right. Sex wasn't enough. But he'd treated her with a respect that was important to her. With him she was a full partner, her skills honored, her thoughts fully considered. Odd that she should realize what had been missing only now that she'd met a man who had no trouble seeing her as an equal.

Not that she had suffered a whole lot of overt sexism. The military disapproved of that. But being free of the smaller judgments, the ones that even she hadn't always been able to identify as sexist, now made it clear to her how much she had endured in subtle ways. Of course, to be realistic, it hadn't always been subtle. There had been a few idiots during her career.

"You're a special man," she said finally. "Thank you."

"For what?"

"Treating me like an equal."

He shook his head a bit. "I've seen what you're talking about, but I don't get it. And I've told you why. People should be judged as individuals, not members of some group or other, and certainly not by stereotypes."

"Not many could honestly say they do that. And you did have a moment."

He laughed quietly. "I did. But I wasn't putting you in the class of all women, just the class of one female partner who caused me a whole peck of trouble. And who uses pecks anymore?"

"Beats me." She let her head come to rest on his shoulder again. "This seems positively sinful, to be relaxing like this when there's a killer out there."

"We worked hard today. Especially you. Right now we're at a standstill. By tomorrow we might be wishing for one."

It was true. The instant things heated up, they might not take a deep breath for days. Right now, all she had was a vague suspicion about one man, and until Gage checked him out, there was little more they could do. Gage at least had access to his employment application. She and Cade had already done everything else they could without a warrant.

Part of her wanted to stay exactly where she was, but the itch was coming back. As if he sensed it, Cade let go of her and reached for the two plates of untouched coffee cake.

"Grab the mugs," he said. "Your obsession is returning."

She froze. "Is that how you think of it?" She didn't like the sound of that.

He stood, looking down at her with his patented crooked smile. "I'm the one who just got up. Seems I share the obsession."

Feeling better, she grabbed the mugs and they headed back to the kitchen table. Maybe Lew had come up with something else. Maybe there'd be a useful email. Certainly Gage hadn't called yet. He probably didn't feel he could drag out employment applications or do a background check at night without drawing attention, and considering that he was trying to let as few people as possible know anything, she could understand that.

She just didn't like it. She understood the need for caution, understood the need for warrants, but when her nose was twitching like this, she hated it. She could blow an entire case by crossing the wrong line. She'd seen it happen. Evidence got thrown out because it wasn't obtained legally. No, she was not going to risk that.

Her nose would just have to keep twitching.

A couple of hours later, the night had deepened and no new light had emerged from their investigation. Cade was staring off into space, clearly lost in thought. DeeJay was about ready to give up thinking about anything. She seemed to be running in circles now, studying the same things over and over.

"You know," Cade said, startling her a little because he'd been quiet for so long, "the guy you met today. Calvin Sweet."

"Yeah?"

"Maybe he seems trustworthy to the kids because of his job."

"How so? They wouldn't know much about the crisis line."

His gaze returned to her, focusing. "He might have given talks at the school about it. Kids sometimes need someone to talk to. Sometimes they need it even more than adults."

Excitement crawled across her nerve endings. "Maybe. And since the hotline is under the sheriff's department, he might seem doubly safe."

"Exactly." He sighed. "Dang, there's so much we need to know. Now I should add to the list whether any of these kids were having the kinds of problems that might have made them feel they could talk to Calvin. Who the hell is going to admit to that now?"

"Nobody," she said. "Gage would have to talk to school authorities who'd be reluctant to release any information about these kids, dead or not. The parents wouldn't admit to any problems. They might not even have known about them. God, I'd do it, but I'd hate asking those parents if their kids were troubled in some way."

"Me, too," he admitted. "It's an awfully slender thread, anyway. Doesn't even qualify as a real clue. Putting those parents through an emotional wringer would be downright cruel, and it still wouldn't prove that those children had talked to Sweet."

She nodded, looking down at the mess on the table. "Still, Gage would probably know if he'd given any classroom talks. We'll ask him in the morning. In the meantime..."

She put her chin in her hand and regarded him. "I've worked some difficult cases over the years, but this one beats all. I'm grasping at straws."

"Might not just be straws. Regardless, you grasp what you can when you have nothing else." He leaned forward, putting his elbows on the table, heedless of the papers beneath. "If there's one thing I've learned about investigation, it's that the perp is either such an absolute idiot that you've got him locked up in twenty-four hours or you've got a truly smart perp who eludes you for a while. But sooner or later, DeeJay, they all make mistakes."

"He needs to make one before another kid disappears."

"Clearly. But that's not in our control. Which makes this the rottenest case I've ever had to work."

She couldn't disagree with that. "Sweet is all we have. That means I need to take him up on his offer to visit his ranch. At the very least, I might be able to dismiss him as a suspect before we waste too much time on him."

"Agreed. But make that *we*. You're not going alone."

She didn't answer because she had every intention of taking the first opportunity to check the place out. Whether Cade liked it or not.

"You know, if it *is* Sweet, he might just have made his first mistake."

"Mentioning where he'd lived before?" she asked.

"No, asking you out to his place. We've got his driver's license info, right? Let's see if we can figure out where this ranch of his is."

Her excitement returned. "What if it's close to where he hung the first bodies?"

"Exactly. What if the only time he'd need a vehicle would be to transport the bodies, but he could hike up there any time to admire them and relive the experience? Now that would make sense to me."

It would to her, as well. When Cade unfolded the map, she pulled up Sweet's physical address.

Then, rising, she pulled her chair around and sat beside Cade as they pored over the map.

Calvin lit a couple of electric lanterns in the barn so he could view his boys. Instead of the usual thrill he got when he studied his accomplishments, his mind insisted on wandering.

That woman, DeeJay. The need to take her was becoming an audible hammering in his head. His skull felt as if it was splitting. He hated it when the urge became this strong, because there was only one way to get rid of that headache. It could force him to lose control.

He tried to keep one step ahead of the worst, by acting before the hammering in his head began, and usually he managed. He was proud of his self-control, and while he'd acted more frequently when he left here, it remained that even through the pounding need he recognized the danger in moving too swiftly. He'd heighten the search, and worse he might slip somehow and give himself away.

He still had too much to do to allow that. So many kids had to be cleaned before it was too late for them. But he also wanted that woman.

She walked through his mind almost constantly now, limned in a bright aura of color that indicated she was chosen. Most people just looked dull to him, but his chosen ones always gleamed with the beauty of what they would become through him. Perfect angels.

He looked down at his hands and saw they were shaking. The pile driver in his head narrowed his vision. Sitting with his boys wasn't going to help, and he'd better get down from this loft and back to the house before he couldn't see at all.

Once his vision left him, all he'd be able to do was think about his next move. *Who* was already a settled question. *How* was the one he needed to answer.

He climbed down the ladder carefully, reminding himself to pause to lock the barn. When he got back to the house, he had tunnel vision, a narrow area that he could see. Just enough to get to the medicine chest and take something for his headache. Some of those strong pills he'd found here when he came to bury his mother two years ago. Putting her in the ground had been one of the most satisfying yet saddest events of his life.

He was past trying to sort through those mixed feelings. He had more important matters to worry about.

Like DeeJay. He could already envision her wrapped up and hanging among his boys, like a mother. Yes, she would be a mother to them, unlike the other women he'd taken.

A mother. How fitting. Boys needed a mother to control them, even his purified ones.

As for her husband…he needed to plan that out, too. If both of them disappeared, not a soul would look for them. Everyone would just assume they'd finished their job.

But he must not make a mistake. His mother had taught him that and the lesson had served him well.

He closed his eyes as the last of his vision faded, and then, as the medicine began to make him drowsy, he forgot about everything.

Elsewhere and much later, Cade and DeeJay felt drowsy, too. Having parsed all their too-slender evidence yet again, until they felt brain-fried, they had tumbled into bed together for some glorious lovemaking.

Now they lay side by side, holding hands beneath the covers, replete and trying not to think about the looming threat.

Cade stirred. "You think about the future much?"

DeeJay rolled onto her side, still holding his hand. "How so?"

"Well, we're a pair of workaholics, that's obvious. I wondered if you had any long-term goals besides becoming the director of the FBI."

That surprised a tired laugh out of her. "Really?"

"Really." He paused, and when she didn't say anything, he volunteered an answer. "I told you about my hobbies. I like camping, hiking, skiing. You?"

The sad thing was she'd never looked beyond surviving the next day, solving the next case. "I read." That much was at least true. "And work out."

"Right. Me, too. But that's day-to-day stuff. One foot in front of the other kinds of hobbies. I meant longer term. Even if you become director of the FBI someday, what do you see apart from the job? There has to be something apart from the job."

She rolled over a little more, ignoring the fact that she was now lying on their arms and hands, and rested her other arm across his chest. "I've been too busy fighting to really think about it." Even as she said it, she knew it was true.

"That's kind of sad. I'm not saying you're wrong, it's just kind of sad. Sometimes I actually get around to thinking longer term. That's why I was engaged once long ago. I figured that someday there would be kids, and when I was old I could watch the sunset on my own porch with grandkids playing around me."

She released a breath. "That sounds beautiful."

"Yeah, it does. It really does. Eventually. I'm getting closer to forty, and the closer I get the more I think about the parts of life I've missed. That's why I asked. Because something about this case has made me start thinking about it."

She raised her head a little, trying to see him in the dark, then let it fall back on her pillow. "The kids?"

"I don't know. And I think these two workaholics have spent enough time on that damn case for right now. So let's talk about something else. You ever think about having a family?"

"It's crossed my mind," she admitted. "Once or twice. But like I said, I've been so busy..." She trailed off. "That's a lousy excuse, isn't it?"

"I don't think so. Look at us right now. We're so busy trying to get a handle on this case we barely have time for anything else."

She ran her palm across his chest, feeling the nubs of his small nipples. "We found time for this."

He laughed quietly. "Yeah, we did. But don't evade. I'm into some serious self-exposure here."

"Sorry."

He released her hand, rolled onto his side and drew her into a hug. "There's more than work. I've been filling a lot of time and finding my escape in the woods, in traveling a bit. You were probably busy most of the time in the army, but now you're here and, believe me, you won't see that kind of constant action. So what else would you like to do? Move on to a busier job or something else?"

She didn't know how to answer. Her biggest long-range plan had been getting her college degree. And then when she had become an officer, getting her own command. Life had truncated that. Well, to be fair, she'd truncated it herself by refusing to follow an order to let go of an investigation. Rightly or wrongly, she had done it and had known what the consequences would be. Had she been wearying of the army?

"Let me think for a few," she finally said.

"You don't have to. I was just curious. For some reason I've been starting to feel that I've been too job obsessed. Doesn't mean you have to feel that way."

But he'd hit on something she had never really thought about before. It was okay to be a cop 24/7 if that's what satisfied her. But eventually that would go away. Retirement was inevitable if she didn't get herself killed. She'd left all those possibilities hanging out there as some kind of amorphous thing that would take care of itself in time.

"I haven't made any plans," she said slowly.

"I didn't ask about plans, really. Just…I don't know, longings. The way you'd like things to wind up eventually. I get the family part, but I'm sure doing little enough to make it happen."

"Same here." And as she said it, she realized it was

true. In some way she had always assumed there would eventually be a spouse and kids, that it was just part of human makeup. She hadn't done a thing to make it happen, though.

And if you did nothing, you got nothing.

"Oh, boy," she said.

"What?"

"Heavy thoughts here. I've been assuming in a vague way that things would take care of themselves. But they won't, will they."

"Not if we remain workaholics." But amusement laced the words. "We're a pair."

"I guess so." She liked cuddling with him and wondered why he'd brought up this entire subject. It made her uneasy at some level even as she acknowledged the justice in his point. Was he wondering if she was looking at him as potential mate material?

Was she?

Not for the first time she wished she could read minds. Maybe her focus on work had been nothing but a smoke screen to conceal the other lacks in her life. Surely her biological clock ought to be ticking like mad by now. She'd heard other women talk about it but had never experienced it, probably because she didn't leave room in her life for it.

But even though she couldn't read Cade's mind, it hardly seemed important when she couldn't read her own. What *did* she want long-term, aside from the job? Realizing that she had no real answer to that was as disturbing as the question itself.

Cade held her comfortably and was disappointed. Evidently he'd invested more of himself into this prickly pear than he'd realized. He wanted more from her than a fling that would end as soon as this case was resolved.

He wasn't sure it had risen to the level of wanting marriage and a family with her, but it had definitely become a lot bigger than a fling. He liked her, respected her and wanted to keep her around.

Apparently, the thought hadn't even occurred to her. His ego took a ding from that, but so did his heart. Well, what had he expected? She'd been job focused from the start, so intensely that he was surprised they'd managed to tumble in the hay.

It wasn't that this case wasn't important to him. He cared about those kids, and he cared intensely about catching the killer. But he also knew how to take occasional breaks to refresh his mind. More often than not he'd had to remind her how important that was.

He wondered if it was really obsession on her part, or hiding. Given that she had been raped and then treated despicably by those who should have helped her, he could understand if she refused to look beyond her job. She might have built a shell around herself, created by keeping her focus always in one direction.

People had all kinds of methods to protect themselves. His had become avoiding women partners. Hers may have become avoiding all the rest of life.

If so, that was damn sad. He wanted to break her out of that shell, but knew that doing so could conceivably hurt her. After all, he wasn't ready to make any promises and maybe she wouldn't want him anyway. You couldn't just waltz in and break down someone's defensive walls then waltz away.

All he could do was what he was doing: making it safe for her to be vulnerable with him. Beyond that, he didn't dare tread.

It was odd, though, that for the first time in his life he felt he'd met a woman who suited him in every way.

They shared a passion for their work above the ordinary, and the rare times they left work behind they fit well in every respect.

But he'd better not let it grow any more. She had just said she wasn't ready to go beyond the job. Her shield and lance high, she would focus on work and shut everyone out.

Including him.

Chapter 12

A new deputy showed up at their door in the early morning. Introducing himself as Micah Parish, he was a large man who did indeed wear his Cherokee ancestry proudly. The years had been pretty kind to him. Tall and straight with dark eyes and black hair that was just beginning to show threads of gray, only weathering had added to his age.

"Gage told you I'm okay, right?"

DeeJay nodded and invited him in. "News?"

"Maybe. Been talking to our old sheriff, Nate Tate. He and I go all the way back to Vietnam. A lifetime ago, it feels like. Then sometimes it feels like yesterday."

DeeJay and Cade had been indulging in coffee cake for breakfast. Micah was happy to accept a piece.

"The thing about Nate," Micah said while he ate and sipped coffee, "is that nobody sneezes hereabouts that he doesn't get wind of it. Gage is clued in, but Nate goes past that to a level that's almost scary. So Gage put your concerns to him about this Calvin Sweet."

DeeJay leaned forward to hear better. Cade, on the other hand, seemed to settle back, watchful and waiting.

Micah's voice was deep, his manner almost deliberate.

"So Nate did some ruminating and called me this morning. If he's forgotten anything about the people around here, you couldn't prove it by me. He said Sweet didn't rise to radar level very often. Quiet boy, caused no problems. His father committed suicide when he was a youngster, so his mother raised him. Nate remembered the mother pretty well, called her a sour, disapproving prune who had little to do with anyone around here. No family, no friends. Said he felt sorry for anyone who was raised by her. Anyway, there were a couple of times, just a couple, when teachers questioned the boy about whether he was being mistreated at home. He denied it and while it came to Nate's ears, there was no evidence to pursue. Some felt he wasn't getting enough to eat, but there were no signs of physical abuse. You can't go all Dirty Harry on someone because a couple of times some teachers *felt* there might be something wrong."

"And that's all?" DeeJay asked.

Micah smiled very faintly. "Depends on what you're looking for. A good kid who never made waves, who appeared too thin for his age. But there was one time he wound up in the emergency room with a severe concussion. They both claimed he'd been fooling around in the barn loft and fell. He was released a few days later, and seemed fine. Nate tried to get more information about the accident, because he'd heard from the teachers who were concerned about the boy's treatment. Nothing. Sweet and his mother both explained it away well enough. Accidents do happen."

Now DeeJay was holding her breath. She looked at Cade, who nodded, his expression intent.

"Head injury," she said. "Very often involved in these cases."

"But not enough for a warrant," Micah said flatly. He looked at DeeJay. "Gage said you got an invite to go out to Sweet's ranch."

"I did. I was thinking about it."

"Well, hell. You don't need me to remind you what kind of line you'd be walking. You're a law officer, not a civilian. You're limited to what's in plain sight unless you have a warrant. You don't suppose some killer is going to show off his victims to you, do you?"

"No."

"Then what are you hoping? That he might attack you?"

DeeJay bridled a bit. "It appears he may have killed at least two women in the past—both of them fitting my description."

"Then this is even crazier." Micah apparently didn't believe in tiptoeing around. "You want to be bait? I had a case of that a couple of years ago, and it was a damn good thing I was on a rooftop with a sniper rifle. That's easy to arrange in town, but a hell of a lot more dangerous out on a ranch. I don't care what kind of training you've had. I spent twenty years in Special Ops and I wouldn't walk into that alone. Assuming we've even got the right guy."

The justice of his words sank home. But she still had a stark reality to face. "Some other child could be at risk right this minute. He could accelerate. Most of these killers do and from what the FBI said, he may have accelerated in the past. For all we know, he's making friends with some boy right now, luring him."

Micah lifted a brow. "You think he lures them?"

"How else can you explain that nobody ever notices

anything when these kids disappear? He must gain their trust enough to get them to come to him. I want to know if Sweet has been giving talks at the schools. How he could meet these kids and persuade them he's trustworthy."

Micah nodded slowly. "I can see it. But what about you?"

"He asked me out to his ranch. I'm supposedly here to write about the resort, but he asked me out to his place, promising spectacular views of the mountains to photograph. That's a lure."

"It could be."

"Or maybe not," said Cade. "I don't want her going out there alone, either, so maybe we can go as a couple."

Micah sighed and finished his coffee. "Which is going to undo the whole bait thing." He rose. "I'm as worried about these kids as anyone, but I know the limits of the law as well as you do. Let me talk to Gage and Nate. Maybe we can work out some way for DeeJay here to go in and still be covered. God knows, I don't want to see anyone else dead. And keep in mind, before you go haring off on your own, that right now there isn't enough to build a case. You might just be wasting your time. Right now, our guy could be almost anyone in this county."

DeeJay couldn't deny it. But her nose was twitching. "Intuition is telling me something else."

"Maybe so. And you might be right. But, damn it, we need something more, and preferably without your body providing the evidence. You read me?"

"Loud and clear."

He gave a short nod. "One of us will get back to you. I'm not sure how far Gage has gotten looking into Sweet's background."

"We don't have much, either," Cade said. "And we've been looking, too."

"Same resources." Micah frowned. "We need to find something."

"Maybe Gage will find it in Sweet's job application."

"We can hope."

Someone might notice. Someone might put two and two together. That was a risk they'd been studiously avoiding so that the killer wouldn't be on the lookout for either of them. Yet they'd had one deputy after another, the former sheriff and Gage Dalton visit them. Some cover, if someone on the street noticed and mentioned it.

DeeJay stood at the front window after Micah left, and she was chafing. He was right: as an officer of the law, she was far more hampered than a civilian. Any one of the people on this street could go snooping at the Sweet place and bring evidence back, but not a cop. A cop needed a warrant. Hell, a cop couldn't even *ask* anyone to do the snooping.

She didn't usually object to that stricture. Indeed, she mainly approved of it. People had a right to be protected from intrusion into their privacy by the law. Evidence had to be gathered according to the rules.

But she chafed anyway.

Cade spoke from behind her. "The devil and the deep blue sea," he remarked.

She turned and found him holding out a fresh mug of coffee to her. She took it, thanking him, and returned to staring out the window at the snow-covered world. "He could be gaining some boy's confidence right now."

"Yeah. On the other hand, if it really is Sweet, maybe he's got his sights set on a female victim right now. Namely you. I called Gage again."

"Anything?"

"He's still trying to find the job applications for the

crisis center. Somebody did a lousy filing job. Anyway, I told him I wanted a photo of Sweet's mother."

"How much difference will that make?

"If she looks like his two other female victims, if she looks like you at all…" He didn't complete the thought. He didn't need to.

She set her coffee down, feeling a burst of frustration, and whirled around to look at him. In an instant, a seismic shift occurred inside of her. In one single moment, as she looked at Cade, she forgot everything but him. Inside, she softened and the world went away. The reaction was so strong she couldn't even fight it. Didn't want to fight it.

"Cade?"

"Yeah?"

"If we get through this…"

He waited, then finally prompted her. "What? If we get through this what? And I don't like your phrasing. You promised you wouldn't do something stupid, and you're not a stupid person, DeeJay."

"I'm being stupid right now."

"Oh, hell," he said. He put his coffee down and took a step toward her. "You're not going out there alone."

She shook her head. "Quit obsessing about the case." She almost smiled as she saw his eyebrows lift.

"And you're not?" he demanded.

"I'm obsessing about you." There, she'd said it. And now she was hanging on painful tenterhooks, awaiting his response.

Slowly, so very slowly, he started to smile. "In what way?"

"After this is over, can we have a date? A real date?"

He stepped even closer. "Like with dinner, and flowers and all that stuff?"

"You can skip the flowers. I'm not a flowers girl." Her

heart had begun to hammer until she couldn't quite get enough air. She felt emotionally naked, so exposed that any wound now would run deep and last long. She was terrified in a way she had seldom felt before. Having a gun pointed right at her hadn't been this scary. "Actually, I'm the kind of girl who'd probably give *you* the flowers."

His smile widened. "What brought this on?"

"When I looked at you just now, I forgot everything else. You make the obsessions go away, Cade. I'd like to explore that."

He reached her and slid his arms around her loosely. "Best reason for a date I've ever heard," he said huskily, then kissed her.

It wasn't a demanding kiss. In fact, it was almost comforting, but it invited her to lean into him, to lay her burdens down and just be in the moment. When he broke the kiss, she let herself do something she had never done before: she snuggled into his embrace and rested her head in the hollow of his shoulder. His arms tightened, feeling like a bulwark but not a prison.

"I don't know what we've got here," he said a little while later. One of his hands began to run up and down the curve of her back, soothing her. "I don't know if it'll mean anything when we're done. But I'd sure like to find out. So yes, we'll date. More than once unless you discover you can't stand me. We'll find out where this might go."

"Probably all to hell," she said almost sadly. "My other relationships have."

"So have mine. I guess neither of us is a good bet. But I'm willing to see."

She tipped her head a little but could only see the underside of his strong jaw. "It's scary," she admitted. That left her even more exposed.

"I think anything that really matters is scary," he said

slowly. "I also think that you have even more experience than I do of staring fear down."

"I don't know, but I've had to do it more than once." He was right about that. Giving in to fear, that one time in her life, had cost her a lot. She'd vowed never to do it again.

"After the rape," she said.

"Hmm?"

"I was young, but maybe that's no excuse. I allowed myself to be ruled by fear. Fear of what the command structure would do to me if I didn't shut up. Play by the boys' rules, if you follow me. I was a coward, and I've never forgotten it."

"Grab your coffee and let's go sit on the couch. I want to hear about this."

They settled together, his arm still around her. "Tell me."

"I think I already have. I could have fought them. I could have become such a pain in the butt that..."

"They'd have found a way to get rid of you. Like they did after your last case."

"Frankly, while I wanted a career in the army, I was more afraid of getting myself killed." It hurt to admit it, that fear she hadn't wanted to face even inside herself. Now she was laying it bare. "Accidents happen. They happen in training, and they happen at other times, like when you get shipped to Iraq or Afghanistan. Or any other troubled place. I don't think my NCO or CO would have done anything like that, but there was the guy I accused and his friends."

He cussed quietly. "I don't guess you felt very well protected."

"No." She'd become a nut about studying self-defense of every kind. It had helped her as an MP, but it had never erased her original cowardice.

"I don't think you were a coward. I think self-preservation is an overwhelming force in all of us. You did what you felt you had to in order to survive. I'm glad you did. My life would have been a lot poorer if I'd never met you."

Her mood shifted a little, bringing a smidgen of amusement. "You'd never have known if you never met me."

"Don't go all logical on me. Some things just aren't logical." But his tone, too, sounded faintly amused.

She smiled.

"So," he said, "you got over being raped, as much as anyone can, but you never got over what you think was cowardice?"

"It still bothers me." Not often, but from time to time it haunted her.

"That explains a lot, including throwing your career away over one case. So let me be clear here. You have nothing to prove, certainly nothing that requires you to walk into a trap alone. Understood?"

"God. Can no one drop that?"

"I haven't heard any promises, and that worries me." He caught her chin with his hand and tipped her face up. "This is something you don't have to face without backup. If your instincts are really pointing at Sweet, then I suggest we make ourselves available for another approach from him. Note that I said *we*."

"Noted. But he might not make the invitation again if you're always around."

"Then so be it. We'll find another way to catch this guy. We've put Gage onto a number of things, like whether Sweet gave talks at the school, things like that. I assume he's got someone poring over the phone logs at the crisis center to see if any of the missing boys ever called there,

and if so who took the calls. If he's not, I'm going to insist on it."

"That could take forever."

"A lot of things could take forever. But we've got to
try everything."

"And so we come back to our obsession."

He laughed. "Inevitably. Told you I was a workaholic.
But after this is over, I'm buying you the best dinner ever
and we're going to find out if we've got more than a case
to keep us together. Fair enough?"

It was fair enough, she thought. She straightened so
Cade could pull out his cell and call Gage. He explained
that the boys might have called the crisis center, listened
a moment, then said, "Great." When he disconnected, he
looked at her.

"He's already on it. You apparently pushed him into hyperdrive yesterday. He pulled the call logs, claiming they
needed to provide data for funding, and he put Sarah Ironheart on it. She's working her way back. As for whether
Calvin ever spoke to classes, no."

"So it had to be the hotline." Assuming it was him, of
course. But now she believed it more than ever. "Think
what a tool that crisis line could be for him."

"I am, and it's making me sick." He rubbed a hand
over his face.

It made her feel the same, to think of youngsters in
some kind of trouble, reaching out to a stranger on the
phone only to fall into a sticky spiderweb.

If it turned out to be Calvin Sweet, she wanted his
blood.

Calvin Sweet didn't think anything when he saw that
Cherokee deputy come out of the house where DeeJay
was staying. The whole damn town seemed to be trying

to put on its best face for these writers, so why wouldn't that include the sheriff's department?

He almost giggled as he trudged through the snow toward the house and Micah Parish drove away. The cops were probably busy showing how caring and alert they were, what a safe place this was…and hoping like hell the writers didn't focus on the fear and the missing kids.

He liked walking around town these days, feeling all the fear, watching the way people tried to keep their children close, knowing he had caused it all.

So, yeah, the writers had to have heard about it. And the sheriff was probably busy making it look like cops were on top of everything around her.

But they weren't. They'd never been. They sure as hell hadn't saved *him* and he had always wondered why. They must have known what was going on, even though he denied it. He'd been questioned about it, but nobody ever took it any further.

That made them lazy. Maybe it even made them evil. They'd turned a blind eye even when they got suspicious. His mother had certainly thought they were evil and had wanted nothing to do with any of them.

This whole place lived in some kind of fantasy world, where the only bad things they wanted to know was who was cheating on whom. Well, he'd taught them before and he was teaching them again.

Blind. They were all blind. And now they were afraid.

So, yeah, the sheriff was probably trying to minimize the whole thing so these writers wouldn't trash the town. Giving them personal attention from the police to convince them that nobody had superior law enforcement.

Calvin knew better.

But he was teaching all of them a lesson and, more importantly, he was carrying out the mission left to him by his mother. Purifying those boys.

And now it was time to purify a woman. The surety of it had become his current driving force. He was past questioning the wisdom of anything he was doing. He only knew he *must* do this.

It was time to lure his prey.

Sometimes the confusion of his own thoughts troubled him. He was saving these boys, and these women, so why did he see them as prey? But once the hunting urge took over, the confusion and questions vanished. He was on a mission. That one conviction never deserted him, not even in moments of confusion.

He walked up to the front door of the house and knocked.

Cade opened the door and faced a slender, dark-haired man, possibly in his early thirties, who had a face so smooth and perfectly shaped that it appeared almost angelic.

But he also felt a jolt of recognition, one that made his stomach twist into knots. He didn't need to hear the guy identify himself to recognize the resemblance, however slight, to the photos he'd seen of the boys and women who had disappeared. This guy fit the victim profile in every way except age. Now he knew for sure why DeeJay kept saying her nose was twitching.

He had long experience of appearing impassive, so he was sure the jolt didn't give him away. He summoned a look of mild inquiry. "Yes?"

"I'm Calvin Sweet. From the crisis center. I met Dee-Jay the other day."

"Oh, yeah. She mentioned you. Cade Denton." He offered his hand, and Sweet shook it. Cade was surprised that anyone with such an unmarred face could have hands that felt as if they did rough work.

Calvin smiled. "Nice to meet you. I invited DeeJay out to my place to take some photos. Great view of the mountains. I've got some time tomorrow and wondered if you both would like to do that."

Cade smiled back. "Are you that proud of your view?"

"You bet."

"Well, come on in. Do you like coffee? The two of us were just getting ready to go out, but we haven't turned it off yet."

Already his mind was racing like mad. All that stuff spread on the kitchen table. He had to keep this guy from following him out there. He waved toward the living room to direct Calvin that way and wondered how to handle this.

"I won't keep you long," Calvin said as he walked into the living room. "I've got to go to work in a few hours anyway, but I just wanted to set up something with Dee-Jay, if you guys are interested."

Cade knew a moment of relief when Calvin took the armchair. Now what about the dang coffee? He decided not to ask again. Best to make sure there was no opportunity for him to go to the kitchen.

"DeeJay?" he called.

"Be there in a second." It sounded like she was in the kitchen.

"I would like that coffee," Calvin said.

God, thought Cade, how could a monster have such a sweet smile? But maybe he wasn't the monster. He had to keep that in mind.

Not that he believed it was likely any longer.

He crossed the narrow entry to the kitchen and halted in the doorway, waiting to see if Calvin followed. The sight that met his eyes, however, almost made him smile.

DeeJay was in the process of gathering up the last of their papers. A kitchen cabinet was open, and he could see the bulk of them already stashed up there.

"You're quick," he said, keeping his voice to a murmur so Calvin couldn't hear.

"You betcha." She scooped up the last items and stuffed them into the cabinet.

"He wants coffee."

"I'll get it. You just keep him entertained."

Back in the living room, Cade sat across from Calvin. "DeeJay's bringing the coffee."

"Thank you." Calvin was still smiling, although to Cade his dark eyes held something not nearly as angelic as his face or smile. He dismissed it as imagination. He cast about for something to say.

"DeeJay was pretty impressed with your crisis center. It must be difficult work."

"I like helping people," Calvin replied. Cade felt another jolt as he recognized the absolute sincerity with which Calvin spoke those words. "I can't imagine, though, why the sheriff thought travel writers would want to know about it."

A prickle crept along Cade's neck. Was that fishing or an innocent question? And what the hell did he himself know about writing a travel piece? He sought for something that sounded sensible in answer. "People are going to spend a lot of money to come here," he said slowly. "They like to know about important services."

Calvin's smile widened. "What, are they afraid they'll be in the middle of nowhere?"

Cade managed a chuckle. "This part of Wyoming probably looks like that to a lot of them."

"Then why would they come?"

Dang, thought Cade. He hadn't prepped for this exam.

"Because it's new and different. But they still want to know they'll have a hospital, police, that kind of thing."

"So they want to be in the middle of nowhere and still have all the conveniences?"

This time Cade's laugh was genuine. "Apparently so."

Calvin flashed a grin, then looked over as DeeJay joined them. She carried a tray—where the heck had she found that, Cade wondered—with three mugs, the coffeepot, a small pitcher of milk and some sugar. She set it on the end table.

"Nice to see you again, Calvin," she said brightly, offering her hand.

He shook it—hanging on a little too long for Cade's comfort—then spoke. "I was just wondering if we could set something up for you to come take pictures from my ranch. You should see those mountains in the dawn light. Takes your breath away."

"Help yourself to coffee," DeeJay said, and came to sit beside Cade on the couch. "We were talking about that, weren't we, Cade?"

"We were," he agreed. Although not in the way Calvin probably thought. "Early-morning light?"

"That's best," Calvin said. "The air is so clear, the detail so sharp that you can see every little thing. At this time of year, with the sun so far south, there are enough shadows to give you a feeling for the ruggedness. Anyway, I know DeeJay said you'd have a professional come out here, but I thought you guys could give him some ideas."

Cade's neck prickled again. He glanced at DeeJay and saw her face was perfectly smooth and pleasant. Oh, man, now he understood why she'd been almost positive that Calvin was their man. He was pushing this jaunt as if he'd get wealthy from it. Or as if his future depended on it.

So he decided to be blunt. "What's in it for you?" he

asked. Then, as Calvin's face started to darken, he spoke swiftly. "That isn't meant to be critical. It's just that most of the helpful people we meet have a horse in the race, if you follow me. Like the resort folks, for example. You're being very generous."

Calvin's face relaxed again. "I just want to be helpful. If that resort will be good for the people around here, then I'll do what I can to make it a success. There's a lot of beauty outside of town. That's all."

His own little Chamber of Commerce, Cade thought. Not bloody likely. In fact, come to think of it, the area merchants hadn't put on the dog for the travel writers. This town was still undecided about this resort and whether it would be good for them. And they were certainly more worried about the missing boys.

Cade looked at DeeJay. "What do you think, honey?"

"It won't hurt to go and snap a few shots," she said as if she were thinking about it. "I mean, we're trying to make this sound like a place people should want to come for a variety of reasons. Like hiking and camping as well as the resort. And those mountains *are* beautiful."

Calvin smiled happily. "Good. You can at least give your photographer some ideas."

"He'll probably want to come back in the summer, too," DeeJay said. "For a different look. Is that okay?"

Calvin's hesitation was so infinitesimal that Cade nearly missed it.

"Of course," Calvin said finally. "So…tomorrow morning? Sunrise?"

"Just a little before," DeeJay said.

"That's great. Cade said you were about to go out, so I should be on my way. A few errands to run before work."

He stood, politely shook their hands, thanked them for

the coffee, then left. They watched from the window as
he disappeared down the street.

"Why didn't he just park out front?" DeeJay wondered.

"No obvious connection with us for the neighbors to
remember if we disappear."

Her head pivoted sharply toward him. "You think it's
him."

"I made up my mind when I saw him. He looks like
one of his own victims. And now we'd better go and let
Gage know."

"Calvin might see us."

"Better that he sees us popping in there and a few other
places than that he sees another deputy stop here."

Her brows lifted. "You think he saw Micah?"

"I don't see how he could have missed him."

Gage asked them to wait a couple of hours as he was
involved in another case. Cade didn't tell him much on
the phone, which left DeeJay wondering if things could
have moved faster.

"You should have told him," she said irritably.

"What exactly? At this point, we've got no case against
Calvin Sweet. Gage is tied up with something and, anyway, I don't want to give him extra time to come up with
a million objections."

Still she fumed. And finally she realized what bothered her. "You should have talked to me before you called
Gage." Her truculence was unmistakable and deserved
exactly the response it got.

"Did I step on those toes of yours?"

Her temper flared. "Yes, you did. We're partners, right?
I should have some say on how things are handled."

"You've had plenty of say." Now *he* was looking irri-
tated. "What is it with you, DeeJay? Do I have to walk on

eggshells every single minute with you? Like you haven't done some stuff on your own?"

"Eggshells?"

"Eggshells," he repeated. "I've been walking on them since we met."

"So this nice guy isn't the real you?" She threw up a hand. "Fine. Have it all your way. I'm used to that."

"You could fool me."

They glared at each other, but DeeJay realized something else was working beneath her anger. Standing there almost toe to toe with Cade, she knew she was about to break something. The way she had with other guys she had dated. Smashing every potentially good thing because... because she couldn't trust a guy. Just simply couldn't. Sudden, unexpected self-understanding hit her in the gut. In a flash, she saw herself, and what she saw didn't make her proud or happy.

"Oh, hell," she said, but the words emerged quietly as she turned. "I'm doing it again."

"Doing what?"

She didn't want to tell him, didn't want to admit the truth, even as she finally admitted it to herself.

"DeeJay?" His tone had changed to something softer. "A squabble isn't the end of the world."

"For me it is." And, boy, was she good at starting them.

All of a sudden she felt him take her shoulders from behind, a gentle grip. Instinct made her want to shrug off his touch, but a stronger feeling made her afraid to lose it.

"Tell me," he said quietly. "Please."

She closed her eyes, wrapped her arms around herself and struggled internally. It was like facing a parachute jump off a plane, unable to take that first step but needing to. She'd already exposed so much to this man. So much.

She must trust him, at least to some extent. But trust was so difficult for her.

He said nothing, simply continuing to hold her shoulders as if offering support. She recalled their lovemaking, the way he'd understood her so often, his kindness. He wasn't like anyone she'd known before. Or at least not anyone she'd let herself know. Maybe the few men she'd chosen to date in the past had been selected simply because she knew it wouldn't work.

This time she didn't know if it could work but, damn, she wanted to find out.

She swallowed. "I just realized something."

"What's that?" he asked quietly.

"I protect myself by picking fights. I blow things up before they can blow up on me."

"I see. Do you want to get rid of me?"

"No!" The word burst out of her. "But Cade, it's so hard for me to trust."

"Ahh." He began rubbing her shoulders gently. "Have I done anything to make you distrust me?"

"No. But you will. Sooner or later…"

He spun her around suddenly, his blue eyes boring into her. "Sooner or later you're going to learn I'm exactly the man I seem to be. And you can go kicking and screaming if you want, but I'm not ready to end whatever is happening between us."

"You don't have the right…"

"We're not talking about rights here. We're talking about giving things time. Do I scare you that much?"

He terrified her, she realized. He terrified her as much as anyone she had ever known because she knew he could hurt her so badly, worse than anything in her life. And the longer she was with him, the more he could hurt her. All because she was truly coming to care for him, something she had never really let herself do before.

Hiding behind her emotional walls kept life from dealing devastating blows. But in just a few days, Cade had shown her some of what she'd been hiding from, and she honestly wondered if she wanted to keep missing so much.

She'd taken a lot of risks in her life, but the one thing she had never risked was her heart.

A long, long time ago, she had vowed she would never cry again. She'd kept that promise to herself, but now, with Cade, the possibility of crying hot tears of anguish once again had become a possibility.

Why had she ever let him come this close? And now that she had, what choices remained? Sooner or later this was going to hurt.

He drew her close, wrapping her in his arms.

"Just hang with me, DeeJay. That's all you have to do. Just hang in. We'll solve this case and then see."

He made it sound so easy, but deep in her heart she knew that nothing ever was.

We'll see? That was a hell of a risky proposition.

Chapter 13

They set out a short while later, stopping in a few places to check them out as if they were just looking for things to write about. People welcomed them a little more warmly now that everyone had heard something about them, and Melinda at the bakery sent them on their way with a bag of fresh rolls to try.

"This travel-writer gig could have some advantages," Cade remarked after they stepped out onto the street. Dee-Jay laughed while they walked to the sheriff's offices.

The sidewalks were clear but wet from the melting snow that created berms between them and the street. Every few feet, shop owners had carved an opening in the snow so people could cross the berm as needed. Between the snow and the cars that needed to park away from it so that people could get out the passenger side, she figured the street had narrowed to about half its usual width.

The day felt warm after the past few, though. She didn't know if it was actually warmer or if she was just getting used to it, but before they reached the sheriff she unzipped her jacket. Certainly she felt no need for the ski mask today.

They stepped into a quiet hive of activity at the sheriff's. Deputies were on the phone. The dispatcher, an elderly woman who croaked like a frog and defied all possible laws by puffing on a cigarette, spoke to patrol cars. Whatever had been happening earlier to delay Gage had settled down.

The dispatcher eyed them. "He's in the back waiting for you." Then she went back to annoying some deputy about his bowling game the night before. On the radio.

Apparently, things operated differently here. At least when they were quiet.

Cade led the way back to a narrow hall, which was framed by closed doors with plates on them, everything from individual names to designations like Interrogation and Janitorial.

DeeJay figured this building must run behind many of the storefronts that framed the street facing the square. It was certainly much bigger than it looked from the outside.

One door was open, however, and there sat Gage behind a loaded desk. Between heaps of paper and the computer, the man was almost invisible. He had a phone glued to his ear and waved them to seats while he listened and talked.

At another gesture from Gage, Cade closed the door behind them.

"Okay, got it. Thanks." Gage hung up the phone. He leaned back, grimacing faintly. "I've got some news for you. Who talks first?"

Cade looked at DeeJay. After what she'd said to him such a short time ago, she realized he was going to let her decide the agenda. She almost blushed with embarrassment. On the other hand, he was reminding her that he trusted her judgment.

She looked at Gage. "You've probably got more than we have, information-wise, so you start."

"Okay." Gage nodded. "Sweet's job application, first of all. He worked for a crisis line in Boston, got a stellar recommendation from his last boss. He didn't just visit Houston—he lived there for over a year also working for a crisis line. The interesting thing is that he didn't mention being anywhere else. A big gap in his résumé. But the point is, he lied about only having visited Houston. I have a deputy working on finding out if he lived in those other cities the FBI told you about."

DeeJay nodded. "I'm betting he did."

"I won't be surprised at this point. I've had Sarah Ironheart going over the phone logs for the hotline. There's no personal information about the nature of the call in them, but I can tell you she found one thing, and she's got a whole lot more to go through. I didn't realize the service was that busy. Anyway, to get to the point, the last boy who disappeared called the line and talked to Sweet three days before he vanished. Just one call."

DeeJay felt her heart flip. Then her stomach turned over. "My God," she whispered. When Cade had brought it up earlier, it had been just a speculation, and they'd been doing a lot of speculating. Her emotional reaction had been milder before because she didn't know if it was true. It was entirely different to discover that that man had actually been setting his lures by holding himself out as someone who could help these kids.

"Makes you sick, doesn't it?" Gage agreed. "Gain their trust and then go from there. You were right, DeeJay. Absolutely right. He lures them."

Being right didn't make her feel any better. Not one

bit. "It was just one call. We still don't have anything for a warrant."

"Not a thing," Gage agreed. "But when this many pieces start to fit, you know that you've got a good theory. Now we have to catch the bastard somehow."

"And that's what we're here about," Cade said. Again he looked at DeeJay, and now she felt about an inch tall. She didn't want him deferring to her all the time. Damn her and her native distrust and her stupid blowup earlier.

"You go ahead," she said. "You were the one who saw it."

"Saw what?" Gage demanded.

"Calvin Sweet came to see us. He wants us out at his place by dawn tomorrow to take some photos of the mountains."

Gage leaned forward, putting his elbows on the desk. "My, my, he's a little eager to get you out there. *Both* of you? Why not just DeeJay?"

"I've been wondering about that," DeeJay said. "Then I asked myself a question. We're supposedly here to write a travel piece. Would anybody give a damn if we just didn't show up again? Even our landlord wouldn't wonder for a while. But Cade would, if I didn't come back."

Gage swore quite inventively. DeeJay hadn't heard anyone cut loose like that since she left the army, and she couldn't help grinning.

"What's there to smile about?" Cade asked.

"I'd like to introduce you both to a master sergeant I used to know."

Both men smiled as they understood. But then Cade returned them to business.

"The thing is, for me this was all theory—good theory but still just theory—until I met Sweet."

Gage's brow lifted. "What convinced you?"

"You know him, maybe too well to see it. But he looks like he could be the brother of any one of his victims."

Gage closed his eyes a minute, then his face seemed to sag. "You're right. Damn it, you're right."

"It jolted me the instant I saw him. Maybe because I've spent so much time looking at the photos of those boys and hadn't met Sweet before. Did you ever find a photo of his mother?"

"Not yet. The woman didn't know anyone, didn't go anywhere. If a photo of her exists anywhere outside the Sweet house, we haven't found it. She was a true recluse."

"Well, the female victims resemble him, too, although not as strongly. I assume when he goes for a woman, he's going for his mother."

"It would fit," DeeJay said.

Gage drummed his fingers. "Didn't I say you looked like his victims?" he reminded her. "I wasn't actually serious, just a little disturbed at the time. I didn't know then that he sometimes takes women. Just a moment of uneasiness that hit me. Well, double damn it."

"So we're going out there in the morning," Cade said. "I don't think we should wait."

"Hell no," Gage answered. "I'd love to tell you to put it off a few days. Some time would be nice. But Sarah found something else. Two days ago, Sweet talked to a ten-year-old boy on the hotline. We may not have much time. It was only a few days between the time he talked to the last victim and the day that kid disappeared." He paused. "I put you off this morning because I went out to check the kid. He fits the victim profile."

DeeJay looked at Cade. Her mouth had gone dry, and her heart thumped painfully. "We've got to go in. I may be the only thing distracting him from taking that boy right now."

Gage spoke. "That and the fact that I gave the mother some money to take the boy out of town. They're leaving in the morning. I didn't tell them why, but I didn't have to do a whole lot of explaining. Everyone's scared. They'll get him out of here."

"Thank God," DeeJay murmured.

"So that leaves you two," Gage said. "And what the hell are we going to do about you? There's not a whole lot of cover out there. The snow makes it hard to hide, leaves tracks anywhere anyone goes…" He glanced at his watch. "And you're telling me I have seventeen hours."

The boy, Andrew, called Calvin from school. Calvin could hear the sounds of young voices in the background, but experience had taught him how to filter out the background noise.

He, too, was on his cell phone. Once he was interested in a boy, he always gave them his private number for subsequent calls, a number that he'd picked up with a false name in another town with a well-stocked card to pay for minutes. He wasn't a fool.

He'd checked out Andrew yesterday and had seen the aura around him. He was one of the chosen.

Andrew was upset that he was being bullied again. Calvin listened with sincere sympathy, promising the boy that he'd help him take care of the problem in a few days.

Damn, he had the woman to deal with first, and taking a boy so soon… Yet this one had wandered into his web as if put there by fate. He couldn't ignore such a perfect offering or risk delaying his mission.

"I need a few days," he told the boy gently, yet again. "Can you hang on a little longer?"

"I have to," Andrew finally said. "I just hope I don't get beat up."

"Be sure to stay in sight of a teacher. Maybe I can find a way to meet you tomorrow? Just to talk some more?"

When he was done with Andrew, he went to work, but for the moment he'd forgotten the boy. He'd made a bold move asking for DeeJay's husband to accompany her in the morning and he needed to figure out how he could eliminate the guy so he could have DeeJay to himself.

It unnerved him a little that he hadn't planned ahead before persuading them both to come. He wasn't usually sloppy. But even as he worried the problem uneasily, he felt a growing confidence that he would figure it out.

Later that evening he got another call from Andrew. This time the kid sounded happier. "I won't see you tomorrow," he said. "Sorry."

"Did something happen?"

"Yeah, it's really cool. My mom's taking me skiing for a week. It's a surprise for my birthday next month."

Calvin felt confused. The boy was leaving? But he'd been chosen. "Isn't that kind of early for a birthday present?"

"Yeah, but we have to take the trip this week. She won it, she said, and if we don't go this week we lose the prize."

Andrew sounded ecstatic. Calvin felt a huge pressure growing behind his eyes. He had to act. He had to take DeeJay and he had to take the boy. They were both chosen and he couldn't afford to lose either of them. He didn't know what would happen to him if he ever missed a chosen one, but he was sure it would be dire.

His head throbbed, making thought difficult, but he reached hard to gain some control over the impulses. He had to work this out or fail.

He must not fail.

"Well, that's great," he said, and cleared his throat.

"Listen, maybe we can meet before you go. Can you get out for a walk tonight?"

The boy didn't answer for a few beats, maybe thinking it over. "Sure. I guess. After my folks go to bed, I can come down to the county road."

"Tell me when and I'll be there."

Andrew hesitated. "Midnight? Nothing wakes them up at midnight."

"Cool. I'll meet you there. Your drive at the county road?"

"Yeah."

"I'll bring a little present for you, too. Even if it's early."

The pressure in his head eased when he hung up. The feeling didn't entirely vanish, but it told him he'd done the right thing.

Two at once. He'd never done that before, but a sense of his own power grew in him. He'd take the boy tonight while his family slept. Then he'd take the woman in the morning, and he'd figure out what to do about her husband. Remembering the medicines he kept hidden in a case under his bed, the paralytics he injected, the sleeping pills he could liquefy and put in beverages, he began to form a plan.

Micah Parish squeezed into Gage's small office and closed the door. He leaned back against the filing cabinet, arms crossed, his dark eyes leaping from Gage to DeeJay to Cade.

"Okay," Gage said. "You've got about sixteen hours to organize the best operation of your life. Anybody else you trust with Special Ops background, bring them in. Everyone else is out of the loop…in case."

"In case what?"

"In case we've got the wrong guy. In case somebody

talks before this is over." He sketched the situation with additions from DeeJay and Cade, and Micah began to nod, his gaze growing distant.

"Civilians?" Micah asked. "I may need a couple with the right background. A few SEALs come to mind. Say Nate Tate's son, Seth Hardin, for one."

Gage looked at DeeJay and Cade. "Your asses are going to be hanging out and we called you for your expertise. What do you think?"

DeeJay spoke. "I've had a lot of dealings with Special Ops. Mostly Rangers, but some SEALs, too. If Micah has people he trusts to observe secrecy and do this job, go for it."

Micah nodded and straightened. "I'm on it. I'm going to need one of the choppers to overfly the Sweet ranch today for a terrain check, and I'm going to have a team ready early tonight." He looked at DeeJay and Cade. "It may go against your instincts, but let me handle this part. I'll be in touch when we've got a plan and fully brief you."

"Micah?" Gage spoke. "Remember, we don't have enough for a warrant. One crisis hotline phone call isn't enough to prove probable cause to a judge. Lots of people call the hotline, and lots of them talk to Calvin Sweet without getting into trouble."

"I get it. The primary thing is to be ready to act if he tries to harm either of these agents. I'll have us ready. They won't be alone for long."

Later, Cade and DeeJay walked along the streets of Conard City. For some reason Cade reached out and took DeeJay's hand. Well, they were supposedly married, and she didn't feel the least urge to pull away from the touch.

"The waiting is going to drive me nuts," she said.

"I hear you. So you think these guys can do it?"

"I've had the privilege of seeing Special Ops in action more than once. It's even more amazing than what they let you see on TV. If I have to put my life in someone's hands, they're it."

He nodded. "Okay then. This goes against my grain."

She gave a mirthless laugh. "Mine, too. Action, that's me. But our turn comes in the morning."

"Yeah." He gave her hand a small squeeze. "Maybe we should stop and take a picture from time to time. I don't know much about being a travel writer, and the folks around here probably don't know much, either, but I doubt that we'd just be taking a stroll if we were working."

"Good idea." She pulled out her cell and snapped a photo of the shops along the street. "You know, this place has some real charm. Worn-out charm, but real. I hope the improvements the resort plans don't ruin it."

Overhead, one of the rescue choppers flew, the *whop-whop* of the blades loud.

"There they go," Cade remarked.

"I guess Micah's moving fast."

"He needs to."

She took a few more photos, and when they resumed their stroll, he again took her hand. She found his touch comforting, something she desperately needed right now when she felt cut out of the operation, with no input of any kind. She wasn't used to that.

"It's killing me that I can't be in on the planning," she admitted. "I want to be in the war room."

"Did you used to be, in the army?"

"Usually. When we were planning a takedown in a big case, yes, I was there. Nothing like this, though." She sighed. "I get that Micah is the best person to plan this."

"And we're just here in a supporting capacity. Profilers, doing our part by getting proactive. Local authority rules."

"I understand that, too. It's not what I'm used to, but I'd better get used to it."

He laughed and squeezed her hand again. "We'll have our own big cases, trust me. Statewide investigations. You'll be in the war room again. Just don't expect it to be frequent."

"It was never frequent. Yeah, we did some big investigations, but most of them were the types that cops do everywhere. I'm not expecting major ops around every corner."

"Good, because most of our work is considerably quieter than this. But I have to admit I'm edgy, too. I don't like relying on anyone blindly."

"Ha. You sound like me." She glanced up at him in time to see him smile faintly.

"Okay, so I like to be in charge," he admitted. "I'm not the only one suffering from that deficiency."

She couldn't disagree. "I guess there's no sense to just walking around town. I'll take a few more pictures, and since we left those rolls at the sheriff's office, maybe we should stop and get some more. Friendly gesture, and I want a sandwich. Not a steak sandwich, just a plain old ham sandwich."

"And then what?" he asked as they turned a corner in the general direction of their house.

"I'm going to chew my nails to a nub until we hear from Micah."

"Well," he said, and flashed her a devilish look, "there's another way we could relax."

The laugh that escaped her came easily and naturally for the first time that day. "You're on."

By the time the early winter night settled over the world, distraction was a thing of the past. The two of them were pacing the house, waiting for a phone call.

"He hasn't had enough time to set things up," DeeJay said yet again.

"Nope," Cade agreed as he passed her.

Their time in bed earlier had been wonderful but rushed because they'd both been listening with one ear for a phone call. Neither wanted to be at a point where they couldn't stop when that phone rang.

DeeJay tried to distract herself by remembering that all-too-brief hour, but great as it had been, larger worries wouldn't leave her alone.

She had pulled out all the papers again, all the files, and had tried to reread them from a different angle, looking for indicators that she'd made a mistake somewhere, but she kept coming back to Calvin Sweet and the way he was so insistent that they come out to his ranch.

If she was wrong, if they were all wrong, absolutely nothing would happen in the morning. Then they'd be hunting again with possibly less to go on and a whole lot less time if that boy didn't leave in the morning.

It was seven in the evening when the phone finally rang. DeeJay grabbed it and was almost disappointed to hear the familiar voice of Lew Boulard from the FBI.

"Thought I'd check in," he said. "The cases you had me search for? We sent out an information request to law enforcement for similar cases. I hate to tell you, but he's killed more than I originally told you. Over the last year, this guy appears to have been striking with increasing frequency, sometimes only a few days apart. I can't say for sure, because we have missing persons, too. No bodies. But when I sent out a composite of his victim type, the missing-persons cases started rolling in, as well. You don't have a whole lot of time."

"We just learned that here." DeeJay told him about the call to the crisis line. "He may be stalking a kid right now.

The sheriff has the mother taking the boy out of town in the morning."

"Good. And you?"

"I'm going in as bait."

She listened to silence from Lew. Then, he continued. "DeeJay, be careful. I got tox reports on several of the victims, three boys and one woman. He used a medical paralytic, vecuronium. No side effects, other than paralysis, and it's long acting. I don't know how the hell he got it. I do know it has to be mixed and injected, so don't let him get close."

"I won't."

She barely had time to fill Cade in on what Lew had reported before the phone rang again. This time it was Gage.

"Micah's about ready to roll. Here's how it's going to play out, okay?"

"I'm listening."

"Calvin gets off duty tonight at ten. I'm going to have someone undercover follow him home to make sure he gets there and doesn't divert. We'll call you as soon as he's heading out of town. Then both of you get over here so we can fill you in."

"We'll be there."

When she hung up and told Cade, she asked a question. "Is there any antidote for that paralytic? Can we get it?"

"I suppose there must be, but I don't know." He glanced at his watch. "I'm going to call our forensic pathologist."

Ten minutes later, he had the answer. "The antidote has to be administered by IV. So let's keep our distance."

Shortly after ten, they got the call and hopped into the car to drive over to the sheriff's office. From the street, it looked almost deserted. A different dispatcher manned the desk, and only one deputy was visible through the window. A quiet night in Conard County.

In the very back everything changed. A large room had been turned over to a team. Gage was there, as was Micah. Cade and DeeJay were introduced to five other men, but only one name stuck: Seth Hardin, probably because Micah had mentioned him earlier.

All the team members were dressed in black, but winter camouflage was heaped on nearby chairs. Sniper rifles with scopes lined the wall on a rack. Radios had been laid out on a long table to one side, along with various other implements from knives to garrotes. This was a team preparing for anything.

A map lay spread out on the big central table.

"All right," Micah said. "We're ready. We'll be in place by 4:00 a.m. but we're not going until we're sure that the subject has turned in for the night. Here's the deal. I surveyed as much as I could today. You need to try to draw him toward the woods if you can, assuming you find any evidence, because that's the safest place for us to hide out. But I'm still going to have a couple of guys near the house. There's a gully that runs along here, and we can use it to approach. Still, the woods aren't that far from the house, so we won't be out of reach. Given the lay of the land, though, we'll be at least ten minutes away. Maybe fifteen depending on the snow depth out there. And we can't do a damn thing unless something goes down. You know that. So you'll have to let us know."

DeeJay nodded, studying the map.

"Unfortunately, we're going to be blind on the north side of the house and barn, except for what we can see from the woods. Try not to go that way. If you go inside and something happens, we won't know unless you signal us. Clear?"

DeeJay and Cade both nodded.

Micah went on. "I checked it out and cell phones work out there, which is good because it'd look weird to go out there with satellite phones. Give Seth here your cells. He'll set them up to call us immediately with a one-number punch. Any number."

DeeJay felt impressed. "I didn't know that was possible."

Seth Hardin, a tall, good-looking man, smiled faintly. "A little modification to the auto dialer. You may need a new phone when I'm done, but regardless, you'll still receive calls."

"Go for it," she said, handing over her phone.

Cade passed his over, as well.

"It all looks simple," Micah said, "but these operations are usually straightforward once everyone is in place. So that's what you need to know. If something happens, we're going to need ten to fifteen minutes." He paused. "That's long enough to kill you. Don't forget that."

"Here's something *you* need to know," Cade said. "We just got another call from the FBI. This guy is using a paralytic on his victims. I checked it out. It works fast and it lasts for up to forty-five minutes. We're not going to get close to him if we can avoid it, but if we do… Well, if we don't come out of that house or barn in fifteen minutes, you come in. Because we're supposed to be there to take pictures and I have no intention of staying inside for very long."

"I'd prefer not to go inside at all," DeeJay said. "But if we get the opportunity, I'm not going to turn it down. We might see something."

Micah and Gage both nodded. They didn't need to be reminded of the plain view doctrine. Once Cade or Dee-

Jay was invited inside, anything in plain view became evidence.

A radio crackled from the table and Gage picked it up. "Bluebird," he said.

"Red is in the nest," came the response.

"Eyes on."

"Copy."

"Okay," said Gage. "He's home. Now we wait."

Everyone sat around drinking coffee. Apparently they were all too keyed up to think about sleeping, but conversation was almost nonexistent. The plan was in place, the details hashed out as much as they could be. Everyone just wanted to get going.

Then, at around eleven-thirty, the radio crackled again. "Red left the nest. Going toward town."

Gage looked at DeeJay and Cade. "You two better get home and make sure your car is in plain sight in case he's checking you out."

They took off fast. When they reached the house, they darted inside to sit in the darkness. For all the world a house asleep.

The minutes dragged by on leaden feet.

At three, the phone rang. It was Gage. "Deployment under way. But I gotta warn you, we don't know where he went after he left last night. The man I had tailing him slid into a ditch and couldn't get out. All we know for sure is that our guy got back home an hour later. Something's going down. Nobody takes a midnight drive on these roads for pleasure. Watch yourselves."

A little while later, Cade reached out across the table in the dark and found DeeJay's hand. She curled her fingers with his and held on tight.

As her nerves stretched, a kind of clarity came to her.

She didn't want to die today. She wanted the opportunity to get to know Cade better.

All of a sudden, she wanted all the time in the world, just as her timeline was narrowing to a matter of hours.

"We'll be okay," he said.

She hoped so. She really hoped so. For the first time in a long time, she wanted a future, one that didn't depend on her job.

For some reason she remembered the historic words of Sitting Bull, and paraphrased them. "Today is *not* a good day to die."

Chapter 14

Cade was driving. DeeJay studied the eastern sky, which showed the first predawn lightening. She figured they were only a mile from the Sweet place. Her stomach, which had been a mess for hours, had settled into a hard, tight knot she was familiar with. It was time to act, and they just had to make sure they did everything right. "Fruit of the poisonous tree," in legal terminology, could prevent prosecution of Calvin Sweet even if they found bodies on his property. Everything now had to be by the book.

She suspected the only way they were going to get any further was if he attacked one of them. Up under her jacket she had secured a telescoping baton. Both of them wore shoulder holsters under their parkas.

"If he wants me, he has to get rid of you," she said to Cade.

"I figured that out."

"Sorry."

"No, I'm sorry. I'd be lying if I denied I'm tense. I feel like a spring that's been compressed a little too far."

"I hear you. Plain view, damn it."

"Plain view," he agreed.

Then her phone rang and the nightmare truly began. She listened with growing horror, gave only a brief response and then hung up.

"What?" Cade demanded.

"That boy Andrew? His mother said he went to bed last night but when she got up this morning to take him on his trip, he was gone. He must have let himself out, because the side door was unlocked."

Cade swore inventively. "Okay," he said as they neared the entrance to Sweet's ranch. "Not only eyes on, but ears on, as well."

Hyperalert, she thought. As if she wouldn't be anyway. But the knot in her stomach hardened even more. Now they knew where Sweet had gone late last night. Somewhere a boy might be clinging to life. This had shifted from an exercise to get information to one to save a life.

"Let's get the bastard," she said as they bumped their way toward Sweet's house.

Sweet had evidently heard them coming. He was waiting on his front porch. DeeJay pulled down the zipper on her parka enough to be able to reach her baton or her pistol without revealing either. She saw Cade do the same as soon as he switched off the ignition.

"Ready?" he asked.

"As ever."

They climbed out. DeeJay plastered a smile on her face. The sky was still lightening but not enough yet to take pictures. Calvin came down from the porch, grinning, and shook their hands.

"Thought you might change your minds," he said. "Wait here, I've got some coffee to take with us."

So he wasn't going to invite them inside. DeeJay wondered how they could get around that. But as she looked past the house, she saw the barn and wondered if that wasn't the place they really needed to get into. And as far as Calvin knew, they were out here alone, miles from anywhere.

He wouldn't be afraid of them if he had a plan to take them down. He also wouldn't be expecting them to have backup. She wondered how she could provoke him into doing something stupid.

Glancing at Cade, she suspected his thoughts were following the same path. His face had an almost grim set to it.

Calvin returned, carrying three insulated bottles in his arms. "Help yourselves," he said.

Letting them choose which bottle they took? That would seem to indicate he wasn't trying to slip them a Mickey, but she didn't trust it. He could have put a sedative in all three of them and just wouldn't drink himself. She thanked him as she took a bottle and looked at Cade. He arched a brow and gave an infinitesimal shake of his head.

So he suspected the same thing.

When Cade had his bottle, Calvin led them away from the house. "The view is best once the barn is out of the way."

"I like your barn," DeeJay said. "It has character."

"It's old and keeps me busy," he said. Damn, he sounded so natural. "Drink some coffee. You guys must be having trouble waking at this hour."

"It *is* early," DeeJay agreed. "So you have to plow a path to your barn? I thought you said you weren't working this place."

"I'm not, but I store a lot of things out there. I never know when I might need something."

She felt a moment of horror as Cade unscrewed his coffee bottle and poured some into the plastic cup. Had she misread him?

But she noted that he barely lifted the cup to his lips. He wasn't really drinking, but Calvin mistook it and smiled. "Good coffee, huh?"

"The best," Cade agreed. "You can make coffee for me anytime."

"Have some more. You can have mine if you want. I get up early sometimes, and I'm pretty full of caffeine already."

DeeJay moved around until she was on the far side of Calvin, forcing him to turn away from Cade. Behind Calvin she saw Cade dump the coffee and use his boot to cover the stain with a heap of snow. The crunch of his boot in the heavy snow sounded loud to her ears. She spoke quickly to keep Calvin distracted.

"Calvin," she said, "let me take pictures of your barn, okay? Really, it's the kind of charm we need along with the mountains."

Calvin looked toward the hulking, weathered structure. "I never thought of it that way before. Sure, go ahead."

So she darted forward and pulled out her phone, taking pictures as she moved around. Calvin watched her, but kept glancing at Cade, who appeared to be on his second cup of coffee.

Then she heard it. A faint cry. The back of her neck prickled with awareness. "What's that?" she asked.

"Barn owl," Calvin answered smoothly, but she saw a change in his face. He hadn't expected this. Something around his eyes tightened.

So the boy might well be in the barn and waking up early.

"A barn owl? Is it in the barn?"

"It flies in and out."

"Can I see it?"

Calvin froze for an instant. "Maybe in a few minutes. Anyway, when you go in there, it almost always flies out."

"Why do you let it in?"

"Mice," he said. Some of his smooth veneer was vanishing, and he kept looking at Cade as if he expected something. Finally, he asked, "You feeling okay, Cade?"

Cade looked fine to DeeJay but then he rocked slightly on his feet. Just a little. "I'm fine," he answered. "Just tired. I don't keep rancher's hours."

"Well, have some more coffee," Calvin said.

Pushing it just the way he had pushed them to come out here. DeeJay heard the soft cry from the barn again. Her heart began to race. Impossible to tell if it was human and her mind scurried down legal avenues, wondering if that cry would justify her walking into the barn on the imminent danger doctrine. If an officer suspected someone was in danger, they could break down doors if necessary to get to them. But she had a man standing here telling her it was an owl, and she couldn't be sure.

"I really want to see that owl," she said. "Just let me peek."

Calvin's expression was no longer pleasant. His face had stiffened, become hard. "It's just a damn owl," he said. "I told you, it'll fly away the minute I open the door."

She looked at the barn, debating her options, then heard a sound from behind her.

She turned. Cade had dropped his bottle onto the snow.

"God," he said, "I'm all thumbs today. You'd better take the photos, DeeJay. I'll lose my damn phone in the snow."

"I got it," she said. Calvin seemed fixated on Cade, as if expecting something.

"I'm getting cold," Cade remarked.

Calvin immediately opened his own bottle and poured more coffee, then passed it to Cade. Cade reached for it, but let it slip through his fingers to the ground.

"Is he sick?" Calvin asked. It sounded like a perfectly reasonable question, but DeeJay didn't believe it for a minute.

"Why don't you stay here?" she said to Cade. "Calvin can show me where to take the pictures from, then we'll get you home."

She saw something flare in Cade's eyes. He didn't want her walking away with Calvin alone. But she needed this guy to do something untoward, and she needed him to do it fast. If that sound from the barn was the missing kid, time might be of the essence.

She left her own coffee bottle on the ground near Cade, believing it might turn out to be evidence. Best to keep it away from Calvin, who might be able to get rid of it if things went awry. Then she touched his arm. "Be right back, honey. Drink some more coffee if you need it."

Cade simply sat down on the snow, hard, as if his strings had been cut. For the first time she worried that he might have taken a sip of the brew, and there might be enough sedative in just a little amount to seriously affect him.

But she still had no choice. She had to provoke Calvin in some way. He had to do something that would give her an excuse to react. Until she had cause, she couldn't go in that barn unless he invited her.

Unfortunately, Calvin led her around the north side of the barn, out of sight of the team that lay in wait. The sun rode the horizon now, casting a rosy glow over the mountains just west of the ranch. The trees climbing up the mountains still guarded mysterious shadows, but the light, roseate though it was, held an amazing clarity. Holding her phone up, she took some more photos.

"You were right," she told Calvin. "This is breathtaking. It's amazing how fast those mountains just rise up."

"Well, we're in what's essentially a high valley. The foothills are farther east. It's kind of like Denver, you know?"

She nodded. Then, hearing the faint sound from the barn again, before he could stop her she darted over to a dirty window and peered in, using her hand to cup one side of her face. Little light penetrated the interior.

"Hey," said Calvin surprisingly mildly. His steps approached, crunching on snow.

She turned quickly, trying to look apologetic, making sure he couldn't get close without her knowing. "Can't see a thing. I hoped I might see the owl. Sorry."

That's when she noticed he had removed a glove. He was carrying something she couldn't quite see.

And he kept bearing down on her.

"Calvin? Is something wrong?"

He smiled, looking incredibly angelic except for his eyes. Those dark eyes seemed hard as obsidian.

"Not a thing," he answered, closing the distance between them.

She shifted, moving to the side, trying not to get backed up against the wall.

"You're special," he said.

"Who, me?"

"You look like my mother, you know. I recognized it the first time I saw you."

Her mouth went dry. Still no cause to summon help. She hoped Cade was on his feet again and just around the corner waiting, but she hadn't heard any sounds of movement. The damn snow made enough noise that surely she would have heard something.

"Did you hear?" she said, not caring that it was such a non sequitur it might tip him off. She *had* to provoke him. "Another boy went missing."

He just smiled. "He's special, too, I guess."

Still not enough. He was now within arm's reach. He lifted his ungloved hand and she saw it held a needle.

She hit numeric button on her phone and dropped it, as she sidestepped yet again and slipped her hand inside her jacket to pull out her baton. With one flip she opened it.

He stopped. "What's that for?"

"A lady never goes anywhere without protection."

"I'll protect you," he said. "Really. I want to."

"Protect me from what?"

He didn't answer. She was watching his face, and recognized the moment he had gathered himself enough to spring. The instant he drove that needle toward her neck, she swung the baton and caught him in the upper thigh.

The needle fell from his hand, but he was past feeling the pain. He charged in. When she tried to swing the baton again, he lowered his shoulder and pushed it away before she could gain any momentum.

An instant later, he'd head butted her in the stomach and shoved her to the ground. He fell on top of her, and from the corner of her eye she saw the needle, still glistening on the snow. She had to get it before he did.

Either that or her baton, now lying in the snow on the other side of her. She hadn't had time to slip the loop over her wrist.

Damn, the snow was a bad surface, too soft. She couldn't get enough leverage to push him over as he straddled her. As she fought, he wiggled upward, fending off her fists with his forearms until he knelt on both her arms.

Trapped. Completely trapped. And he was reaching for the needle now.

She closed her eyes, summoning reserves of strength she hadn't needed for a long time. Digging her foot into the snow, she managed to roll. It wasn't easy but it was enough to put him off balance.

Then a gunshot sounded clear and loud on the morning air.

Cade's voice followed. "Get off her, Sweet, or you'll be dead in the next five seconds."

But something seemed to have blinded him and deadened him. He fought viciously, and DeeJay had to fight back. She knew Cade couldn't get a clear bead on him while they were this close. The accuracy of a pistol was about six feet anyway.

She kept pushing and rolling, ignoring the way he pummeled at her arms. He was no trained fighter, but she was. She finally got enough leverage to hit him hard in the side of the head.

The blow stunned him. He went limp just long enough to let her scramble to her feet and grab her baton. Cade came running up and stood near him, pistol aimed.

"Backup is on the way," he said.

"I need to get into that barn," DeeJay said, struggling to keep her balance in the churned-up snow. "You heard it, too?"

He nodded. "I know what a barn owl sounds like. I heard a human cry of distress."

The all-important words.

"Don't let him near that needle." She pointed. She gave one last look at Calvin, who was glaring furiously at her, then trotted to the nearest barn door.

What she found inside would remain with her forever.

* * *

Andrew had been carted off to the hospital in a helicopter, still alive but suffering from an undetermined drug cocktail. He was just coherent enough to say that Calvin had hurt him.

The entire Sweet ranch had turned into a beehive of activity, with crime-scene techs and more deputies than DeeJay would have believed the county had. The barn, yard and house were roped off to prevent contamination of the scenes.

Calvin himself sat in the cage of a patrol car, cuffed in the very plastic ties he preferred to use on his victims. DeeJay battled an urge to give him a bit of his own paralytic to see what it was like.

But under the circumstances, neither she nor Cade could get anywhere close. They had become witnesses, and their work was done. Time to let the locals and their experts take over.

"Say," said Cade as they sat in the car waiting to see where they might be needed next. The heat was blasting, but DeeJay still felt cold to the bone.

"Yes?"

"Do you like sushi?"

"Love it."

"Well, I know this absolutely great place in Denver. You up for it?"

For the first time in endless hours, she actually felt like smiling.

Chapter 15

A few weeks later, Cade opened the shower door as Dee-Jay stood beneath the hot spray. At last they had managed to get away, and Cade had gotten them a suite at one of the best hotels in Denver. DeeJay wasn't used to such luxury, but she was enjoying it.

"Those bruises are looking better," he said.

She'd gotten more banged up than she had realized in her fight with Calvin and was covered with healing bruises on her arms and side. "Kind of an interesting shade of green and purple," she agreed.

He reached out and touched her arm, running his fingers lightly down it. "Want me to wash you?"

"Cade, you're dressed! Just go wait for me. I won't be long."

"Ah, you are getting better." He smiled and closed the door. For a while after she'd battled Calvin, she'd needed his help washing her hair and back because she was so sore. Cade, as she well knew, had enjoyed it entirely too much.

Days of paperwork and questioning had been wearying, but they had spent their nights together, pushing all the bad things into the background, discovering each other.

DeeJay was sure she had never felt so complete and happy. Except for the dreams. She wondered if she would ever be able to bury her memory of what she had seen in that barn. Seeing those boys for real had been entirely different from seeing photos of an old crime scene.

She had dealt with murders before, had even seen battlefields, but the cold-blooded quality of this had struck her to her very core in a different way. Kids. Just kids. Not even old enough to have done anything really wrong. Deprived of a chance to experience life, through no fault of their own.

Sweet's eyes haunted her, too. Dark and hard in those last moments she had spent with him, they had seemed inhuman. But as well she knew, he was perfectly human. People wanted to believe serial killers were different, but she knew better. They were humans, not demons. Badly twisted humans, but they did nothing the species hadn't done before in one way or another.

Still, his eyes haunted her.

Sighing, she turned off the water and stepped out onto the mat, reaching for one of the thick, fluffy towels the hotel had provided. They were luxurious, too.

Her thoughts turned to Cade, and an increasingly familiar uneasiness filled her. She'd had the feeling that he'd withdrawn from her in some way. Oh, he was with her every night, but something had changed, and it worried her. Had he decided they weren't a long-term thing?

She couldn't blame him if he had. She knew she wasn't easy to get along with, and she had already warned him she had a habit of picking fights to break up relationships. Maybe they'd been living in a state of distraction until after they had solved the case, and now they were facing reality again. All of it. Maybe he didn't think they fit well.

And maybe he was right. She'd lowered the guard on her heart but not all the way. She didn't even know if she was capable of it. He had to sense that, so maybe he felt he couldn't trust her.

She supposed she was going to find out and probably very soon.

An hour later they were seated in an elegant Japanese restaurant. He wore a suit with a string tie, and she wore a red satin sheath with long sleeves. The color set off her dark hair and eyes, and she knew it. Strutting her stuff to try to hold off the inevitable, she thought sadly as she pretended to smile and laugh, when she knew the end must be near.

Cade ordered way too much sushi. She figured he was making it their meal. She was perfectly content with that, and complimented the flavors. The fish was fresh, the wasabi biting and the pickled ginger out of this world.

For dessert, they received small plates of fresh fruit and tiny bowls of lime sherbet. She began to lose her appetite as she grew more aware of a tension in him.

Finally, she asked, "Cade, what's wrong?"

He put down his spoon and pushed the sherbet aside. "What makes you ask?"

"I feel like you're tense. And I've been feeling as if you're trying to pull away from me. Do you want to end this?"

He stared at her from inscrutable eyes, then astonished

her by calling their waiter. As soon as the check came, he placed cash on the tray.

"Better to discuss this someplace more private."

She was right, she realized. He didn't want her to make a scene. That could mean only one thing.

They took a cab back to the hotel in silence and rode up to their room without a word. At last they were alone, facing one another across the suite's sitting area, a space that suddenly looked like an immense gulf.

Her nerves felt stretched to breaking. Finally, she said, "If you're done with me, just say so. I can handle it."

"I'm sure you can."

The words fell into her heart like stone. Here it came.

"The problem," he said slowly, "is you."

"Me?"

"I don't know what you want. I'm not sure you do, either. You let me just so close but no closer. I need you to let down those walls."

"Why?" Pain pierced her. "So you can hurt me?"

"No." He shook his head a little. "So I can love you."

She felt as if she'd just gone over a sharp bump in the road and left her stomach behind. Her knees suddenly felt weak, and she reached out to steady herself against the back of a chair. "Love me?" she repeated, her voice thin.

"Love you. All these weeks we've known each other, you've been focused on the job. I get that. I have, too, but when we're alone together, even when you talk to me about yourself, I feel there's this place inside you I can't reach. That nobody can reach. I want to reach it, DeeJay, because I'm out of my mind in love with you. But you have to let me in."

A hot tear rolled down her cheek as understanding slammed home and left her speechless.

"It's okay," he said quietly. "You are who you are. But it's up to you. If you want me, I'll hang around and try to get past those walls however I can. I don't want to lose you. But I feel I've haven't won you. Or even really found you."

She saw him start to turn away, and the sight made her feel as if huge hands were tearing her heart in two. "Cade?"

Galvanized, she stepped toward him.

"I didn't mean to make you cry," he said, his back to her.

"Cade, look at me."

He turned and waited.

"You have found me. All of me. I know I'm broken, but I don't want to be. And I'm scared to death of losing you. Please...be patient with me. I'll die if I lose you."

He tilted his head a little. "Really?"

"Have I ever lied to you? You got to see the scared, scarred parts of me I've never shown anyone. Don't you get how much I trust you?"

"I've been feeling you don't."

"Then you're wrong." She stepped closer. "Cade, please."

Now he stepped toward her, and his expression was softening. "You trust me?"

"Completely. I didn't want to. I admit it. I was so afraid of being hurt again. I'm still afraid. Terrified. But I let you in anyway, and I wasn't kidding when I said I'd die if you left me. I couldn't stand the pain of losing you."

He closed the distance to wrap her in his arms and hold her so tightly she almost couldn't breathe. "I won't leave you unless you tell me to. But DeeJay?"

"Yes?"

"Do you think you might ever love me?"

Her heart split open the rest of the way, and understanding filled her with absolute certainty. "I already love you. I am in love with you."

As she spoke the words, she knew they were the truest she had ever spoken, and when his mouth sealed her words with a kiss, she knew that somehow everything was going to be all right.

With Cade, the future seemed full of promise.

"I love you, DeeJay," he said when he let her catch her breath. "Don't you ever try to get away, because I won't let you. Fight with me all you want, but remember this."

"Mmm?"

"That no matter how many fights you pick, I'm going to stay."

Joy rose in her then, a feeling she'd been without for so long she had forgotten how it felt. Blinding, healing, warming joy.

When he swept her up in his arms and carried her to bed, the shadows of her past remained behind. If they ever returned, she knew now how to banish them—in Cade's arms.

* * * * *

REQUEST YOUR FREE BOOKS!
2 FREE NOVELS PLUS 2 FREE GIFTS!

⊞ HARLEQUIN®

ROMANTIC suspense

Sparked by danger, fueled by passion

YES! Please send me 2 FREE Harlequin® Romantic Suspense novels and my 2 FREE gifts (gifts are worth about $10). After receiving them, if I don't wish to receive any more books, I can return the shipping statement marked "cancel." If I don't cancel, I will receive 4 brand-new novels every month and be billed just $4.74 per book in the U.S. or $5.24 per book in Canada. That's a savings of at least 14% off the cover price! It's quite a bargain! Shipping and handling is just 50¢ per book in the U.S. and 75¢ per book in Canada.* I understand that accepting the 2 free books and gifts places me under no obligation to buy anything. I can always return a shipment and cancel at any time. Even if I never buy another book, the two free books and gifts are mine to keep forever.

240/340 HDN F45N

Name _____ (PLEASE PRINT) _____

Address _____ Apt. # _____

City _____ State/Prov. _____ Zip/Postal Code _____

Signature (if under 18, a parent or guardian must sign)

Mail to the **Harlequin® Reader Service:**
IN U.S.A.: P.O. Box 1867, Buffalo, NY 14240-1867
IN CANADA: P.O. Box 609, Fort Erie, Ontario L2A 5X3

Want to try two free books from another line?
Call 1-800-873-8635 or visit www.ReaderService.com.

* Terms and prices subject to change without notice. Prices do not include applicable taxes. Sales tax applicable in N.Y. Canadian residents will be charged applicable taxes. Offer not valid in Quebec. This offer is limited to one order per household. Not valid for current subscribers to Harlequin Romantic Suspense books. All orders subject to credit approval. Credit or debit balances in a customer's account(s) may be offset by any other outstanding balance owed by or to the customer. Please allow 4 to 6 weeks for delivery. Offer available while quantities last.

Your Privacy—The Harlequin® Reader Service is committed to protecting your privacy. Our Privacy Policy is available online at www.ReaderService.com or upon request from the Harlequin Reader Service.

We make a portion of our mailing list available to reputable third parties that offer products we believe may interest you. If you prefer that we not exchange your name with third parties, or if you wish to clarify or modify your communication preferences, please visit us at www.ReaderService.com/consumerschoice or write to us at Harlequin Reader Service Preference Service, P.O. Box 9062, Buffalo, NY 14269. Include your complete name and address.

HRS13R

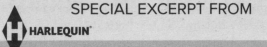
Elizabeth just found out she's pregnant after a one-night stand with her boss's son. And she's the sole witness to her boss's murder. The only one who can protect her is the last man she wants in her life…

Read on for a sneak peek at Marie Ferrarella's 250th Harlequin installment,

CARRYING HIS SECRET

After getting out of his car, Elizabeth crossed to her own, taking careful, small steps as if she was afraid that tilting even a fraction of an inch in any direction would send her sprawling to the ground.

Discovering her boss's body the way she had had thrown her equilibrium into complete turmoil, and she found herself both nauseous and dizzy.

Or maybe that was due to the tiny human being she was carrying within her.

In either case, she couldn't allow herself to display any signs of weakness—especially around Whit.

At the last moment, just before she got into her car, Elizabeth turned and looked in Whit's direction. "If you need to talk—about anything at all," she emphasized, "call me. You have my number."

"I won't need to talk," Whit told her flatly.

He wouldn't call, Elizabeth thought, sliding in behind the steering wheel of her vehicle. She closed the door and tugged her seat belt out of its resting place. The man could be unbelievably stubborn, but there was absolutely nothing she could do about that except to express her heartfelt sorrow and regret. That and be there if Whit discovered that he did need someone to turn to.

Would Whit take over the corporation? Would he just pick up the mantle and act as if it was all only business as usual?

His manner just now indicated that most likely he would, but the man wasn't a robot or an android. He was going to have to make time to grieve over his loss. If he didn't, eventually it would catch up to him and cause a breakdown.

Whit was too good at his job to allow that to happen. But she was still uneasy. After all, he was a man, not a machine.

She had to find a way to make sure that didn't happen. For his sake, as well as for the memory of Reginald Adair… and the life of her child.

**Don't miss Marie Ferrarella's
250th Harlequin installment,
CARRYING HIS SECRET!**

**Available February 2015,
wherever Harlequin® Romantic Suspense
books and ebooks are sold.**

Love the Harlequin book you just read?

Your opinion matters.

Review this book on your favorite book site, review site, blog or your own social media properties and share your opinion with other readers!

Be sure to connect with us at:
Harlequin.com/Newsletters
Facebook.com/HarlequinBooks
Twitter.com/HarlequinBooks

HARLEQUIN®

A *Romance* FOR EVERY MOOD™

JUST CAN'T GET ENOUGH?

Join our social communities
and talk to us online.

You will have access to the latest
news on upcoming titles and special
promotions, but most importantly,
you can talk to other fans about your
favorite Harlequin reads.

Harlequin.com/Community

f Facebook.com/HarlequinBooks

🐦 Twitter.com/HarlequinBooks

📌 Pinterest.com/HarlequinBooks

JUST CAN'T GET ENOUGH
ROMANCE
Looking for more?

Harlequin has everything from contemporary, passionate and heartwarming to suspenseful and inspirational stories.

Whatever your mood, we have a romance just for you!

Connect with us to find your next great read, special offers and more.

Facebook.com/HarlequinBooks
Twitter.com/HarlequinBooks
HarlequinBlog.com
Harlequin.com/Newsletters

H HARLEQUIN®

A *Romance* FOR EVERY MOOD™

www.Harlequin.com